Acclaim for

TORCH

"I love R.J. Anderson's faery books: they're emotionally rich, morally deep, and hugely fun. If like me you have been hungry for more about Ivy and Martin, I promise *Torch* will make you very happy."

— ERIN BOW,

Governor General's Literary Award-winning author of *Stand on the Sky*

"Poignant, engaging, and masterful—a wholly satisfying conclusion to Ivy's story."

— JOANNA RUTH MEYER,

author of *Echo North* and *Into the Heartless Wood*

"R.J. Anderson's storytelling sparkles in *Torch*, a compelling conclusion to The Flight and Flame Trilogy. This tale of piskeys, spriggans, and fairies was delightful from start to finish."

— LINDSAY A. FRANKLIN,

award-winning author of *The Story Peddler*

TORCH

Books by R.J. Anderson

No Ordinary Fairy Tale Series
Knife
Rebel
Arrow

Uncommon Magic Series
A Pocket Full of Murder
A Little Taste of Poison

Ultraviolet Series
Ultraviolet
Quicksilver

The Flight and Flame Trilogy
Swift
Nomad
Torch

TORCH

THE FLIGHT AND FLAME TRILOGY BOOK 3

R.J. ANDERSON

Torch
Copyright © 2021 by R.J. Anderson

Published by Enclave Publishing, an imprint of Third Day Books, LLC

Phoenix, Arizona, USA.
www.enclavepublishing.com

ISBN: 978-1-62184-158-6 (hardback)
ISBN: 978-1-62184-160-9 (printed softcover)
ISBN: 978-1-62184-159-3 (ebook)

Cover design by Kirk DouPonce, www.DogEaredDesign.com
Typesetting by Jamie Foley, www.JamieFoley.com

Printed in the United States of America.

For Deva
who was there from the start
and for all the patient readers
who never lost hope for the ending

1

She'd only just found him again, and now he was gone.

Ivy sat on the front step of the house—not *her* house, a crude human cottage could never be home to a piskey-girl, but right now it was all she had—hugging her knees and staring gloomily into the night. The lights of a delivery van swept the front garden of the farmstead, turning toward the nearby village; on the hedge by the road a rook perched, watching her with a shrewd, glittering eye. Inside the house Mica still raged and stamped about, but Ivy was past caring what her brother did. The pain of losing Martin sat like a lump of cold slag in her chest.

His face had shone as he'd changed out of owl-shape to greet her, soft with joy and an almost reverent wonder. He'd stepped up to Ivy, reaching for her hand . . .

"Get away from her, you filthy spriggan!"

And just like that, she'd lost him. One look at Mica charging toward them, and Martin had vanished like a puff of wind.

Not that she blamed him. The last time Martin fought her brother, he'd ended up in a dungeon with iron around his ankle. But how could he and Ivy ever be together if he kept deciding the better part of valor was to run away?

"Well," said a gruff female voice beside her, "that could have gone better."

Ivy rested her chin on her knee, trying not to shiver. She'd been so furious at Mica, she'd stormed outside without a coat.

Thorn crouched on the corner of the step, rubbing her calloused hands together. "So that's your brother, is it? Can't say I regret not having one. How many have you got?"

"Only Mica," said Ivy. "But that's enough."

The faery woman snorted. "You said it." She blew into her cupped hands and stuffed them into her armpits for warmth. "I'm guessing Broch and I won't be welcome in the house, then. Should we make ourselves scarce until you sort this out?"

She spoke briskly, but Ivy knew it was no light offer. The two faeries had come to Cornwall as ambassadors from their queen, Valerian of the Oak, and if Ivy couldn't find room for them they'd have nowhere to go.

Like everyone else in her life, it seemed.

"There's nothing to discuss," Ivy told her. "Mica can shout all he likes, but you're my guests and it's not his house. Besides, our mother's a faery, so he's not got a pick to dig with."

"Martin's a faery too, but that didn't stop your brother chasing him off."

Half faery, Ivy almost reminded her, but held her tongue. Thorn knew the secret already, but it was safer to talk as though *spriggan* was nothing more than the insult Mica had intended, instead of the literal truth.

"I thought I'd never see him again," Ivy said, picking a bit of gravel off the step. "When he turned himself over to your queen, he was sure she'd execute him."

"Valerian's not the sort to kill people," said Thorn. "No matter how much they deserve it."

Ivy didn't protest. She knew Martin's crimes as well as he did, and he wouldn't want her to make excuses. "Maybe not, but letting him go? I don't know your queen well, but that doesn't seem like her either."

Thorn shrugged. "I don't know and I didn't ask. All I know is that when Rob dragged Martin in, Queen Valerian sent everyone away and spent half the night talking to him. The next day she called us back and said she'd decided to pardon him, as long as he swore to go straight to Cornwall and never leave it again."

An oath he'd taken, obviously. But how had Martin convinced the faery queen to trust him? He'd never lied to Ivy, or at least not about anything that mattered, but he'd deceived nearly everyone else in his life at some point, as many of Valerian's people could testify.

Besides, the queen didn't know Martin like Ivy did. She hadn't found him chained up at the bottom of a mineshaft, half-crazed with guilt and remorse; she hadn't saved and been saved by him, or spent weeks tramping about Cornwall in his company. She hadn't shared Martin's memories, or learned the secrets of his long-forgotten past. And she certainly didn't love him, as Ivy had grown to love him.

So why had Valerian let him go?

Ivy's eyes stung, and she rubbed them furiously. Martin would have told her, she was sure of it—if only Mica hadn't come storming in to interrupt them.

Thorn cleared her throat. "I was wondering."

"About what?"

"I thought your people lived in that old mine—what's it called?"

It hurt even to say it, Ivy missed her home so much. "The Delve."

"Right. So where did all the piskeys in the barn come from?"

So that was where Thorn had slipped off to while Ivy and Mica were arguing. Though she must have turned invisible first, because if the knockers guarding the barn had spotted a strange faery, they'd have hefted their thunder-axes and gone after her at once.

"It's because of my Aunt Betony," Ivy said. "She was our Joan—what we call our queen—for years. But she was obsessed with keeping our people safe, and she thought making all the women and children stay underground was the best way to do it. Only the mine was poisoned, so we were getting sick."

"I know that much," said Thorn. "I heard you tell Queen Valerian. You tried to warn Betony but she didn't believe you, and the other piskeys were too scared to go against her. So what changed?"

"A few days ago, I went back to the Delve and challenged Betony. My best friend stood up for me." Ivy closed her eyes, remembering Jenny's face in that moment. She'd never looked more beautiful, or more brave. "And Betony burned her to ashes. In front of everyone."

Thorn let out a low whistle.

Swallowing grief, Ivy went on. "I wanted to kill her. But I—I couldn't. Her fire went out when Jenny died, and our people were so shocked . . . she was losing them, and she knew it. So she threw herself on my sword."

"Killed herself, you mean? Or tried to?"

"She wanted people to believe I stabbed her on purpose, so they wouldn't follow me either. And it worked, mostly." Ivy shifted on the concrete step, cold creeping into her muscles. "Mica and a few others left to join me aboveground. The rest are still in the Delve, waiting for Betony to heal and get her fire back."

And maybe her aunt would, eventually. Though it would be nice to believe some unseen judge like the Great Gardener of the faeries or the spriggans' Shaper had punished Betony by taking her powers away, Ivy feared that was too much to hope. After all, Betony had burned Ivy's mother nearly to death only two days earlier, but she'd still had enough fire to kill Jenny.

"But the piskeys who left, they follow you, don't they?" asked Thorn. "So you're their Joan."

"No!" Ivy burst out, loud enough to make Thorn scowl. She flushed and added more quietly, "The true Joan can make fire at will. That's why she's called the *Wad* in the old language, the torch that lights our people's way. I can't do that. I'm just giving them a place to live until we find something better."

"Hmph." Thorn wrinkled her nose. "Maybe it wasn't the best time for Broch and me to come, then. Not much good trying to make a truce with your people if they can't even say who's their leader."

Ivy gave a reluctant nod. Much as she owed the faeries for saving her mother, perhaps it would be better if they left. If Thorn and Broch went back to the Oak now, Ivy wouldn't have to worry what her fellow piskeys would make of them.

"On the other twig, though . . ." Thorn stood up, rubbing her stomach absently. "We just got here, and I'm not keen on going back without a good reason. I'll go talk to Broch." She shook herself, changed to her tiny, winged Oakenfolk form, and flew away.

Mica must have calmed down or left the house, because Ivy couldn't hear him ranting anymore. Maybe Cicely, their little sister, had talked some sense into him: she was one of the few people who could crack his tough shell.

Even so, the thought of going back inside gave Ivy no pleasure. Glad as she was for a place to live, this clumsy box of a house with its patchwork stones was nothing like the cozy tunnels and snug caverns she'd grown up in.

Yet Ivy had spent months on the surface now, so she'd had a chance to get used to it. The twenty-odd piskeys camping out in the barn had no such advantage. Unlike Ivy and her mother, who could easily pass for human and often did, most of them stuck doggedly to their usual piskey size and refused to wear anything but the old-fashioned clothes they'd brought from the Delve. They'd settled into the barn well enough, but they kept the windows shuttered and seldom went outside unless they had to. And though Ivy had offered to share the house's comforts with any piskey who needed them, even the oldest aunties preferred to huddle around a fire in the barn corridor than stay in a strange, human place.

Ivy had hoped to save her people by leading them up to the surface, away from the poison. But until they found a new home where they could dig for gems and refine metal to their hearts' content, they'd always mourn for the Delve they'd left behind.

"Ivy! Ivy!" Quartz, Jenny's imp of a little brother with his bright eyes and mouse-brown hair, came pelting across the darkened yard toward her. Even at human size Ivy was small, but the piskey boy stood only halfway to her knee. Hurriedly she got up and shrank to match him.

"What's going—" She broke off with a gasp as Quartz flung his arms around her and squeezed. He was only twelve, barely older than Cicely, but he had a knocker's blood and the strength to go with it.

"Good news!" he exclaimed. "Come and hear!"

Bewildered, Ivy let Quartz tug her across the cobbles to the barn. Inside, the first box stall was taken up by Dodger, a shaggy bay pony who'd been there longer than any of them, while the next two were full of slumbering piskey families. But at the end of the corridor a small peat fire burned in a stone brazier, and Gem and Feldspar sat with hands cupped around bowls of a late and apparently well-earned dinner. The smell of roast rabbit mingled with the earthy scent of the pipe Hew was smoking on the other side of the stall. Ivy gave the old knocker a respectful nod, which he returned gravely, as Quartz dragged her over to the other men.

"Tell her," he urged. "About the mine."

Feldspar cleared his throat. "We checked it out tonight,

Gem and me, and it doesn't look bad. Usual mix of killas and granite, a few decent pockets of ore. The shafts were mostly flooded, but if we dug a few more adits for drainage, like . . ." He looked up at Ivy, his broad, earnest face creased with hope. "We can show you, if you want to take a geek."

She couldn't blame the piskey-men for being excited. They didn't know what she'd found out days ago, that all the nearby shafts were tainted with the same poison as the Delve, and no amount of pumping or digging could make them safe again. "Is it the one in the wood?" Ivy asked. "By the fork in the bridle path?"

Gem's face fell. "You know it, then." He nudged Feldspar with an elbow. "That means it's no good."

"Ayes," said Feldspar glumly, and the two of them went back to eating.

Even if they both owed their lives to her—and they did—it made Ivy's head whirl to be treated with so much respect. Especially by two of the Delve's best hunters, grown men with children only a few years younger than herself. "I'm sorry," she said. "We're still too close to the Delve here. But I'm always looking for mine shafts, wherever I . . . fly."

It was hard not to stammer on that last word, knowing how her people felt about shape-changing . But after growing up wingless, Ivy could never regret learning to take bird-shape, no matter how unusual it might be. "Don't worry," she went on more firmly. "I won't give up until I find us a safe new home."

"We know that, me lover." Hew took his pipe out of his mouth and grinned at her, displaying several missing teeth. The poison had aged him, like it had so many other piskeys, and he looked decades older than he should. "You're not your aunt, with her stubbornness and haughty ways. Your father was a fine knocker, a hero—"

"Rest his spirit," said Feldspar, raising his bowl solemnly.

"—and you're Flint's daughter, through and through." Hew

tapped the ashes out of his pipe and stamped on them. "All you need's a good fellow to be your Jack, and you'll make us a fine Joan some day."

Heat rushed into Ivy's face. Mica had told her there was a rumor that she was the next Joan, but she'd never imagined any but the youngest piskeys would take it seriously. "But I can't . . ."

"O'course you can," said Feldspar. "The power'll come to you, we've no doubt of it."

"As soon as you've got rid of Betony," Quartz chimed in with relish, and the older men nodded, as though this were common knowledge.

Ivy took a step back, shaken. "Good night," she stammered, and vanished.

Cicely didn't jump when Ivy landed in their shared bedroom; she was used to her older sister appearing out of nowhere. But she sat up sharply at the sight of Ivy's face. "Did Mica go after you? I told him—"

"Not Mica." Ivy sank onto her side of the bed, pulling a pillow against her chest. Martin wasn't here, and she needed to hold on to something. "The others. Cicely, they think the only reason I can't make fire is because Aunt Betony's still alive. And I think . . . I think they expect me to kill her."

Cicely looked horrified, and Ivy felt a rush of gratitude; at least one person understood how she felt about killing Betony. Once, in an agony of grief, she had tried—but only because she'd given up hope and cared for nothing but vengeance. She was no longer that bitter, despairing girl, and she never wanted to be again.

"I know," Ivy said. "I won't do it. Aunt Betony may be evil, but . . ." She hugged the pillow tighter. "I've seen what murder does to people. There has to be a better way."

"But do you think they're right?" her little sister asked, twisting her braids with anxiety. "Not about killing her, but the fire thing?"

Ivy had never heard of anyone inheriting the Joan's power without the Joan's consent. But then she'd never heard of a Joan losing her fire the way Betony had, either. She gave a helpless shrug.

"Have you tried it?" Cicely persisted. "Lately?"

There was a red mark on Ivy's palm, still tender, from two nights ago. She'd lit the biggest candle she could find in the house, the one with three wicks, and tried to cup its flame—but the pain had stung tears to her eyes, and she'd snatched her hand away. She couldn't even touch fire, let alone summon it. "I've tried. Nothing happens."

And worse, Ivy didn't know anyone else who could make fire either. When the last Joan was dying all the older piskey-women had failed the test except Betony, and the few who remained were too young, too timid, or too busy with their own families to even consider it. The only one who'd seemed fit to become the next Joan was Jenny, but she was gone.

"Well, maybe you'll work it out," said Cicely. "Or Aunt Betony might die anyway. Mica said she was wounded pretty badly, and Yarrow can't heal her with magic like Broch healed Mum."

Perhaps not, but Yarrow's skill with herbs and potions was almost as impressive. And the Delve's healer wouldn't give up on Betony without doing all she could to save her. Wearily Ivy put the pillow aside and reached for her nightgown.

She'd barely started changing when a tentative knock sounded at the door. "Ivy? Are you asleep?"

Cicely made a face and vanished under the covers. "Not yet," Ivy said. "What is it?"

The door cracked open, revealing their mother with her waves of honey-brown hair and dark, haunted eyes. "Come to my room when you're ready. There's something I need to tell you."

"What is this?" demanded Ivy, staring at Marigold's freshly made bed and the open suitcases lying on it. Both were full, while the wardrobe in the corner stood empty. Ivy's mother had never owned many clothes or trinkets, but she'd packed up everything she'd brought to the house, and now her room might have been a stranger's.

"I can't stay here, Ivy." She closed the first suitcase and clicked it shut. "Not after . . . It's not safe. If Betony comes back . . ." Her lips trembled. She pressed them together and looked away.

Of course she was terrified. She knew better than anyone, even Ivy, what it felt like to face Betony's fire. "But it's different now," Ivy reassured her. "Mica's here, and Mattock and all the others. We can protect you."

"I know you think that, my darling, but you shouldn't have to. I should be the one protecting you and Cicely. And I can't do that, not here." She turned pleading eyes to Ivy. "Come with me."

Ivy sat down on the edge of the bed, a numb feeling creeping over her. "You're going to London, aren't you. To be with *him*."

It shouldn't have come as a shock: she already knew her mother and David Menadue, the house's human owner, were in love and eager to marry. But Ivy hadn't expected it to happen so soon.

"It's not just for me," Marigold insisted. "It's for Molly. It's not safe for her to come here, now Betony knows where to find us. But David's bought a house, a nice big one. We could all be together. As a family."

David's daughter was one of Ivy's dearest friends, so the idea should have been tempting. But unlike Marigold, who'd spent years living in the human world, Ivy couldn't be happy pretending to be something she wasn't. Especially not for the rest of her life.

"What about Mica? He's family too." Even if she'd like to strangle him right now— but it wasn't the first time, and it surely wouldn't be the last either. "What about the other piskeys in the barn? I can't just fly off and leave them!"

Marigold sighed. "Mica wants nothing to do with me
or David. He says he's a piskey and he'll die like one. But
you know better, don't you?" She moved closer, taking Ivy's
hands. "You can't help those people any more than you've
done already. You worked so hard to bring them here, but it's
only a matter of time before Betony comes to take them back."

Ivy wanted to deny it, but deep down she feared Marigold
was right. While Betony lay wounded, her consort Gossan had
exiled Mica and all the other piskeys who'd defied her. But
Ivy's aunt was hard as diamond, and once she recovered her
strength, she might well overrule the Jack's order. It was one
thing to banish lone troublemakers like Ivy, but twenty-two
piskeys were too many for her stubborn pride to lose.

"Please," whispered Marigold. "Cicely says she'll only
come if you will. Can't you do it for her sake? And let Mica
deal with whatever happens here?"

Ivy searched her mother's face, taking in the wide eyes and
delicate features that were so like her own. Then at last, gently,
she drew her hands away.

"I don't blame you for leaving," she said. "I hope you and
David are happy together, and please give Molly my love. But I
won't leave my people." Or Martin, for that matter. How could
she go anywhere he couldn't follow?

Marigold's eyes brimmed, but she nodded. She closed the
remaining suitcase and gave Ivy a sad smile. "Take good care
of Cicely," she said. "I'll ring you on the weekend."

For six lonely years Ivy had longed to see her mother again.
She'd taken wild risks and braved terrifying dangers, first to
find her and then to save her life. But she sounded so human
now, as though the years she'd spent in the Delve had never
happened. As though she'd never been a piskey-wife, or even
a faery woman, at all.

"All right," said Ivy, forcing the words past the lump in her
throat. "I love you. Stay safe."

When she got up the next morning, leaving Cicely still burrowed under the covers, Ivy expected to find the rest of the house empty. But as she stepped out of the bedroom, Broch's voice floated down the hall toward her.

"You can't hide it forever. She's bound to find out eventually, whether you tell her or not."

"Not if we stay here," Thorn countered. "A few more months, and no one'll be the wiser."

"No one? Queen Valerian knows. Wink knows, and she's not the best at keeping secrets. And you can't expect the piskeys not to notice."

"What if they do? They don't care about us. They've got their own troubles to worry about."

Curiosity roused, Ivy was tempted to go on listening. But sneaking about and eavesdropping wasn't the piskey way. She followed the faeries' voices to the kitchen and found them sitting at the breakfast table, helping themselves to jam and bread.

If Marigold were here she'd probably ask them how they'd slept, but to Ivy's embarrassment, she'd forgotten to make up a room for either of them. Broch could take bird-shape, so he probably didn't need a bed, but she should at least have offered Thorn the sofa, or the foldaway cot in the study. "Have you decided to stay, then?" Ivy asked. "If so you'll be welcome, but I should introduce you to the other piskeys. I don't want them to think I'm hiding you."

"We're staying," said Thorn firmly. "At least for now. If your people won't listen to us, that's their crop to harvest. But

I'll be blighted if I go skulking back to the Oak without even planting a seed."

Ivy picked the crust out of the breadbasket and dropped it into the toaster. Cicely wouldn't eat it, so somebody ought to. "All right. I'll take you over after breakfast."

The faeries nodded, and they fell into a companionable silence until Thorn spoke up again. "I see your mother's gone."

A statement like that, Ivy had learned, was Thorn's way of asking a question she wasn't sure she had any right to ask. Faeries had an elaborate system of bargaining for favors, and even information, that made little sense to piskeys. "She's marrying David," Ivy told her. "And staying with him in London. She can't fight Betony anymore."

Thorn's brows went up. "You don't seem surprised."

"That's because I know what she's been through." And so did Cicely, even if she had shed a few tears last night. "It's only Mica who blames her, but he's still angry she left us six years ago."

"Even though she would have died if she'd stayed in the Delve?" asked Broch.

Ivy had tried to explain that to her brother, but it hadn't made any difference. He seemed to think everybody had to be as tough as he was, or else they were cowards. "You'd have to ask Mica," Ivy said, helping herself to an orange. "Or Cicely— she's the only one besides Matt who can make sense of him."

"Matt?" Broch looked puzzled.

"Short for Mattock," Ivy explained. "He used to live next to us, in the Delve." Though he was far more than just a neighbor, to be sure. The knocker boy had been Mica's best friend since the two of them were children, and his steady calm had smoothed over many a family quarrel. It was almost a shame that Ivy couldn't bring herself to marry him, especially since half the piskeys in the Delve kept teasing her about it. Like Hew had last night.

*All you need's a good fellow to be your Jack, and you'll make
us a fine Joan someday.*

Matt was unquestionably a good fellow, but was Martin?
Not by piskey standards, for certain. The Jack O'Lantern, the
Joan's consort, was the chief example of what a piskey warrior
should be. He had to be strong, brave, and honest, as well as
unfailingly loyal, and Martin was seldom more than two of
those things even when he cared to try . . .

"I think you can eat that now," Broch remarked, and Ivy
blinked out of her reverie. She'd not only peeled the rind off
her orange, she'd torn all the segments to bits as well.

"Sorry," she said, pushing the bowl away. "I was thinking.
If you're finished, we should go."

"This is Thorn," Ivy told the other piskeys as they gathered
around her in the barn. "She's come to us as an ambassador
from Queen Valerian of the Oak."

With news like that, a few suspicious looks from the men
were only to be expected. Ivy's people mistrusted faeries,
and not without reason. But the women studied Thorn with
interest, and their children nudged one another excitedly.
Standing at their height, strong-boned and thick-waisted with
her glassy wings hidden behind her, she looked more like a
piskey than Ivy did.

"And this is Broch," Ivy continued, gesturing to the slim,
bearded man. "The healer who saved my mother's life. He
comes from the Green Isles of Wales and knows all kinds of
wonderful stories."

"I'll warrant he does," grumbled Hew, and Ivy felt like
her heart had dropped down a mineshaft. How could she be

so stupid? Hew's father had been the Delve's droll-teller for years, and Hew's son Keeve had seemed likely to follow him. But Keeve had died at the hands of a vengeful faery, and his granfer had passed away soon after. The last thing Hew wanted was some jumped-up faery scholar trying to replace them.

But Ivy couldn't afford to hesitate. If she wanted her people to trust Thorn and Broch, she had to show how much she trusted them herself. "I know that in the past, the piskeys and faeries of Cornwall were enemies. But the Oakenfolk live in England, far east of the Tamar, and they have no quarrel with us. All Queen Valerian wants is an opportunity to show her goodwill and make us an offer of peace."

She stepped back, and Thorn cleared her throat. "I'm not a flowery talker," she declared, "so I'll keep it short. I don't mind if you're suspicious; you've a right to be. I'm a stranger, and you don't know anything about me. But only faeries who spend a lot of time with humans are good at lying, and I'm not one of that sort. So if you ask me a question, you'll get an honest answer, and we'll go from there."

The men kept their eyes narrowed, but the effect of Thorn's speech on the women was extraordinary. Hew's wife Teasel whispered to Mattock's mother Fern, and the two of them started to quake—not with fury, but with the sparkling eyes and tight-shut lips of suppressed laughter.

Ivy had no idea what that was about, but she chose to take it as encouragement. If her people could find Thorn funny, they were more than halfway to accepting her.

"I *am* a flowery talker," Broch announced with a wry smile. "But I am trying to learn better. As Thorn says, you have no reason to trust us, and we have no right to expect you should. But if you will give me a chance to prove myself, I am a skilled healer and will gladly treat anyone who comes to me for help."

There was an uncomfortable pause when he finished, and

Ivy was wondering what to say, when a small voice piped up, "I hurt my finger."

Her mother made a shushing noise and reached for her, but the little girl ducked away and trotted to Broch, thrusting out her hand. He knelt and considered it gravely, then touched her finger with his own.

The girl's face brightened. "You fixed it!" She scampered back to the other children. "Look, the hurt's gone! See?"

The older piskeys stirred and muttered, but it sounded less like hostility and more like hope to Ivy. Her people might not trust the faeries, but if they could find them useful, perhaps . . .

"I've a question for you," called Teasel, looking pointedly at Thorn. "Boy or girl?"

Thorn turned purple, and Ivy stood speechless. Despite her cropped hair and mannish clothing, surely anyone could tell the faery was a woman? Broch winced, and Ivy feared an explosion. But then Thorn's hand dropped to her stomach, and she mumbled, "Boy, if you must know."

"I knew it!" crowed Teasel, as Fern began to giggle. "And your first babe too, by the look of you. What a droll-tale!"

Ivy stared at them, flabbergasted. No wonder the piskey-women weren't afraid of Thorn: they weren't seeing her as a soldier of the faery queen but as an awkward soon-to-be mother. Someone they might even take under their own moth-wings and help, if Thorn could unbend enough to let them.

"And you're the father, no doubt," said Gem slyly to Broch. But if he'd thought to make the faery man blush, he was disappointed. Broch stepped up and took Thorn's hand in his own.

"I am, and I'll welcome any advice you can give me. As my wife will, if she doesn't burst from embarrassment first."

Of all the outcomes Ivy had imagined when she brought the faeries to the barn, she'd never imagined this. Fortunately, she didn't have to say anything. The piskey-women came crowding around Thorn, all chattering at once, while the men ambled off to light their pipes and quarrel amiably in private. They didn't invite Broch, but he didn't seem to mind. He only watched, lips quirked with amusement, as Teasel and the others inspected his wife, poked the slight swell of her belly, and peppered her with personal questions.

"You've got piskey blood in you somewhere, no doubt of it," declared Fern, squinting up and down at her. "Your mother's side, d'you think? Or your father's?"

"I don't have a mother *or* father," Thorn protested. "I hatched from an egg sixty years ago—"

"Sixty!" exclaimed Daisy, Gem's wife. "You look younger than I do, and I'm thirty." She touched her mouth wistfully, tracing the faint creases there. "And did you say *egg*?"

"It's a long story," Thorn told her. The color in her cheeks was still high, but easing; she seemed resigned to the piskeys' curiosity, instead of outraged as Ivy had feared.

Thrift, the little girl Broch had healed, tugged at Thorn's breeches. "Are *you* going to lay an egg?"

"Great Gardener, I hope not!" said Thorn fervently. There was a shocked pause, then all the piskey-women burst out laughing, and after a moment, Thorn chuckled too.

It was a marvel. No, a miracle.

"You never told me you were married," said Ivy to Broch. The piskey-wives were giving Thorn advice now, some of it earthy enough to make her blush all over again.

"That was Thorn's wish," he replied. "My wife may speak bluntly, but she keeps her own business private."

Ivy couldn't help smiling. "Maybe in the Oak she did. But not anymore."

Despite the winter chill it was a beautiful morning, the sun gleaming like white gold in a near-cloudless sky. Ivy crossed the yard toward the house, her heart so light she felt like skipping. Introducing Thorn and Broch to the piskeys had gone better than she'd ever dared to dream.

"You'll never believe this," she called, as Cicely came out to take Dodger for his morning ride. All the piskeys loved horses, but her sister and the bay pony had a special bond, and by now he was prancing with impatience to see her. "Did you know Thorn—"

"Ivy," said a soft voice, and she turned in surprise to find Mattock behind her. For such a broad-shouldered, squarely built young man, he could move with eerie quietness when he chose.

"What is it?" Ivy asked.

Matt glanced at Cicely, who was watching with bright interest. "Do you mind?" He made a shooing gesture toward the barn. "This is private."

Cicely's steps faltered, and the corners of her mouth pulled down. Then she dropped her gaze and strode on without a word.

Ivy looked up at Mattock, apprehensive, but he shook his head. "Don't worry, it's not that kind of private. I know how you feel about me, and I'm not slurry-brained enough to think I can change that by arguing with you." He took off his cap, eyes solemn beneath his thick, rusty brows. "I've got news from the Delve."

Ivy's breath caught. "About Betony?"

Matt nodded. "I took Mica to Redruth last evening, to get his mind off things, and we ran into Shale. You remember him?"

One of the younger hunters, with a gormless grin and ears that stuck out like elbows. He was likeable enough, but not known for good sense or discretion, and it was a wonder Gossan had let him out of the Delve without an escort. "Yes," Ivy said. "Go on."

"Well, he seemed friendly, so I bought him a pint and he gave me an earful. Betony's mending, but slowly, and no one sees her but Gossan and Yarrow. The folk in the Delve are worried she won't be up in time for the midwinter Lighting, and some fear she can't start the wakefire even if she does."

That would be dire for the piskeys living underground, especially the women. The all-night Lighting ceremony not only gave them a much-needed taste of fresh air, it renewed the magic that made them able to glow. "What are they going to do, then?" Ivy asked, her pulse quickening. "Did Shale say?"

Matt shook his head. "He just looked gloomy about it."

Ivy's mind raced, leaping from one possibility to another. If Betony couldn't light the wakefire for her people, they'd be more than disappointed—they'd be desperate. But if Ivy could give them what Betony couldn't . . .

"Gather the others," she told Mattock. "We need to plan a Lighting."

"I want to help," Cicely urged, running after Ivy as she crossed the yard. "There must be *something* I can do."

Ivy stopped and put a hand to her forehead. Where had she been going? Her thoughts kept sliding away from her like gravel. They only had one more day to prepare for the Lighting, and it wasn't nearly enough to make a proper job of it. "I thought you were helping the little ones make decorations."

"I was, but Bramble said we were chattering too much, so she chased me out and took over." Cicely made a face. "Why do old aunties have to be so fussy?"

Someone has to be, Ivy almost said, but held her tongue. Cicely meant well, even if she often struggled to concentrate and found it easier to start things than finish them. "What about Teasel and Fern? They could probably use help in the kitchen."

Cicely shook her head. "All they ever let me do is turn on the oven and show them where to find things. And I'm tired of sitting around."

Ivy sighed. To her relief, the others had seized on her Lighting plan with enthusiasm and thrown themselves into hard work as only piskeys could do. But they were so determined to get their tasks done right and quickly, they had no time to be patient with someone like Cicely who was still learning. And Ivy had too much on her mind already to waste time convincing them.

"Go around and ask who needs help, then," she said. "I'm busy. I have to talk to . . ." Who was it? She couldn't remember. "Somebody."

Cicely's lip quivered, and Ivy felt a pang of remorse. She reached out to her, but Cicely spun away and fled.

She'd get over it, Ivy told herself, watching her sister go. It might even be good for Cicely to work things out on her own instead of always looking to Ivy, or . . .

Mica! *He* was the piskey she had to talk to. They had needed a crowder for the dancing, and he was the only one who could play the fiddle. Ivy quickened her pace, heading for the house.

As she walked in, the smell of fresh baking greeted her, and Ivy paused to savor it. The hunters had snared rabbits and bagged a pair of fat ducks while the old uncles foraged for mushrooms and wild garlic, and yesterday Ivy had gone to the nearby city of Truro and bought the other ingredients they needed: saffron, currants, sharp cheese, fresh pilchards, and several sacks of flour. Fern and Teasel were two of the best cooks in the Delve, and once Ivy had coaxed them into the kitchen and convinced them to turn human size, they'd set about preparing a proper Lighting feast.

She would have stopped to greet them, but by their harried and somewhat shrill voices, they weren't in a mood for interruptions. Ivy slipped past the kitchen, heading for the bedrooms.

Mica had shut himself up in Marigold's room, which was now Ivy's—she'd offered it to Thorn and Broch, but they'd chosen to stay in the study. As she reached the end of the corridor, she could hear him scraping away at a six-hand reel and cursing when he made a mistake. As usual, he'd left practicing until the last minute.

"Matt said I'd find you here," Ivy said, opening the door cautiously. "Is everything all right?"

Her brother stopped playing with a screech that made her wince. "Oh, you're talking to me now? I thought you were done trying to chisel sense into my great useless lump of a head."

She should have known he wouldn't forget their quarrel so easily. Ivy shut the door behind her and leaned against it. "I was angry then. I'm not now. Mica, can't we let it go? The Lighting's tomorrow, and—"

"Are you still talking to that spriggan?"

To him it was only an insult, but the word made Ivy's heart skip every time. "Stop calling him that. You don't know anything about him."

Mica made a sour face. "I know you think you love him. That doesn't mean you should. Not when there are piskey-men worth a thousand of that . . . faery fellow, and at least one who wants to marry you."

"You can't argue me into marrying Mattock," Ivy said irritably. "He's a good man, but I don't love him that way."

"Then you're stupid. What does that faery—"

"His *name* is Martin."

"—have to offer you? The only reason you even met him was because Matt and I caught him camping in an old adit, half-starved and jumping at shadows. He barely even put up a decent fight. That's no man worth having, whatever you think of his fine talk and pretty face. He can't protect you or provide for you. He doesn't even have a home!"

Martin would have, though, if he hadn't given up his share of the house so that Ivy and her family could live there. It was the hoard of the Gray Man, his long-dead father, that was paying most of their rent.

But that was Ivy's secret and none of Mica's business.

"Neither do you or Matt, right now," she retorted. "If you meet a fine piskey-maid at the Lighting, what have you got to boast of? Do you think she'll want to come back here and live in a stable?"

"That's not the point. I know how to hunt and barter and dig ore, and if I had to make my own way in the world I could do it. Your precious *Martin* can't do anything but turn into a little bird and fly away." He made a scornful flapping gesture. "And it doesn't make it any better that he taught you to do it too."

So he still disapproved of her shape-changing. Even knowing that turning herself into a swift or a peregrine was the only way Ivy would ever fly, Mica blamed her for not sticking to tradition and refusing to change at all.

"If he hadn't," Ivy snapped, "you and every piskey in the Delve would be dead by now. Or have you forgotten how I saved you all from the Claybane?"

Mica flung his bow aside in disgust. "You really don't see it, do you? That's why this is important! Our people look to you, Ivy. If you don't choose a man they approve of, you'll lose them." He passed a hand over his face, and when he took it away he no longer looked furious, only tired. "And then they'll go back to the Delve and die with Betony, because they think they've got no other choice."

Ivy stood rigid, disbelieving. Surely Mica didn't think . . . He couldn't mean . . .

"I'm only seventeen," she said at last, thickly. "And I can't be the Joan without fire. I don't have to *choose* anybody."

"So you won't? Good. Finally something we agree on." He started to his feet, but Ivy held up a hand.

"You have to stop interfering, Mica. Even if you're older and you think you know better than me, I can't help our people if you keep barging in to tell me that everything I do is wrong."

"I never—"

"Yes, you do." She held his black eyes with her own, willing herself not to flinch as he stalked closer. Mica wasn't quite as big as Mattock, but he still loomed over her like a boulder poised to fall. "You've been doing it so long you can't see it, but everyone else does. If you're so worried about our people losing faith in me, you'd better start showing a little more faith yourself."

Mica's hand clenched on the neck of the fiddle. His mouth worked, as though he were chewing all the words he had to swallow. Then he gave a curt nod, picked up the bow, and went back to playing.

Ivy soared over the old Engine House in falcon-shape, her keen peregrine eyes scanning the gorse bushes, bracken, and rocks that littered the hillside for signs of life. But apart from a wandering fox and a few mice, the land around the Delve stood empty. She swooped to land by the barred-up entrance to the Great Shaft and cocked her head to listen, but no sound floated up from the depths below.

"All quiet," she called to Thorn, who had made the three-mile flight with her on her own faery wings and looked a bit peevish about it. But the older woman had never been to the Delve before, and she refused to let Ivy carry her, so there'd been no other way. "Are you ready?"

"As long as we don't stir up a whole bees' nest of angry knockers, I am," said Thorn. "Where do you want me?"

"I'll start from here and work down." Ivy gestured to the Engine House. "And you can come up from the wood."

Thorn gave a brisk nod and flew off. Concentrating hard, Ivy walked a slow, widening spiral outward from the Great

Shaft and around the Engine House, willing the wards into place as she went. Usually it was the Joan's duty to lay the net of illusions and protective charms that kept the Lighting safe from intruders. But Betony wasn't here, and none of the other piskey-women knew how to do it, so the task had fallen to Ivy.

What her people didn't realize was that Ivy had learned all she knew about warding from the faeries—and that when Martin healed her a few months ago, he'd accidentally lent Ivy some of his strange spriggan magic as well. She could only hope no one would sense the difference.

"Done," Ivy announced when she and Thorn met in the middle of the slope. Their spells might be flimsy compared to Betony's, but for one night they ought to be good enough. "I appreciate your help. With everything."

Though the words hardly seemed adequate, after all the faeries had done. While the piskeys scurried to prepare the Lighting feast, Thorn had borrowed David Menadue's carpentry tools and turned a pile of wood scraps into three handsome and solid tables. Broch had worked hard as well, gathering fuel for the wakefire and helping Hew turn his scrambled recollections of old droll-tales into stories that actually made sense. But they'd chosen to stay away from the Lighting so as not to offend the Delve folk, which showed how unselfish their efforts had been.

Thorn, however, only shrugged. "I like woodworking," she said. "And Broch can never get enough stories, for some reason. But now I think of it, he overheard Quartz and Pick's boy—Elvar, isn't it?—plotting to prank your little sister. You might want to keep an eye out for her tonight."

It wouldn't be a Lighting without at least one good prank, so Ivy wasn't surprised. But Cicely was still moping and not in a mood to enjoy it. "I will," said Ivy.

"I'll fetch the tables, then," said Thorn, and vanished.

The twilight was deepening, and soon it would be full

dark. Ivy brushed the gorse prickles and dried bracken off her skirt and climbed back up the trail to the Engine House. A few minutes later, she'd just finished dragging the last table into place when her fellow piskeys arrived, lugging packs and driving handcarts loaded with supplies for the feast.

"I've got a surprise for you," said Gem, winking at Ivy. With a flourish he pulled a bottle out from behind his back. "Can't have a proper Lighting without piskey-wine!"

Ivy's eyes widened. "Where did you find it?"

"Brought it from the Delve when we left. It was the last of Dad's old stock, and I couldn't leave it behind for just anyone. D'you think it'll be enough?"

"Ayes, if you don't drink the lot before it gets to the rest of us," said Feldspar, poking him in the ribs as he passed by.

"'Scuse me," said Gem, thrusting the bottle at Ivy and swiping at his hunting partner. The other man ducked, chortling, and in seconds the two of them were pelting around the Engine House like wild hares while the other piskeys whooped and cheered them on.

They were making quite a commotion, but that was all for the better. Soon the sounds of music and laughter would reverberate all the way down the Great Shaft, and their underground neighbors would come creeping up to see what was going on. Once they found the bonfire lit and their fellow piskeys feasting and dancing, surely they'd be eager to join in?

If Ivy could get the piskeys who'd left the Delve and the piskeys who'd stayed behind talking to one another, good was bound to come of it. Especially if they could do it while Betony was still too weak to interfere.

Tucking Gem's bottle into the crook of her arm, Ivy turned to study the woodpile stacked by the wall of the Engine House. Thanks to Broch and a few of the younger piskey-boys they had a fine heap of branches, big enough to burn all night. But at a proper Lighting the Joan would start the wakefire with her magic, and Ivy had only a box of matches.

Should she light the fire now, while no one was looking? That would be easiest, but it didn't feel right to Ivy somehow. Usually the Joan gave a speech, and the Lighting began with great ceremony. And though Ivy wasn't the Joan, she feared her people might be offended if she didn't give at least a nod to tradition. "Cicely," she said, turning to her little sister. "I need your help."

Her sister glowed—literally, even, since she'd spent plenty of time aboveground and didn't need a wakefire to do it. "You mean it? You're not pranking me?"

"No prank, I promise," said Ivy. "I need to start the fire and say the blessing. Will you pour this bottle of piskey-wine into that big bowl over there and hand it to me when I ask for it?"

"I can do that," said Cicely, seizing the bottle eagerly. "I'll do it right now."

By the time her sister got back, the other piskeys had spotted Ivy by the woodpile and hurried to join her. Ivy gazed around the semicircle, stomach fluttering. She had to say something, but what?

"I'm not Betony," she told them, clearing her throat, "and I can't do all the things she did to make our Lightings special. But I'm glad to be here with all of you and for all the work you've done to make this feast happen. What our neighbors in the Delve will make of it, I don't know. But I hope this will prove our goodwill to them and remind them that we are all piskeys, no matter where we live or who we follow." With a tentative smile she turned away, struck a match, and dropped it into the pile.

A gust of cold wind swirled past, and the tiny flame guttered. Hastily Ivy lit another match. It tumbled into the kindling—

And with a *whoof*, the whole wakefire sprang alight. Ivy

stumbled back from its surging heat, dazzled. How had it gone
up so fast?

"She's done it!" Mattock exclaimed. "Ivy's made fire!"

Alarmed, Ivy started to protest, but Mica cut her off. "Three
cheers for our Joan!" he announced, and all the piskeys began
shouting, their skins glowing with joy and renewed hope.

None of them seemed to notice the sickly sweet smell of
petrol wafting off the woodpile. Ivy shot an incredulous stare
at Mica, but he made a cutting gesture and shook his head.
Don't say it. Don't say anything.

Was this his idea of a prank? She hadn't meant to fool her
fellow piskeys, hadn't even tried to hide the matches as she
struck them. But she'd stood with her back to the crowd, and
perhaps the darkness had hidden more than she realized.
They really seemed to think she'd lit the wakefire by magic.

"You did it!" Cicely squealed. "You finally did it!" She flung
her arms about Ivy in a jubilant hug, then picked up the bowl
of piskey-wine and thrust it at her.

Should Ivy explain that this was all a misunderstanding?
She'd have to at some point, or her people would be angry
at her for deceiving them. Yet she didn't want to embarrass
Mattock and Cicely in front of everyone, either. Maybe she'd
better keep silent for now.

Ivy lifted the bowl, willing her hands and voice steady.
"This is the Draft of Harmony. Let us drink and be one in
heart, so that our enemies can never divide us . . ."

She knew what ought to come next, or at least what Betony
had always said: *A blessing on the Delve, and a curse on faeries
and spriggans.* But she couldn't say either of those things
anymore. Ivy took a deep breath. "And that we and all our
friends may live in peace."

The piskeys looked blank, but Mattock called out, "To
peace!" and one by one the others joined in. "To peace," they
echoed, then louder as they gained confidence, *"To peace!"*

Ivy handed the bowl to Teasel, who stood on her right side. The older woman started in surprise, then took a sip and passed it to her neighbor. Little by little the draft made its way around the circle, until it came back to Ivy.

No wonder Teasel had hesitated; the Joan usually drank first. But Ivy wasn't the Joan, and it wouldn't be the first tradition she was breaking tonight. She lifted the bowl, drained it, and shook the remaining drops into the fire.

"Time to eat!" she announced, and the piskeys hurried to snatch up plates and load them with food from the tables. It was a modest feast compared to most Lightings, all of it cold except a few dishes Broch and Thorn had brought over by magic at the last minute. But judging by the enthusiasm with which her people were digging in, nobody minded.

Ivy turned slowly, her gaze searching the Engine House. Was that a glimmer of eyes in the darkness, on the other side of the fire? She wasn't sure at first, but when a shadowy figure tiptoed past the window, her doubts vanished. "All are welcome at our wakefire," she called. "Come and join us, and bring as many friends as you please!"

The shape froze, then dropped out of sight, and boots crunched on gravel as the piskey sprinted away. But was he running to invite his neighbors or rouse the Delve to attack?

Well, they'd find out soon enough. Ivy could only wait and hope the feast wouldn't end in disaster.

Once the piskeys had finished eating, Mica picked up his fiddle and struck up a dancing tune. Nobody wanted to sit and shiver, so they all linked arms for a lively winter chain-dance, while Mattock tossed more branches onto the fire. They were halfway through the third reel when a line of figures crept through the doorway of the Engine House.

They were mostly knockers by the shape of them, powerfully built piskey miners with picks and thunder-axes in hand. Ivy waved at Mica, and he stopped playing. "Do you come as friends?" she called. "If so, you'll find us friendly. Step forward, and warm yourselves by our fire."

Please, she prayed silently. Her followers were unarmed except for a few hunting knives, and if the knockers attacked, they'd have to flee or die.

There was a long, wary silence as the two groups of piskeys stared at one another. At last one grizzled old knocker lowered his thunder-axe and propped it against the wall. "Do you fancy yourself the new Joan, then?" he demanded.

"I don't claim to be anyone but myself," Ivy replied. "We're not here to make trouble."

"But she did light the wakefire, Copper," Gem shouted from behind her, and Feldspar added, "Ayes, she did!"

Copper waved a hand at the other men, who lowered their tools. The last ran to the door of the Engine House and returned with a nervous-looking group of women and youngsters, huddling close and casting longing glances at the fire. An old auntie coughed, the chesty rasp that came from breathing the Delve's poisoned air, and Jenny's mother Moss hurried over to take the woman's arm.

"I know how that feels," she soothed. "It's a dreadful cough, isn't it? Come sit by the fire, and you'll soon feel better."

And with that, the tension broke. The Delve folk swarmed the wakefire, holding out their hands to its warmth. Fern fetched a platter of saffron buns and offered them to the newcomers, while Hew refilled the blackened kettle and set it on for tea. Mica struck up a hornpipe, and Elvar began to dance it, skinny legs flailing as the older men cheered him on.

Ivy's followers were barely more than twenty, and the piskeys who'd come up from the Delve to join them were perhaps fifteen more. Which meant there were still over two hundred of Ivy's people underground—including all the children ten and younger, and the old ones too feeble to reach the surface. They'd made a start, but there was still a long way to go.

White wings shirred the darkness at the corner of Ivy's eye, and with a leap of her heart she spun about. A barn owl landed silently in the window of the Engine House, its heart-shaped face tilted like a question. Then it launched itself into the night.

Longing swelled in Ivy until she could scarcely breathe. She glanced at the bonfire, where her fellow piskeys were dancing. Would they notice if she slipped away for a few minutes? Would it worry them even if they did?

She'd told Mica she didn't have to choose anyone. What he didn't realize was that her choice was already made, and the only way to unmake it was to unmake herself. Backing into the shadows, Ivy changed to falcon-shape and flew after Martin.

She found him at the far edge of the wood, where the trees sloped into a little valley, and the moonlight glimmered on the slow-moving brook below. He looked pale as hoarfrost, but when he saw Ivy gliding toward him, his smile blazed up like the wakefire itself. Ivy dropped out of falcon-shape, hit the ground running, and threw herself into his arms.

Martin caught her easily and swung her around with a laugh that made her shiver. "Well," he said, dropping his hands to her waist, "there's no need to ask if you're glad to see me. May I?"

"Please," breathed Ivy, and raised her face to his.

Their first—and until now, only—kiss had been a desperate, hurried impulse, clumsy with grief and the knowledge that others were watching. This one felt like a new beginning, a secret treasure for just the two of them to share.

"Ah, Ivy," Martin murmured, a timeless moment later. "You've no idea how long I've dreamed about that sweet mouth of yours."

Her cheeks flamed, but she wouldn't let him fluster her so easily. "I know exactly how long," she retorted. "You didn't dream at all until I gave you back your memories, and that was barely two weeks ago."

"I meant daydreams, you impertinent minx. And you know better than to take anything I say literally."

"Or seriously?"

"That, either. Except for this." His voice lowered. "I love you, Ivy of the Delve."

After all he'd suffered for her sake, Ivy had no reason to doubt it. But hearing the words was enough to still her blood and take her breath away. She opened her mouth, but Martin stopped it with a gentle finger.

"Don't steal my dramatic moment," he said. "Or make promises you might not be able to keep."

"It's not fair," she whispered, dropping her face against his shoulder. She could feel his ribs even through the fabric of his jacket; whatever he'd been eating as an owl or an ermine, it wasn't enough to sustain him for long. "I want us to be together."

"You understand, then. Why I couldn't stay."

"Of course." She tightened her arms around him, trying to share her warmth. "I know you're not afraid of Mica—"

"I absolutely am. Have you *seen* your brother?"

"Hush," she said irritably. Yes, Mica was big even by piskey standards, and Martin disliked physical combat. But he had unusual strength for his size, and if he hadn't been exhausted the first time they'd fought, her brother wouldn't have won so easily. "I know you left for my sake, and I'd be a fool to blame you for it. You're right that Mica doesn't understand, and the rest of my people wouldn't either. But . . ." She drew back, gazing into his face. "That doesn't mean there's no hope."

"Ivy," he began, soft with pity, but she cut him off.

"My people are starting to change, Martin. They're learning better. The way they've accepted Thorn and Broch—the way they've accepted *me*, even knowing I can change shape—and look what's happening right now, here, tonight!" She shook him for emphasis. "They *will* understand, someday. We just have to give it time."

"You never give up, do you?" He kissed her again, lightly. "Well, I won't argue with you. I don't know about your people changing, but you weren't wrong to hold out hope for me."

She'd seldom seen Martin look so serious. "What happened?" she asked. "Why did Queen Valerian let you go?"

Martin took her hand and led her to a fallen log, where the two of them could sit together. "I don't know. When Rob dragged me into her council chamber, I thought execution was the best I could hope for."

He rubbed his face wearily. "I *tried* to make her do it, Ivy. When she asked if I deserved punishment, I told her I did. When she asked what I'd done to deserve it, I told her every sin I'd ever committed—the lies, the betrayals, the murders, all the filthy things I did to serve the Empress and save my own wretched skin. I thought if she knew all that, she'd decide prison was too good for me and have Rob cut off my head."

And from what Ivy knew of Rob, he'd probably have been glad to do it. He'd never forgive Martin for killing the kindly old man who'd taught him music, even if the evil faery Empress had left Martin no choice but to obey.

"When she asked what I'd do if she pardoned me . . ." Martin's voice roughened. He was shivering now, with cold or with memory, so Ivy put an arm around him. "I thought she was mocking me. I was angry enough to spit, until I looked up and saw her face."

He stared out into the darkness, gazing at something Ivy couldn't see. "She wasn't anything like the Empress. It never crossed her mind to offer me hope and then snatch it away. She meant it, Ivy. She was giving me a chance to start over."

"So you swore you'd come back here and never leave Cornwall again?"

"Not exactly." He gave a shaky laugh. "First, I fell on my

knees and bawled like a mooncalf. Then I told her I'd do anything she asked. She said, 'Will you give me your name?' and it felt like she'd ripped my guts out. But I crawled up to her and whispered it, I was that desperate. And instead of using it to enslave me like the Empress did, she gave it back to me. Forever."

"Gave it *back*?" Ivy had never heard of such a thing. Knowing a faery's true name gave you the power to command them absolutely, and that didn't seem like something Queen Valerian could forget even if she wanted to.

"I know. I didn't think it was possible. But when she told me I was free, I could *feel* the truth in it. In her." He exhaled slowly, his breath frosting the air. "The Oakenfolk think she made me swear a blood oath not to come back to England. But she only asked for my word. As if . . . that was enough."

No wonder he'd looked so awestruck when he first came back to Ivy. She'd met Valerian only briefly, when she'd begged the Oakenfolk to heal her dying mother, but the queen's wisdom had impressed Ivy then—and her compassion astonished her now. Betony would never have shown such mercy.

"So here I am," Martin said, shifting to face her. "And this time I mean to stay. Will you come with me?"

Ivy recoiled, startled. "Where?"

"I've found a place, one of my father's old troves. It's not much, but I'm making it better. We could hide there, just the two of us, and no one would know."

Ivy gazed at him, aching inside. Martin had changed for the better in so many ways, but he still thought like a fugitive. She couldn't blame him: he was the last spriggan left in the world, and hiding was the only reason he was still alive. But she couldn't follow his example, especially now.

"My people need me, Martin. I haven't found them a proper home yet, and I can't leave until they're safe from Betony. And Cicely's not been happy since our mother left . . ."

"Did she?" He frowned, then his face cleared. "Ah. Of course. David?"

Ivy nodded. "And Molly. The house here isn't safe anymore, now Betony knows where to find it."

"Which means it isn't safe for you, either." His voice was edged with frustration. "Why are you still putting yourself in danger? You've done more than enough for your people already. If they can't see that now, they never will."

"You don't understand. They think I'm their Joan. I know that's not true, but until they find another leader, I'm the best hope they've got."

"Their weakness isn't your problem, Ivy. And even if you think it's your duty to help them, that doesn't prove that you can." He took her hands, thumbs caressing her knuckles. "If Betony comes for your people, how are you going to stop her? Your people might think you can make fire, but we both know better."

So he'd been watching her in the Engine House, long before she noticed. Well, it wouldn't be the first time. "We don't know Betony will get her fire back," Ivy said, trying to ignore the hard clench of her stomach. "And I won't give up on my people until there's nothing more I can do."

Martin sighed. "I knew you'd say that. But you can't blame me for—" His head came up. "What was that?"

For a moment Ivy wondered what he was talking about. Then her ears caught the sound of distant shouting, and the sizzling crack of a thunder-axe jolted her to her feet. "The Lighting!" she gasped, and willed herself back to the Engine House.

As soon as she landed Cicely pelted toward her, braids flying. "They just burst in—we couldn't stop them. What do we do?"

The wakefire still burned, but there was no more merriment in the Engine House. Thorn's tables lay overturned and broken, food and drink spilling across the stones, and Ivy's people cowered back as a rank of piskey hunters advanced on them. Mica, Mattock, and a trembling Elvar had drawn their own knives in answer, and a few of the Delve's knockers stood with them. But they'd left their thunder-axes on the other side of the wakefire, and without them they didn't have a chance.

"Stop!" Ivy shouted, and the leader of the hunters swung to face her. It was Gossan, his handsome face set with fury.

"You. How dare you come to *our* Engine House and offer our people false fire? You're no Joan—you're hardly even a piskey. Give yourself up and tell your people to surrender, or we'll kill you all."

The Gossan she'd grown up with would never have spoken so harshly. He'd always seemed gentle compared to his wife, patient and slow to anger. Had the toxic air of the Delve poisoned his mind?

"We're not here to fight," Ivy said, spreading her hands. "We were only trying to help. Let us leave in peace, and we won't trouble you again."

"You've made nothing but trouble since you were born," Gossan said coldly. He nodded to his hunters. "Take them."

"Wait!" cried Ivy. "We surren—"

Wind blasted through the Engine House, and the wakefire exploded, sparks raining in all directions. Gossan's men yelped and dropped their weapons, slapping their clothes in panic—but to Ivy's astonishment, her people weren't touched by the fire at all. It was as though some invisible shield was protecting them.

The knockers who'd joined her ran for their thunder-axes, while the ones who hadn't bolted. Gossan whirled, eyes wild, as a pair of blurred figures appeared from nowhere, grabbed some of Ivy's followers, and vanished with them. By the time the Jack managed to gather his scattered hunters, there were hardly any piskeys left for them to fight.

"Away, you starvelings," boomed a rich, rolling voice out of the darkness. "You elf-skins, you dried neat's tongues! Would thou wert clean enough to spit upon, thou poisonous, bunch-backed toads! I'd beat thee, but I would infect my hands. Exeunt!"

Oh, blast and smelt it, Ivy thought weakly. It was Martin, and he was thoroughly enjoying himself. He must have leaped to the house to find Thorn and Broch, urged them to rescue Ivy's people while he provided a distraction, and now he was playing the role of the evil giant—or spriggan—with all the melodrama he'd learned on stage.

Meanwhile Mica and Mattock stood their ground, knives drawn, and the remaining few knockers stayed with them. Iron stopped faery magic, so Thorn and Broch couldn't whisk them away. But it didn't matter. By the time Martin finished cursing them, the Jack and all his soldiers had fled.

"Picks and hammers!" Quartz danced excitedly, leaving muddy boot prints all over the barn floor. "How'd you do it, Ivy? That was the best prank I've ever seen!"

"Stop your gabble, boy," Hew told him sternly. "What happened tonight was no joke."

"But the look on Gossan's face!"

"Enough of that. Get on with you." He pushed the boy toward the stall where his mother waited, then laid a hand on Ivy's shoulder. "All right, me bird?"

Ivy nodded, too shaken to reply. She'd come so close to losing all the good people who'd followed her. If Martin hadn't intervened, they'd be captured or dead by now.

"Ah, Ivy-bird, don't look like that." Hew turned her to

face him, his weathered face lined with sympathy. "T'wasn't your fault. You did the best you could, and we're no worse off for it." He gestured to the new arrivals, who were tentatively exploring the barn while the other piskeys made up straw beds for them to sleep on. "And for these folk, it's all the better."

Perhaps, Ivy thought, but for how long? The box stalls were already crowded, so the newcomers would have to sleep in the corridor. She'd invited them to the house, but like the others they'd refused, so the best she could do was offer food and water and the few blankets she could spare. And though Martin had left her with a good pile of human money, she'd spent much of it already. If she couldn't find a new home for her people, she'd soon have nothing left to offer them.

Teasel must have noticed Ivy's troubled look, because she marched up and shooed Hew away. "I'll see to our young Joan," she said firmly. "Off to bed with you. I'll be there dreckly."

I'm not the Joan, Ivy wanted to protest, but how could she? The piskeys who'd joined them at the Lighting had barely settled in yet, and she feared to disappoint them. So she let Teasel lead her to the other end of the barn, where she could confess without being overheard.

But the older woman spoke first, hushed and urgent. "Bless the day you brought those faeries to join us. We'd have been in a right stew tonight if it weren't for them. But how do we repay them? A life-debt's a costly burden, and we've no treasure here fit to give."

Ivy was taken aback. She hadn't realized her people understood faery bargains so well, or were prepared to take them so seriously. "I don't think they'd want gold or jewels anyway," she said. "Only our willingness to help them in turn, if they're ever in need or danger."

Teasel looked relieved. "Ayes, that would be fine. But . . ." Her grip on Ivy's arm tightened. "What of the other one, him who frightened Gossan and his bully-boys away?"

Ivy winced. She'd hoped her fellow piskeys wouldn't guess what had really happened—that like Quartz they'd think Ivy had blown up the wakefire with magic and assume the Shakespearean insults had come from Broch. But Teasel was sharp-eared as well as sharp-witted, and not much escaped her.

"He's . . . a friend," Ivy said, hoping her discomfort wasn't obvious. "And he did it to help me, not to put you in debt. You needn't worry."

Teasel's eyes narrowed, and Ivy braced herself for more questions. But the older woman only sighed. "Get some sleep then," she said, and padded off to rejoin her husband.

For a wild moment Ivy nearly dashed after her. She still hadn't told the truth about the wakefire, and she longed for Teasel's advice. But then she caught sight of Mica standing halfway up the corridor, arms folded and eyes hard as basalt, and her nerve failed. She wasn't up to another clash with him right now.

I'll tell her tomorrow, Ivy promised herself, and hurried away.

Thorn met Ivy coming out of the barn and fell into step with her. "I've put a few more wards about," she said. "Not that we're likely to need them tonight, but it never hurts to be careful. You'll want to make stronger ones, though, in case Gossan and his folk come looking for you."

The faery woman was right, but that too would have to wait for tomorrow. The first pangs of a headache tapped Ivy's skull like a tiny hammer, warning her she'd done enough magic for one night.

We could hide, just the two of us, Martin had said, and she'd refused like the loyal, hard-working piskey she was. But right now Ivy longed to take falcon-shape and fly off to him, if only to forget her worries for a while.

"My people aren't safe here," Ivy told the faeries the next morning, her hands clenched around her teacup. "I know that. But all the mines I've found so far are either flooded too deep to live in or poisoned just like the Delve."

Broch and Thorn sat across from her at the breakfast table, arms folded and heads cocked in matching looks of deliberation; it would have been funny, if Ivy weren't too exhausted to appreciate it. She'd gone straight to bed last night as Teasel suggested, but her thoughts were such a tangle she hadn't slept at all.

"Does it have to be a mine?" Broch inquired. "What about a cave or a burrow?"

Ivy shook her head. "Caves are for spriggans. And burrows are dirty. We're miners, not rabbits."

Though it hadn't always been that way. Long ago, as she and Martin had discovered, the magical folk of Kernow had all lived in peace together. The knockers worked the mines alongside the humans, while the piskeys dwelt in cunningly hidden villages on the surface. But first Ivy's people had fallen out with the spriggans, and then they'd gone to war against the faeries as well. There'd been so much pillaging and slaughter on all sides that it was no longer safe aboveground, so the piskeys had joined the remaining knockers in the Delve—and now they'd lived underground so long they couldn't imagine living any other way.

"What about one of those old mine buildings you've got cluttering up the landscape?" asked Thorn. "You can hardly throw an acorn without hitting one. If we fixed the roof and stopped up the gaps—"

"We'd have to constantly guard it from humans," Ivy said. "And it still wouldn't be big enough for all of us. The Engine House is good enough for a Lighting, but we need more space to live."

"Trees are no use either, I suppose. Not that I've seen any good ones about here." Thorn grimaced. "This *is* a knot in the grain."

Ivy nodded glumly. Right now, the only way she could think of to protect her people was to teach them the magic she'd learned from Martin and the faeries. They'd never agree to change shape, and most of them probably couldn't do it anyway, but they'd all heard droll-tales of how their ancestors could leap from one place to another at will. It wouldn't be easy to convince them, but if the only alternative was surrender . . .

"There's one thing we haven't considered," said Broch. He sounded reluctant—but he'd also said *we*, and Ivy felt a surge of hope.

"What?" she asked, sitting up.

"Fighting back."

Thorn groaned. "I should have known that was coming."

"You disagree?"

"No, I just wish I could. Go on."

Broch put his hand over hers and turned to Ivy. "If moving isn't an option, you need better defenses. Don't let Gossan and his soldiers catch you unprepared. Stand up to them instead of running, and they may decide to leave you alone."

If it were only Gossan in charge, Ivy might have agreed. But she knew her aunt too well to think that Betony would give up that easily. Every piskey who'd left the Delve was a threat to her, and Ivy most of all.

Still, Broch had a point. Ivy and her people might not be soldiers, but they'd be foolish not to try to protect themselves. Patrolling the nearby countryside—and making more weapons—would be a good start.

"I'll talk to the others," Ivy said, pushing her chair back decisively. "We'll see what we can do."

"All clear on the west side," said Mattock, wrestling out of his sopping overcoat. "Not even Betony's mad enough to go out in this weather."

The rain had started early that morning—not the light showers common in wintertime or the drenching mist known as "mizzle," but a heavy, gust-driven downpour that rattled the roof slates and dripped from the rafters. A rivulet snaked down the barn corridor, and the bucket under the biggest leak was already half full.

"Ayes," said Hew, inspecting the bin lid he'd been hammering into a shield. "It's henting down."

"What about Mica?" Ivy asked, as Mattock gratefully accepted a mug of hot chicory from Teasel. "I thought you went out together."

"We split up at the edge of the wood." He glanced around. "You mean he's not back yet?"

Gem put down the whetstone he'd been using to sharpen the hayfork and sat back, rolling his stiff shoulder. "No sign of him."

That was odd. Mica didn't usually wander so far, and since he still refused to travel by magic, he'd have a long walk home—what her people called a "fair stank."

Still, her brother was as healthy as anyone, and a soaking wouldn't hurt him. "I'm sure he'll turn up," Ivy said. "If he'd run into trouble, we'd have heard him bellowing by now."

The older men chuckled at that, and even Mattock cracked a grin. He sat down by the fire and began to unlace his boots.

"Mam, I'm wet!" Thrift jumped up, flapping her skirt. A new leak had started above the box stall. Hastily the piskey-women shuffled to make room for her, while Quartz ran to fetch another bucket.

The creaking above was getting louder, and it worried Ivy. The barn's stone walls seemed solid enough, but the wooden beams and roof trusses were old, as were the slates that covered them. "I think we should move everyone into the house," she said. "At least until it passes and the barn has a chance to dry."

"It's too late for that," Mattock told her. "The little ones are scared enough of the storm without dragging them out in it, and the aunties couldn't go two steps without being blown off their feet. We'll just have to wait."

Surely the weather couldn't be *that* bad. Ivy hurried to the barn door, cracked it ajar—and the wind nearly ripped it from her hands. She caught the edge and clung on, heart hammering. Outside, rain swept the cobbles in sheets, and an army of black clouds was marching up the horizon.

Where could Mica have got to? Even he wasn't fool enough to keep patrolling in this weather. He'd taken to his new guard duties with surprising relish, but he hated being wet even more than Matt did . . .

"Ivy!"

Martin dropped out of owl-shape and sprinted across the yard toward her. "The worst storm in a century, they're calling it," he panted. "It's tearing up the coast. Is everyone safe?"

Dread clutched at Ivy. "Mica's still out there. How much time do we have?"

"Not much. I raced it all the way from Land's End."

No wonder he looked exhausted. "I have to find him," Ivy said. She slammed the door shut behind her and threw herself into the wind.

In peregrine-shape she was a powerful flier, but she'd never fought a gale like this one. No matter how hard she beat her wings, it kept trying to blow her away. Martin flapped after her, barely keeping pace—his barn owl wasn't as streamlined as Ivy's falcon. Soon he dropped to the ground and changed to his ermine form instead.

Thunder rumbled as Ivy zigzagged across the pasture, skimming over the back fence into the strip of woodland beyond. There was a path here, though muddy and half-submerged already, and by its edge she spotted the print of an old-fashioned and inhumanly small mining boot.

Ivy landed in her own shape, and the rain soaked her in an instant. She clung to an overhanging branch as the wind threatened to rip her off her feet. "Mica!" she yelled hoarsely. "Mica, where are you?"

No answer. Ivy changed to swift-shape and darted onward, zooming among the trees. If she went much further, she'd be halfway to the Delve. Surely Mica knew better than to go that way alone?

"Ivy!" Martin shouted behind her, faint with distance. "I've found them!"

Shaky with relief, Ivy veered back to him. She'd missed the spot in her panic, but there sat her brother at the foot of a tree trunk, clutching something—no, some*one*—in his arms. A young piskey-woman, clad in a tattered jacket and mud-soaked skirts. Her face was hidden by the wild tangle of her hair, but it almost looked like . . .

"Here," Martin said, reaching out. "I'll take her back to the barn."

"You're not touching her, spriggan," Mica growled, then yelped as Ivy cuffed him.

"Don't be a dross-wit!" she snapped. "If we stay here we're all going to die!"

"I'll die a thousand times before I—" Mica began hotly, but then his eyes rolled and he slumped over. With one smart tap on the forehead, Martin had put him to sleep.

He was going to be furious when he woke, but right now Ivy couldn't have cared less. As Martin lifted the unconscious girl, she threw her arms about Mica's shoulders and willed them both to the barn.

"Yarrow!" Teasel gasped when the four of them materialized, rushing to help Martin lay the young woman down. "Great diggings, she looks half-dead. Where did you find her?"

"Mica found her," Ivy said, staggering with the effort not to drop her brother into a puddle. "And we just found him. Matt . . ."

"I've got him." Mattock stepped in quickly to lift Mica's weight from her shoulders. "Ugh! He's soaked."

So was Ivy. Her black curls dripped down her forehead, and her wet jeans chafed and chilled her. Only the warmth of her wool coat kept her teeth from chattering. "Will she be all right?" she asked the women bustling around Yarrow.

Teasel, who had covered the girl with blankets and was briskly peeling off her wet clothes under them, spoke without looking up. "Right enough, once we get her warm. Her heart's strong, that's the main thing."

No need to ask Broch to heal her, then. That was a mercy. But to leave the Delve, especially in such weather, Yarrow must have been desperate. What had happened?

Mica might know, but the longer he slept, the better. Martin stood with her, and this time Ivy wouldn't let anyone chase him away. She seized his arm and tugged him into the light.

"This is Martin," she told her fellow piskeys. "He saved my life when I first left the Delve. He led me to my mother, and . . . and now he's helped save Yarrow and Mica."

It was tempting to mention how he'd scared off Gossan and his troops only two nights ago, but whistling up a wind strong enough to blow a wakefire to pieces was spriggan magic. If she let them think Martin was just another faery, though, they might give him a chance. "So I hope you'll make him welcome," Ivy continued, "because I'm not sending him out in this—"

Her voice was lost in a deafening clap of thunder, and the electric lights fizzled out. Dodger whinnied, and the piskey children squealed in terror. They'd never heard storms like this in the Delve.

"It's all right," Ivy soothed. At least she and the other piskeys had their skin-glow, so they weren't totally in the dark. "I know it sounds terrible, but—"

Cold gusted through the barn as the door to the yard banged open. Ivy dashed to close it, Martin racing after her. But they'd no sooner yanked it shut and shoved the latch into place than the roof gave way. A whole line of slates slid off, and the rain came pouring in.

Ivy was already wet, but this was like being drenched in an ice bath. She staggered against Martin, as the slates fell with a tinkling crash to the cobbles outside. The wind caught the roof's corner, and laths popped and splintered as the beam above them began to *lift—*

Martin flung up his hands. "Quick," he gasped. His arms were stiff, fingers splayed wide; he was holding the roof in place with the sheer power of his magic. "Cover the hole."

"Move!" Ivy yelled to her fellow piskeys, who stood frozen with shock. "Patch the roof! Hurry!"

Feldspar was the first to recover, scrambling up the ladder to the half loft. He grabbed the edge of a floorboard and yanked it up, rusty nails popping in all directions. Mattock and Gem rushed to help him, while Hew rummaged through David Menadue's toolbox for a hammer.

Meanwhile Martin stood in the drenching rain, arms upraised and teeth bared in concentration. The howling wind died, and an eerie hush fell over the barn; the only sounds were the crack of wood and the grunts of the laboring piskey-men as they hauled the planks down to ground level.

Martin wasn't just holding the beam in place, Ivy realized with shivering wonder. He was pushing the wind away from the barn at the same time—literally holding back the storm. But the blood had drained from his face, and his legs swayed like a drunken miner's. If he collapsed, the gale would come rushing back and they'd lose the whole roof at once.

Instinct told Ivy what to do, and she obeyed it without hesitation. She flung her arms around Martin, willing her own power into him.

A tremor rippled through him, followed by a wave of sparkling heat. The shadows around them fled as Ivy's skin-glow leaped up to envelop them both. She barely noticed the piskey-men rushing past her, swarming up the wall of Dodger's box stall and onto the splintered beam.

Ivy's magic had never been especially strong for a piskey's. Changing shape was her one extraordinary skill, and even that hadn't come easily. But she'd spent her whole life making up for her weakness with sheer determination, and though Ivy felt her strength flagging she refused to hold back. Her people were counting on her—*Martin* was counting on her. Nothing else mattered.

How long she clung to Martin, Ivy couldn't tell. She felt frozen to the marrows of her bones, and the roof patching seemed to take forever—her people were used to working with stone, not wood, and scarcely knew what they were doing. If only Thorn were here to help! But Ivy didn't dare let go of Martin to look for her, so all she could do was wait and hope.

"Done it!" Mattock shouted, boots clumping as he leaped down. Martin stood for one last moment, rigid with the effort of holding back the storm. Then he sagged against Ivy, and the two of them tumbled to the floor.

She wanted to cover him with grateful kisses, but she didn't dare. Hastily she untangled herself, and turned to her fellow piskeys. "We're safe," she panted. The storm sounded less fierce now, the wind softening and the rain slowing to a patter. "Good work, all of you. All of *us*."

She'd expected smiles from the men who'd patched the roof and relieved sighs from the women. But they all stood silent, glaring at her.

No, not at her. At Martin. He lay on the floor by Ivy's feet, his pale hair plastered to his forehead. His eyes were dull with exhaustion, and in his wet clothes he looked thinner than ever. Nothing like the coldly beautiful faeries of piskey legend, and everything like the enemy her people feared most of all—a ragged, hungry spriggan.

Hew raised his hammer, and the younger men reached for their knives. "Step away, me bird. We'll handle this."

"Are you mad?" Ivy burst out. "He just saved our lives!"

"He'd like us to think so," Pick retorted, adding a terse, "Hold, boy," as his son Elvar started to edge away. "But we know his sort, even if you don't. He won't cast his tricksy spells on us."

"What are you saying?" Somehow she had to stall for time and let Martin get his strength back. Right now he was too drained to sit up, let alone leap away. "You can't think he's a—"

"Spriggan." The voice was Mica's, thick with sleep and rage. He stalked up with their father's thunder-axe over his shoulder, and Mattock stepped back to let him pass. "I knew it. Get away from him, Ivy."

"No!" She moved to block him, arms spread wide. "This is wrong. Even if he is . . . what you say, he's done nothing but help us. There's no justice in treating him like this."

"Ivy-bird," began Hew, pained, but she cut him off.

"If you kill him, you'll be murderers. Is that how you want them to think of you?" She jerked her chin at the women and children huddled at the back of the barn. "Do you think they'll be proud of you for smashing a boy's head in? Especially when he's unarmed and exhausted, and you outnumber him ten to one?"

"He's bewitched you, Ivy." Mattock spoke heavily, his blue eyes dark with anguish. "That's what spriggans do. I know he told you he was a faery, but we all saw what he did."

"Ayes," said Gem. "Only spriggans can charm the wind and weather—everyone knows that. And what's to prove he saved us? For all we know, he brought the storm on us himself!"

At the back of the barn, Thrift began to cry. Her mother stooped to comfort her, but no one else moved.

"You should be ashamed of yourselves." Ivy was so furious she was shaking. "You're so afraid, you can't even see the truth when it's right in front of you. How can Martin be a spriggan, when even Betony agrees the spriggans died out thirty years ago? You should know that, Hew—you killed the last of them yourself!"

The older men shuffled uneasily. They couldn't explain that, and there was no way they'd ever guess the truth. "If there's any doubt that Martin's our enemy, we've no right to treat him like one," Ivy insisted. "It's only fair to give him a chance."

Behind her Martin sat up, pushing the wet hair from his eyes, and the cold fear in Ivy's chest thawed a little. If she could keep her men distracted a few minutes longer . . .

"If there's any chance he *is* a spriggan," Pick argued, "we can't take the risk. Not now he's seen our women and little ones, and knows where we live." He glanced around at his fellow hunters. "All right, boys?"

The men started forward, but Ivy held up her hands. "Stop!"

She had only one hope left to save Martin, and if it failed she'd be ruined with him. But Mica had handed her this coin when he put petrol on the wakefire, and Ivy wouldn't give up without spending it. She drew herself up defiantly. "You called me Joan at the Lighting. Am I your Joan, or not?"

Mica glowered: he knew what she was doing, and he hated it. But he kept his mouth shut. The other men traded uncertain looks, and finally Hew said, "Ayes, you're our Joan now."

"Then it's my right to judge what's good for our people. And letting you kill a stranger just because you think he *might* do something bad is not." She dropped her arms, standing as tall and dignified as she could. "Put down your weapons. Now."

For a few tense seconds no one moved. Then Mica grimaced, lowered the thunder-axe, and set it down. Mattock sheathed his knife, and one by one the other hunters did likewise.

Ivy let her breath out. It was the biggest gamble she'd ever taken, and she'd come dangerously close to losing both Martin and her people's trust. Which was why she had to be careful, very careful, what she did now.

"Martin," she said, keeping her back to him, "I command you to tell the truth. Are you a spriggan?"

His answer came softly, hollow with defeat. "I am."

The piskey-women gasped, tugging their children behind them, and the men gave grim nods as Ivy went on. "Are there any more spriggans in Kernow? Or anywhere else you know of?"

"None. I am the last."

Ivy turned to face him, mouth stern and eyes expressionless. Trying to look like a queen passing judgment, instead of a girl saying goodbye to the boy she loved.

"Well, then," she said. "One spriggan can do little harm to

anyone. But you must leave this homestead and never return so long as my people dwell here. And you must swear not to cast a spell or raise a weapon against us as long as you live."

"Not even to defend myself?" Martin's eyes narrowed. "You drive a hard bargain, lady."

"Harder where there's none," Ivy told him, aching with memory. So much tenderness had passed between them since they last spoke those words to each other, but she couldn't falter now. "Do you want to live? Then swear."

"I swear it." He shifted to one knee and bowed his head before her. "I will go far away, and do no harm to you or your followers even if it costs me my life. I swear it by my blood, my hoard, and my true name."

"If you break your promise," Ivy warned, "my men will kill you. You must never be seen here again in *any* form, do you understand?"

Please understand, she begged silently, hoping Martin could hear her. *I'd rather lose you forever than have to watch you die.*

"I understand." Martin looked up at her, his gray eyes rimmed red. "I will obey you—my Joan." Then he vanished.

"**M**y Joan." Teasel clucked her tongue. "Can you believe the cheek!" She tucked another blanket around the sleeping Yarrow and rose, brushing straw from her skirt. "But you served that spriggan right, I'd say."

Ivy stood silent, her throat too tight for words. She'd never meant to claim the title of Joan at all, let alone so boldly. If she'd had enough confidence she'd have told the truth about the Lighting days ago and let her people choose someone else to lead them—but now she was glad she hadn't, for Martin's sake.

"He'd better not show his pointy nose here again," Teasel went on darkly. "Or he'll find my fist in it. *My Joan* indeed! As if a spriggan had any right!" She patted Ivy's shoulder. "You've had quite a shock, me bird, but it's over now. Go and get dry."

She'd never have dared talk to Betony like that, let alone touch her with such familiarity. But she thought nothing of doing it with Ivy. How could her fellow piskeys obey her one moment and boss her about the next? They might call her their Joan, but they hardly acted as though they believed it. No more than Ivy did herself.

Yet a strange thing had happened when she'd spoken up to save Martin. She'd been playing a role at first, trying to imitate Queen Valerian's grave dignity and imagine what she would say. But as she did so, she'd felt a strange peace inside, and the right words had come to her lips with no thought or preparation at all . . .

"What in the name of all that's green and growing—?" Thorn spluttered. She stood in the doorway with fists on hips, staring up at the clumsily patched roof. "Which one of you pebble-heads made such a crow's dinner of this?"

A roar of laughter rose from the piskey-men as Gem got up and sauntered over, grinning at her. "We're miners, me lover, not carpenters. We'll mend the slates and mortar, if you'll sort the rest."

Thorn only wrinkled her nose at the endearment—she'd got used to the piskeys' Cornish slang and knew better than to take it literally. "The wood needs to dry out first," she said. "And in this weather that won't be easy."

Gem glanced hopefully at Ivy, who pretended not to notice. With any luck he'd think up his own reasons why his Joan might not choose to conjure fire in such an awkward, high-up place, and never guess it was because Ivy couldn't do it.

"As soon as you're ready, then," Gem said with a shrug. "We'll get to the slates dreckly."

Thorn probably didn't know that meant "when we feel like it" instead of "straight away," because she looked mollified and said no more. Ivy was about to take her outside and tell her what had happened with Martin when little Thrift cried, "She's woke up!"

Yarrow had bolted upright, eyes wild and face ghastly. Ivy hurried to her. "It's all right. You're safe here."

Fern and Teasel bustled over to make the young healer more comfortable, while Daisy shut the door of the box stall to keep the other piskeys from peering in. "How do you feel?" Ivy asked.

Yarrow's gaze darted in all directions, as though reassuring herself the barn and the other piskey-women were real. "Like I've woken from a nightmare," she whispered.

"Never you mind," said Teasel, draping a blanket around her shoulders. "You had a fair stank from the Delve in that foul weather, and it's a good thing Mica found you in time. But you were right to come to us."

Yarrow gave a hysterical laugh. "Right? Nothing's right. We'll never be right again."

"What do you mean?" Ivy asked sharply. The Delve's healer had always been calm and levelheaded; this wasn't like her at all. "What happened?"

The healer's face crumpled. "Shale," she faltered, and burst into tears.

It took a long time for Ivy and the women to comfort her: every touch and kind word only seemed to make Yarrow more distraught. But at last she wiped her eyes and stammered out her story.

Last night she'd gone down to Betony's stateroom as usual, to bring the Joan her evening dose of medicine. Her wound was healing, but she was still flushed and slightly feverish, and Yarrow feared she might have an infection. When she reached the Joan's chambers she'd lifted the ring to knock, only to hear a horrible scream from inside. Alarmed, Yarrow rushed in— and found Shale lying on the stones by Betony and Gossan's feet, charred almost beyond recognition.

"She'd burned him to death," she choked. "Just like she did Jenny."

Moss's hands flew to her mouth, and Ivy's stomach twisted in horror. She still had nightmares about Jenny, as did all the people who'd loved her. No one who'd seen her die would ever forget it.

"But why?" blurted Daisy, her hands over Thrift's ears. The little girl squirmed, but her mother refused to let go. "What harm could poor silly Shale do anyone?"

"He talked too much," Ivy said heavily. "He told Mattock what was happening in the Delve."

"I thought it was the poison," Yarrow murmured. "I thought she'd grown sick in her mind, and I pitied her. But she's worse than mad—she's *evil*—"

A sob wracked her, and she buried her face in her arms. Teasel patted her gently and gazed at the circle of women.

"So," she said. "Betony's got her fire back."

And she's angry, Ivy thought, feeling queasy. *Angry enough to kill.*

The road beyond the house was littered with fallen branches, the front garden flat and muddy as a giant's footprint. Ivy stood at the front window, rubbing her arms. She'd dried off and changed her clothes, but she still felt cold.

"I really thought we had a chance," she said to the faeries, who sat on the sofa behind her. "Even if Gossan and his men came. But now . . ."

"You're not doomed yet, by the sound of it," Thorn pointed out. "We're a three-mile walk from the Delve here, and if Betony's still weak, she won't be making it soon."

"Which means there's time to move your people," added Broch, "if we can find a safe place for them."

Ivy let out a slow breath. They were right, but that was a big *if.* And Gossan could still attack at any time, even without Betony's help.

"We could teach your people battle magic," Thorn suggested. "Broch and I know a few spells from when we fought the Empress."

"I don't think they'd let you." Ivy turned away from the

window and slumped into a chair. "Every time I think my people are changing for the better, something happens to remind me they don't really want to change at all."

Thorn sighed. "I'm going to regret saying this, but if Martin's been poking the wasps' nest, then Queen Valerian ought to know about it. I'm pretty sure she didn't spare his life just so your people could execute him instead."

Ivy looked up sharply. "How did you . . ."

"We saw you and Martin by the barn," Broch said. "And when the roof started breaking, we heard the wind change. After hearing all your people's tales about spriggans, I doubt they took well to finding one on their doorstep." His mouth gave a rueful twist. "Literally."

"They would have killed him if I hadn't banished him first." Ivy rubbed her eyes. "He's the only spriggan left in the world, and they're more scared of him than they are of Betony."

"That's because they know what to expect from her," said Broch. "She may be cruel, but she's still a piskey. Spriggans are . . . something else."

"And Martin is *definitely* something else," added Thorn dryly. "Though I'm guessing they don't know how you feel about him, or we wouldn't be having this conversation. Where is he now?"

"I have no idea. All I know is it's a long way from here, and he's alone, and cold, and hungry." Anger flared up in Ivy, and she slapped the arms of the chair. "Why does this keep happening to him? He's spent his whole life running. He's never had a moment's peace!"

"You can't say he didn't earn at least some of it," said Thorn. "He hasn't exactly been a little snowdrop of virtue, either."

"He wouldn't deny that. But he never would have had to live that way if *my* ancestors hadn't murdered his entire clan!" Ivy shoved herself to her feet and began pacing. "And the war between our tribes only started because one jealous knocker killed the Joan and blamed a spriggan for it." Or maybe the spriggan had been guilty, after all. The legend didn't say, and probably no one would ever know.

Broch sat up, alert as a hunting badger. "I haven't heard that story. Where did you hear it?"

"It doesn't matter. My people wouldn't believe it anyway. The last thing they want to hear is that the spriggans used to protect our treasure instead of stealing it, and that the Joan was their queen too." Ivy sighed. "Piskeys have done too many terrible things to spriggans to admit we were wrong to do it."

"They did terrible things to faeries too," said Broch. "But that didn't keep them from accepting us."

Ivy gave a wan smile. "You have a beard like a piskey-man, and you work hard and show respect for our traditions. And Thorn looks more like a piskey than I do. They'll accept you as long as you don't start acting different." She raised a hand to the window, tracing a trickle of rain down the cold glass. "Or remind them how their fathers and granfers treated your people a hundred years ago."

There was a long silence. Then the sofa creaked, and Broch rose to his feet. "I'll find Martin," he said, stooping to kiss Thorn. "If you put some food and supplies together, Ivy, I'll see he gets them."

Ivy blinked, but the faery man had already vanished. "Typical sentimental Green Isles nonsense," grumbled Thorn, but her cheeks were pink and she didn't look half as annoyed as she sounded. "At this rate he'll be singing Martin a lullaby and tucking him in at night, too."

"I found him in an old dolmen, an hour's flight southwest,"

Broch said as they sat down to supper that evening. "If he banished himself any further, he'd be in the sea."

But Martin had taken the food, blankets, and winter coat Ivy had sent him; that was something. And although Broch hadn't looked beneath the quoit that sheltered him, Ivy guessed it was more spacious than it seemed. Maybe even big enough for two.

"I'm in your debt," she told Broch. "We both are."

He shrugged and passed the potatoes to Cicely. "It was not a hard journey. And now that I know the place, I can leap there with a thought. If you have any messages, I'll deliver them."

Piskeys, like faeries, did not say *thank you* except in extraordinary circumstances. So Ivy could only bow her head in gratitude, but Broch's answering smile told her he understood.

"That storm was horrible," said Cicely abruptly. "I watched the news when the power came back, and there were pictures of trees ripped up and cliffs falling into the sea. And barns like ours, with their roofs torn right off." She shivered. "I'm glad Martin was here to help. Even if he is a spriggan."

Ivy's heart warmed. She reached to put an arm around her, but Cicely stiffened. "What is it?" Ivy asked.

"I heard . . ." Cicely clutched her braid. "Someone told me you can't make fire, you're just letting people think you can. Is it true?"

Heat flooded Ivy's cheeks, but with an effort she stayed calm. Thorn and Broch hadn't even reacted: they already knew the truth, after all. "Mica, I suppose?"

Cicely hunched her shoulders. "He made me promise not to tell anyone."

Of course he had. If the truth got out, he'd be in trouble too. Drat Mica and his meddling! "It's only for a little while," Ivy told her, hiding her clenched fists under the table. "Until

I find our people a safe place. Then I'll tell them everything, and let them can decide what to do."

Cicely's gaze slid to the faeries, then to her lap. "Oh."

Of course she was disappointed. She'd been so happy at the Lighting, thinking her sister really was the Joan. "I'm sorry I didn't tell you. There's just been so much going on."

Cicely said nothing, but picked up her fork and started eating. Ivy forced herself to relax, glad the conversation was over. Being reminded that she couldn't make fire was never pleasant. Especially now she knew that Betony could.

Ivy got up early the next morning, when all the others were still asleep and the dawn no more than a seam of pale gold at the tin-black edge of the sky. She dressed in her warmest clothes and stepped outside, shutting the door quietly behind her. Then she took a running leap, transformed to a peregrine, and soared away.

The farmstead fell behind, and the landscape of mid-Cornwall spread out before her, bristling with rusty bracken and clumps of yellow furze. Drystone walls marked the borders of old pastures, lined with ranks of spindly, leafless trees. Ivy flew on, her sharp eyes sweeping the ground, until she'd passed all the abandoned buildings and old mines she'd already searched and the scenery no longer looked familiar. There had to be *somewhere* she could hide her people, even if only for a little while.

But though she stopped to investigate every ruin and old tunnel she saw, none offered enough room to house nearly thirty piskeys. She flew past several carns, the ancient rock piles that marked the sites of old spriggan troves—but she had no way to enter them without Martin, and their buried chambers were too small to hold for more than a few piskeys in any case. The caves Ivy spotted along the coast were too open to harsh winds and rising tides, their rocky mouths too prone to crumbling. And despite all the scattered wreckage of the storm, humans swarmed everywhere. There was no place to escape them except underground, but the mines Ivy visited proved no safer or drier than any of the others she'd seen.

By the time she gave up and winged home, Ivy was exhausted. Desperate for a solution, she'd barely rested or eaten all day. But though the piskeys swarmed her eagerly when she came into the barn, all she could tell them was that she'd look again tomorrow. She'd seen no sign of movement outside the Delve, so they ought to be safe for tonight, but they had no time left to spare.

When Ivy came into the house, Cicely was waiting for her. "Mum rang an hour ago," she said. "Where were you?"

Ivy fought the urge to snap at her. "Out. What did she say?"

"She and David got married today at some sort of . . . *office.* They're having a special party in a few days, and she wants us to come." Cicely clasped her hands under her chin, jittering with excitement. "Can we? She says she'll buy us train tickets, and I've always wanted to ride one."

Martin liked trains, too. But thinking of him only made Ivy feel worse. "I'm not going anywhere. Especially not to some human *party.*" She threw her scarf onto a hook and flung her coat after it. "If she calls again and I'm not here, tell her I'm busy and I'll ring back when I can."

"But we'd only be gone a day or two," Cicely protested. "And it's not like you can do anything to—"

"Enough!" Ivy rounded on her. "You had your chance to go with Mum, and you said no. If you've changed your mind, call her back and ask her to come get you. But I don't have time to play games, Cicely."

Cicely backed away, lips trembling and cheeks red. Then she fled to her bedroom, slamming the door behind her.

The study door opened, and Thorn stuck her head out. "What's going on now?"

"It's not important," Ivy told her wearily. "Never mind."

Ivy spent two more days searching the countryside, but her efforts were fruitless. She found a couple of places that would serve for one night, but nothing better or safer than what they had now. Which left them no choice but to dig deep, as Hew put it, and defend the barn as best as they could.

The first priority was to repair the barn. Copper, the old knocker who'd joined them at the Lighting, slowly puzzled the broken slates together, while the other men mended them with magic and crafted stout nails to hammer them back in place. Inside, Thorn inspected the roof from one end to the other, testing the wooden laths for weakness and replacing them as needed. Soon the broken corner of the roof was fixed, and all the leaks stopped up as well.

Ivy laid wards around the farmstead to alert them to coming danger and flew over the Delve each night to make sure Gossan and his hunters weren't on the march. The piskey-men took to patrolling in pairs, one armed with a knife and the other with a thunder-axe. Yet her people balked at learning any new magic, no matter how Ivy urged them to reconsider.

"It's all right for you to know a few tricks we don't," Feldspar told her kindly, "especially as you're the Joan. But we'll stick to what we know, and no doubt we'll be better off for it."

Ivy doubted that herself, but there was no moving her people once they'd made up their minds. All she could do was hope the crude weapons and armor they'd made would be enough.

She was crossing the yard on the third evening, lost in troubled thought, when Broch flashed into view beside her. Ivy whirled, ready to scold him for startling her, but when she saw the urgent look on his face her resentment vanished. "What is it?" she asked, breathless.

"Martin's found something important," Broch said. "He wants you to come right away."

The quoit stood in the midst of a rocky heathland, its capstone of lichen-crusted granite supported by smaller pillars slumped unevenly together. Once it had been the tomb of some ancient chieftain, robed in earth and moss; but now it stood naked to the elements, with no company but the sea and a few lonely hills in the distance.

Martin stood by the pile of stones, hands deep in the pockets of David Menadue's old coat. Ivy changed out of falcon-shape and landed on the grass beside him.

"It fits you," she said in surprise, and Martin laughed.

"You have the strangest priorities," he said. "But yes, the coat fits—if only because I used magic to make it so. Even a beggar should be allowed *some* vanity."

Ivy put her arms around him, leaning her head on his chest. How he managed to stay clean in such a desolate place she couldn't imagine, but his clothes were spotless and there was no trace of dirt on his skin. "I'm so sorry," she murmured. "I didn't know what else to do."

"No matter." He spoke lightly, stroking her hair. "You saved my life, and that's the important thing. Now, let me show you." Releasing her, he stepped back and changed to bird-shape.

With a twittering cry he shot off across the moorland, angling parallel to the sea.

Bemused, Ivy changed shape and followed, soaring above him to warn off any other birds that might be tempted to see a house martin as prey. They glided over the countryside for several minutes, then down toward a patch of woodland by the edge of a small town. The land shrugged upward here, and the storm had struck it hard: broken branches littered the landscape, and at the foot of the hill two big trees lay torn up by the roots.

Martin landed and took his own shape, pointing at the muddy hole beneath. "Look," he said, as Ivy touched down beside him. "Do you see it?"

She squinted into the darkness, but all she could make out were tangled roots and clods of earth. "See what?"

He crouched, kindling a glow-spell at his fingertips. "What about now?"

"Martin, I don't—"

He caught her wrist, tugging her closer. "Here," he said, and pressed her palm against something cold.

A haze slid away from Ivy's vision, revealing a square of storm-gray, weathered granite. Dirt and old lichen mottled its surface, but it appeared to be carved in a spiral pattern, radiating out from a circle on one side. It was small by human standards, but . . .

"It's a door," Ivy said blankly.

Martin flashed her a smile. He touched the spiral, and with a grating noise the door swung inward, revealing a narrow entrance and a set of steps leading up into the hill. He shrank to near-piskey height, dropped onto the threshold, and slipped inside.

His confidence surprised Ivy: she'd thought Martin hated being underground. But he seemed unfazed by the closeness of the passage, or the weight of earth pressing in. Treading carefully past the broken floor-slates and slab walls streaked with damp, he led Ivy through the entrance and up the stairs.

The first few steps were uneven, just flat stones staggered atop one another. But as they climbed, the stairs smoothed out, and the crude patchwork of rocks around them clustered into patterns, rippling up the walls like sea waves and curling into windy spirals of cloud-white quartz. Ivy had grown up in tunnels decorated with gems and mosaics, but she'd never seen work like this before; it reminded her more of human abstract paintings than anything piskeys would make.

At the top of the stair stood a second door, its spiral curving opposite to the one at the bottom. Martin pushed it, but nothing happened.

"That's as far as I've been able to get," he said, turning to Ivy. "I've spent hours poking at it and trying every spell I could think of, but it won't move. Maybe you'll have better luck." He stepped back, gesturing for her to try.

Chance favored spriggans more than piskeys, and even Martin's so-called good luck tended to be mixed at best. But there seemed no harm in trying, so Ivy stepped up and pressed her palm to the door.

Nothing happened. She traced the spiral with her fingertips, trying to activate its magic, but it stayed dark until Martin slipped behind her, so close she could feel his coat-buttons, and laid his hand over hers.

Silver light swirled around the spiral, glowing through their interlocked fingers. A deep clank echoed through the tunnel, and with a rasp the door slid aside.

Ivy glanced at Martin, astonished. "How did you know it would take both of us?"

"I didn't." He looked equally surprised. "It just felt right, somehow."

Who would make a door that only a spriggan and a piskey together could open? Ivy shook her head, wondering, as

Martin kindled a glow-spell and led her into the strangest place she had ever seen.

It was a chamber, broad and deep, its walls streaked with the same pebbly stonework as the staircase. The floor was thick with sand, flour-white and dimpled with footprints, and every few paces it rose into a soft hummock, as though some enormous turtle had buried its eggs there. Ivy crouched to brush the sand from the nearest, but the lump beneath was opaque and hard as pottery, giving no clue to its purpose.

The stillness of the air made the chamber feel solemn, even sacred. Yet it smelled oddly fresh for a room that had been sealed for decades, perhaps even centuries. Some powerful magic lay over this place.

Martin crossed the room slowly, the light of his glow-spell casting stark shadows across the floor. "There's another door here," he called, and Ivy hurried to join him.

Behind it lay another chamber, slightly smaller than the first. There were more of the egg-like bumps here, but arranged in a different pattern: these ones circled a dark, misty well in the center of the floor.

Like a man in a trance Martin walked to the well, stooped, and reached inside it—and when he raised his hands they were filled not with water, but treasure. Gold chains dripped from his fingers, and silver coins rained back onto the hoard. "This place," he breathed. "It's . . ."

"It belonged to your people," Ivy said, equally quiet. Piskeys didn't use coins, and faeries didn't live underground: there was no other explanation. But she'd never seen a spriggan hoard as large as this, or so well built.

Martin let the treasure fall again and moved to the side wall. "Another door," he said. "How big *is* this place?"

They entered one chamber after another, exploring as they went. First came a storeroom stocked with spears, shields, knives, and leather armor; then a bigger one filled with sacks of grain and sealed jars of oil, preserves, and honey. In a third, thick woolen cloaks hung from pegs, with more clothes piled on the bench beneath them: sheepskin vests and hide breeches, tunics, stockings, and other old-fashioned but practical attire. Ivy fingered a pair of knitted gloves, amazed at how new they looked. It was as though the whole place had lain in stasis for centuries.

All in all they found eight chambers in the underground complex, and Ivy's piskey senses told her there was plenty of room in the hill to dig more. It might not be nearly as large as the Delve, but it was safe, warm, and dry. Best of all, Betony had no idea this place existed, and no chance of finding it—even if her scouts stumbled onto the entrance, they'd never get past the inner door.

"This place is . . ." Ivy started to say as they returned to the main chamber, then bit her lip. How could she ask Martin to help her people, after the way they'd treated him?

"I know what you're thinking." He stopped with his back to her, his eyes on the hummocked floor. "And you're right, it's perfect. But you saw what happened the last time. Your people don't want anything to do with spriggans. Or me."

Ivy stepped up to Martin's back, sliding her arms around him. She knew he must be grieving for the people who had built this place—the spriggans that her folk had banished and then wiped out. "I know," she said softly. "And you've got every reason to hate us for it. But if it comes to choosing life with you or death with Betony, they'll have to change their attitude. There's nowhere else we can go."

Martin was silent. She laid her cheek between his shoulder blades, waiting, until he sighed and turned to face her. "I don't hate them, Ivy. How can I, when I've seen them through your eyes? I'm just tired of finding peace only to have it snatched away. But if you can convince your fellow piskeys . . ." He gave a little shrug. "Let them come."

Tears of gratitude sprang to Ivy's eyes. "I know we don't deserve it," she said thickly. "And we'll never be able to repay you."

"No." He took her face in his hands. "But I've been given a few things I can never deserve or pay for either. I think I can afford it."

His mouth brushed hers then, achingly gentle. She moved closer to return the kiss—and her foot kicked something in the sand. Startled, Ivy pulled away and bent to pick it up.

It was a ball the size of a knocker's fist, sewn from scraps of cloth. She held it up for Martin to see.

"Maybe some spriggan child dropped it, before they left. You saw the footprints."

"Yes, but *why* did they leave?" Ivy gestured around the cavern. "Your ancestors could have been safe here, and warmer than they ever were living in fogous and sea-caves. Why make such a beautiful place and then abandon it?"

Martin's gray eyes turned distant. "Not to mention all the supplies and the spells they cast to preserve them." He circled one of the egg-like bumps on the floor. "And what are these?"

A chilling thought struck Ivy. "Martin, what if it's—"

"A tomb? I thought of that too. But it doesn't seem right." He rubbed a thumb pensively over his lower lip, then knelt to brush the sand away.

Light flickered beneath his fingers, snaked like a bright ribbon over the dome's surface and vanished. Ivy blinked, half-convinced she'd imagined it, but then a second and then a third shining thread appeared. They rippled outward, until the whole half-shell was webbed with radiance.

Ivy backed up and tripped over another bump, only to find that it, too, was glowing. She gasped and covered her eyes as the whole room lit up at once. The chamber echoed with loud crackling noises, and when Ivy dared to look again all the shells had crumbled, revealing a host of bodies inside.

They lay curled up with knees to their chests and heads pillowed on clasped hands, so perfectly preserved that Ivy's revulsion faded at once. They didn't look dead, not really . . .

The figures close to her began to stir, yawning and stretching in all directions. The one at Martin's feet sat up, and with a shock, Ivy saw it was a little boy not much older than Thrift, with bleary eyes and sleep-mussed yellow hair.

"I lost my ball, Mam," he mumbled. Then his eyes focused on Ivy, and he let out a squeak, kicking backward and showering her legs with sand.

"It's all right," Martin said, holding up both hands in a soothing gesture. "We won't hurt you."

Numb with wonder, Ivy knelt to the boy's level and held out the ball. "Here," she said. "My name's Ivy. What's yours?"

The little boy watched her suspiciously, then snatched the ball away and hugged it. "Haven't got one."

Of course not. She'd forgotten that spriggan boys had to earn their names and didn't get them until they were old enough to fight. With an apologetic smile, Ivy rose and turned to Martin.

She'd never seen him so unguarded, eyes wide and mouth slack with awe. He gazed across the cavern, entranced, as the remaining sleepers struggled to their feet.

They were all boys, and there had to be at least twenty. The oldest, a bony youth a year or two older than Cicely, shook out his black hair and squared his shoulders, eyes wary and one hand on his belt-knife.

"I'm Dagger, son of Helm," he said. "Whose son are you?"

Helm had been the name of Martin's protector, the gruff but loyal warrior who'd sent him into the future at the cost of his own life. Ivy caught her breath, and Martin had to clear his throat before he could speak.

"I am the son of the Gray Man," he said huskily, and the spriggan boys fell to their knees.

Waking the spriggans from magical slumber had been miracle enough, but when Martin saw them all kneel to him, he looked thunderstruck. Ivy stepped close and touched his hand.

"Breathe," she whispered. "Talk to them."

Martin exhaled, long and slow. Then he said, "You don't have to do that. Get up."

"But you are the one we were promised," said a lilting voice at the back of the chamber, as a girl stepped into the archway. She was dressed in a sleeveless robe belted with leather, and her red-gold hair hung loose to her waist. "You came to save us, as the Seer said."

In the shock of seeing the boys wake, Ivy had forgotten about the humps in the treasure chamber. But it was the duty of spriggan women to tend their family's hoard, so of course that was where the girls had been sleeping. The boys shuffled aside, their eyes lowered, as the red-haired girl beckoned and nine younger ones padded out of the room to join her.

Thirty spriggan children, thin and pale as driftwood, but miraculously alive. And all of them gazed at Martin like he was the most wonderful thing they'd ever seen.

"What Seer?" Martin asked. "Who put you here?"

The girl looked at Dagger, who puffed up his chest and

spoke. "'Twas my grandmam had the vision, when the Gray Man's son was born. She said—"

"If this one grows to be a man, he'll be the saving of our people," Ivy whispered, echoing him. Helm had told Martin that story, but when he went through the portal he'd forgotten it, like everything else from his past.

"The piskeys and knocker-men were killing us," Dagger went on, "and the faeries would help none but themselves." He flicked a resentful look at Ivy. "So when they heard the Seer's word, our clans banded together to build this place. Every fifth summer they drew lots to choose a child to sleep here, so if they lost the battle at least some of our folk would live on."

"Our people worked as one to cast the spell," the girl added, her clear voice taking up the story. "They drew power from the earth of Kernow and made shells of magical clay to guard our slumber. Then they stopped time within the barrow, so that we would not age or decay before the Gray Man's son came to set us free."

Ivy clutched Martin's hand. Only a few months ago, the faery who called herself Gillian Menadue had used an ancient spell called the Claybane to trap the piskeys of the Delve in waking torment. Now it seemed that same spell had been cast by the spriggans—albeit for a far gentler purpose.

Martin nodded gravely, so calm that Ivy knew he was acting. Despite the dark rumors about his ambition, all he'd ever wanted was to stay alive, and it had taken all his cunning and ruthlessness to do it. Being suddenly in charge of thirty children had to be the most daunting challenge he'd ever faced.

"Well," he said, "here I am. But the world outside this hill is not much kinder than the one you left. So my first command is for all of you to stay here, and not go out unless I say so."

The girl looked stricken. "But how can that be? The door to our barrow was charmed not to open until a piskey, a faery, and a spriggan came here together in peace!"

Martin and Ivy traded glances. It seemed that if they hadn't both been half faery, they'd have been locked out of the chamber as well. "I'm trying to teach my people about spriggans," Ivy told her apologetically, "but they still have a lot to learn."

Dagger glowered at her. "A piskey! Who gives you the right to speak?"

"You will address her with respect, boy," snapped Martin, and Dagger blanched. He cringed back as Martin went on, "Ivy is our Joan. You will obey her as you do me."

The children stared in bewildered wonder. "*Our* Joan?" asked the oldest girl. "But—"

"There is no peace between the piskeys and the spriggans yet," Martin told them. "But with Ivy's help, there will be. You can trust her with your lives, as I trust her with mine." He raised Ivy's hand to his mouth and kissed it, and a nervous giggle went up from the younger girls.

Ivy was flustered. He sounded so confident when he called her the Joan, it was as though he really believed it. But how could he, especially now?

"Wait here," Martin told the children. "Do nothing until we return."

He took Ivy's hand and they left the chamber, heading down the stairs and shutting the outer door behind them. Martin helped her out of the hole, and they sat down on one of the fallen trees together.

She had to say it now, before her resolve failed. Much as it hurt, it was the only right thing to do. "I won't tell anyone about this place. It belongs to your people."

"Ivy . . ."

"They're children, Martin. They need to be safe."

"I know. But your people have children, too." His thumb brushed her neck, stroking away her tension. "Don't give up. They may come around yet."

Ivy looked at him, surprised, and found him smiling—not the sly curve of lips she was used to, but a broad, incredulous smile that creased his eyes and showed all his teeth at once.

"I have no idea what I'm doing," he admitted. "It's a disaster. But they're alive, Ivy. The spriggans of Kernow are *alive.*"

Ivy could have leaped home to her fellow piskeys in an instant, but she chose to fly instead. She wanted to make sure the spriggan hideaway was a safe distance from both the barn and the Delve, but she also needed time to sort out her feelings. The hope that had sprung up in her when she saw the barrow had died when she saw the spriggan children wake, and now she was torn between happiness for Martin and his people and renewed grief and fear for her own.

One thing was clear, though: whatever happened, Ivy had to keep the barrow a secret. She couldn't bring her people there unless they gave up their hatred of spriggans, or she'd betray Martin's trust and put the children in danger as well.

Yet how could she be the Joan of the piskeys *and* the spriggans at the same time? Especially when one expected her to conjure fire out of nothing, and the other was waiting for her to forge an equally impossible peace?

The sky was darkening when Ivy reached the farmstead. She changed shape in the yard, about to head inside for supper, when she heard the sound of piskeys shouting—and fighting. Heart dropping into her stomach, she raced to the barn.

One glance put her worst fear to rest: there was no sign of Gossan or any of his hunters. It was her own people shaking their fists at one another, while two familiar figures wrestled on the stony floor. Mica—and *Mattock?*

"Stop it!" Ivy yelled, thrusting her way through the crowd and grabbing Mica by the collar. "What is wrong with you?"

Mica jerked back, swiping sweat-damp hair from his forehead. His eyes were bloodshot with rage. "Tell them!" he snarled. "Tell them he's lying about you and that—that spriggan!"

Ivy's bones turned to water. "What?"

"Matt says it's *his* filthy hoard that's paying for us to live here." He glared at Mattock, who lay winded beneath him with a bloody lip and one eye half-shut. "He says we've been all been living off spriggan gold!"

"Living?" Copper scoffed, leaning on his thunder-axe. "Thirty of us crammed into this rabbit hutch, and you call it living?"

"Shut your muzzle, you ungrateful old mole!" Fern swatted him with her dishcloth. "Go back to the Delve and die then, if you're too fine to make do with the rest of us! And you"—she jabbed a finger at Mica—"stop talking dross about my son!"

Breathe, Ivy reminded herself. *Talk to them.* "Mica, get off Matt. Who started this?"

Answers poured in from all sides at once. Copper had started it by complaining about his sore back—no, Daisy had done it by using the water Fern had boiled for her laundry—no, it was Mica's fault for snoring too loud and keeping everyone awake at night—

The only thing clear was that Ivy's people were unhappy living so close together, especially with the threat of attack putting everyone on edge. And somehow, in all the quarrelling, Mattock had let slip that Martin had given Ivy some treasure.

"All right, yes!" Ivy snapped. "I helped Martin find an old spriggan hoard back in the summer, and he gave me half of the money he got from selling it. Would you rather I'd refused his offer and let you all starve?"

There was a shocked silence while all the piskeys stared at her. Then Teasel said slowly, "But . . . spriggans don't sell their treasure."

"Or share it, neither," said Fern. "Where did you say he—"

"Wait." Gem held up a hand, his face stony. "You found a hoard with him, you say. So you *knew* he was a spriggan."

She didn't dare look at Mica: she could feel the fury rolling off him in waves. She dropped her gaze to Mattock, whose ears had turned red as his hair.

"I didn't know when I first met him," she replied at last, "and he didn't know it either. His mother was a faery, and he couldn't remember his father. He'd never even heard of spriggans until a few months ago."

"But you knew it when you took his treasure." Mica's voice was deadly quiet. "And you knew it when . . ."

"I knew it when I brought him into the barn," Ivy cut in quickly. If Mica told the piskeys she was in love with Martin, it would all be over. "But I also believed I could trust him not to hurt any of you. And I was right."

Hew shook his head. "This time, maybe. But mark me, that spriggan won't keep his oath, any more than he'll let you keep his treasure. He'll come back, and we'll all pay for it."

"Leave that to me," Ivy said. "It was my bargain, not yours. And even if I banished him, Martin owes me his life."

"Ayes, but you owed him yours first," Feldspar spoke up. "You told us he healed you."

Ivy wanted to bang her head against the wall, but she forced herself to patience. "Yes, but he still owes me more than I owe him." Or at least she thought so. After all she and Martin had been through together, she'd stopped keeping track.

"In any case," she added briskly, "it's done, and there's no use arguing. The question is, what now? I know this barn's too small for us, which is why I'm searching for something better. But I can't do that if this kind of nonsense happens every time I leave you alone. Don't we have enough enemies without fighting each other as well?"

The piskeys stared at the floor, mouths sullen. Ivy was about to give up and order them back to their duties when Hew cleared his throat.

"What we need's a good Jack," he said. "A strong fellow with a level head and a loyal heart to keep the peace and make sure everyone gets what's owed them. Someone who can be here when you're not and do as you'd want things done. Wouldn't you say so, boys?"

The tension eased out of the men's faces, and they nodded. Mica's black eyes met Ivy's, gleaming, and she drew a sharp breath—but he spoke first. "I say we choose Matt."

Mattock rounded on him, indignant, but Mica gave him a shove. "Shut up. We'll sort that out later. The point is," he went on, raising his voice, "Matt already offered for Ivy's hand, not long ago. Isn't that right, Ivy?"

She was going to murder Mica. In his sleep, with a dull knife. "Not exactly," she shot back. "He was thinking about it, but then he changed his mind. Didn't you, Mattock?"

Matt swallowed. "I did."

Good, Ivy thought. If he kept his answers vague, there was still a chance they'd get out of this.

"But . . . I'd offer again, if I thought there was any hope she'd have me."

Ivy shut her eyes, despairing. He was going to tell them she'd turned him down for Martin, and then none of their people would ever trust her again.

"And maybe she would, if I proved myself as brave as she is. I'm willing to wait and see, if she's willing to give me a chance."

Ivy's eyes flew open. Was he saying he'd be her Jack *without* expecting her to marry him?

If so, it could be the perfect solution. Because much as Mica annoyed her, he wasn't wrong about Mattock being the best choice. There were a few older piskey-men who were thoughtful and steady, but they were married, and the Jack's first loyalty had to be to the Joan. He was her chief advisor, her lieutenant, her partner in all things; it made no sense for him to be anything less than her consort—or on rare occasions, her brother. But even Mica knew better than to offer himself as a candidate.

"Will you, Ivy?" Mattock held out his hand to her. "Give me time to show I'm worthy, and then decide if you're willing to marry me?"

"I'm only seventeen," Ivy stammered. "I'm too young to get married."

"But not for a betrothal, surely," Daisy spoke up, bright with eagerness. She tucked her arm into Gem's and squeezed it. "*We* were betrothed at your age."

"But . . ." It made Ivy sick to say it, knowing how it would hurt him. But she couldn't give her people false hope. "I don't love Mattock that way."

Hew chuckled. "Ah, maid, love's a choice, not some girlish fancy. You've been friendly with the boy since you could walk, and it's plain to all of us he'd make you a fine husband, even if it's not yet plain to you. And whatever you think you don't feel now, there's no saying you won't feel it later."

"But even if you don't," Mica cut in, "you're the Joan, and you have to choose a Jack soon. Or folk will wonder."

And you'll have to tell them, of course, Ivy thought resentfully. He'd trapped her, with no more pity than a rockfall blocking up a stope.

"Let her alone, Mica," Mattock warned. "She needs time to think about it. Clear off, all of you."

Somehow he managed to make it sound like a request, rather than an order. Dutifully the piskeys retreated—even Mica, though Yarrow had to tug his sleeve, and he obeyed with ill grace. Matt gestured to the barn door, and reluctantly Ivy followed him outside.

"Now," he said, turning to her, "this isn't what either of us wanted, but we've got to make the best of it. I know how you feel about the spri—I mean Martin, and I know he loves you back . . ."

Ivy's head jerked up, and Mattock gave a rueful smile. "I'm not such a slag-wit as you think, Ivy. You think I could watch him kneel at your feet, look up at you with his whole heart in his eyes, and not know? Whatever Mica and the others say, I don't think you were wrong to trust him with your life. It's the rest of our lives I'm not sure about."

"He would never," Ivy said hotly, but Matt put a hand on her shoulder.

"It doesn't matter. Even if he hates the whole piskey race now, he can't hurt us without hurting you, so he won't do it. I know that. Will you please stop trying to fight me? *I'm on your side.*"

His square, handsome face held no hint of malice, and Ivy's resistance crumbled. "That's . . . good," she said. "But what do you want me to do?"

"I'll be your Jack, or at least I'll do the work of one, but I won't ask you to marry me. Not until I've defeated Gossan—"

Ivy clutched his arm. "Matt, no! You can't put yourself in that kind of danger!"

"I didn't say I was going to march to the Delve and challenge him," Mattock explained patiently. "I mean if he comes to attack us, I'll fight him then. Jack to Jack."

Ivy was silent.

"You don't think I can beat him? I only let Mica hit me because I was furious at myself for blabbing about the treasure.

If I'd fought back I could have tied him in knots, and everyone knows it." His mouth twisted. "Except you, apparently."

"It's not that." Mattock was bigger than Gossan, which no doubt did make him stronger. But Betony's consort was more experienced at fighting, more skilled at magic—and from what she'd seen, far more ready to kill. "I just don't think it's a good idea."

"Look, if I can't beat Gossan, I don't deserve to be your Jack anyway. *Somebody's* going to have to fight him, just as you're going to have to fight Betony." He gripped her shoulder. "You know that, don't you? Win or lose, it's the only chance we've got to free our people. *All* our people."

Much as Ivy dreaded it, he was right. She still hoped it wouldn't come to that, especially since she didn't know how to fight Betony without getting burned to ashes. But she'd have to confront her aunt at some point, and when that time came, she'd need a strong Jack beside her.

This wasn't about her feelings, or Martin's, or Mattock's. It was about doing what had to be done.

"All right," she told Mattock quietly. "I'll make you my Jack O'Lantern."

When Ivy announced that Mattock would be their new Jack, the piskeys cheered up at once. Hew clapped Matt on the shoulder, with a knowing wink that made his ears redden, and even Copper stopped complaining long enough to agree it was a fine thing. Then Daisy and Feldspar's wife Clover rushed to Ivy, eagerly asking what food she wanted for the betrothal feast and what she planned to wear. Ivy cast Matt a desperate look, and as he cleared his throat, all the piskeys came to attention.

"It's an honor to serve as your Jack," he said. "But that's all I'm doing for now. Ivy's risked her own life more than once to save us, and I don't blame her for wanting a man who's not afraid to do the same. So I'm not asking her to marry me until I've beaten Gossan in fair combat, and taken his cap for my own."

Mica folded his arms, his expression skeptical. "And when's that going to be, exactly?"

"As soon as I get the chance," Matt told him. "I'm not fool enough to try and best him on his own ground, but he'll come at us when he's ready. And then I'll be ready, too."

He spoke boldly, but the other piskeys traded dubious

looks. They'd never had a Jack who wasn't bound to the Joan before, and they didn't like it.

"That's well enough if he comes soon," Gem said. "But we can't sit about forever waiting for that rock to fall. And if Ivy's so unsure of you that she thinks you need proving—"

"I'm not!" Ivy protested. If she lost her people's confidence that was one thing, but she couldn't bear to see them lose faith in Matt.

"Then there's no reason not to accept him right now, is there?" Mica raised his eyebrows at her. "Unless there's someone you like better . . ."

It was a challenge, and Ivy had to answer it. "No," she said flatly. "There's no piskey I like better than Mattock, and none more fit to be Jack. But I won't be bullied, Mica. Either you accept my decisions even if you don't like them, or you can go back to the Delve and take your chances with Betony."

Mica's smile froze, and Hew sucked a breath through his teeth. There was a charged silence as Ivy and her brother glared at each other. Finally Mica shrugged. "You're the Joan."

Ivy let out her breath. She'd won that round—but Mica wasn't the only one she needed to convince. Her people had good reason to wonder what their Joan was thinking, and unless she put their fears to rest, there'd be trouble not only for her, but for Martin.

"Give me six months," she told them. "I'll be eighteen come spring. If all goes well, we can be betrothed at Midsummer."

She waited hopefully, but the piskeys only looked glum until Hew stepped forward, pulling off his cap. "Meaning no disrespect, maid," he said, "but six weeks is enough, surely? It's only betrothal, not a wedding, and as Daisy's said, there's been plenty of folk pledged younger."

"Hew's right," said Teasel. "You might not be ready now, but if you can't see Mattock's worth by then, you never will."

Six weeks was a pitiably short time to beat Betony

and Gossan, and find her people a new home. If Ivy could only convince them to make peace with Martin and the spriggans . . . but there seemed little hope of that, either.

"Fair enough," Ivy said, trying to sound gracious rather than defeated. "Six weeks, then."

The sky outside the barn was black and starless, and an icy wind swirled across the cobbles. With leaden feet Ivy climbed the steps to the house and went in.

"You look like I feel," remarked Thorn, striding into the kitchen and reaching to fill the kettle. "I'm having a baby, what's your excuse?"

Ivy hesitated. She longed to pour her heart out to someone, but she'd asked so much of the faeries already—and she wasn't sure Thorn would understand. "It's been a long day," she replied at last. "Where's Broch?"

"Well, now, that's an interesting story. Seems he got tired of waiting for you to tell him what Martin was worked up about, so he went to look for himself."

Ivy tensed, then relaxed again. He could only have gone to the quoit, after all, and when he didn't find Martin there he'd surely have given up . . .

"You *are* in a fine heap of owl pellets, aren't you?" Thorn said. "A barn full of piskeys and a barrow full of spri—" She caught Ivy's wrist, scowling. "What d'you think you're doing?"

She'd tried to clap a hand over the faery woman's mouth, terrified Cicely would hear. But Thorn's grip was like iron, and she clearly didn't like being touched. "Don't," Ivy whispered frantically. "Not another word."

Thorn looked suspicious, but she let go. Ivy tiptoed through the sitting room, where Broch was dozing on the sofa, and leaned down the corridor. The light was on in Cicely's room, but her door was shut.

"All right," Ivy said as she returned to the kitchen, "tell me, but quietly. How did he find them?"

"Martin found him first, as it happens." Thorn's mouth curled. "He was babbling nonsense, and Broch thought he was drunk."

That wasn't surprising: Martin often quoted Shakespeare when his feelings got the better of him. "So he showed him?"

"Only the outside. But . . ." Thorn eyed the electric kettle, then poked it on and snatched her hand back as though it might bite her. "They struck a bargain I'm none too pleased about. He wants Broch to go to London and sell some treasure for him."

Of course. With thirty-one hungry spriggans to feed, the barrow's stores wouldn't last forever. And Martin was too shrewd not to make use of Broch while he could. "Sell it how?"

"That's what I'd like to know," said Thorn. "Broch's never been to a big city, and he knows even less about humans than I do. He'll stick out like a fish in a tree."

That was the least of the problem. Ivy knew only one shop in London that bought old coins and jewelry, and she was quite certain Thom Pendennis wanted nothing to do with spriggan treasure ever again. "But he agreed? What did Martin offer him?"

Thorn threw up her hands. "Who knows? He kept dodging the question when I asked. Which means it's probably a lot of broken pottery, or bits of parchment, or some such rubbish. Broch can't get enough of that kind of thing."

Distracted, Ivy picked up the tea canister, only to find it empty. She was about to add shopping to her growing list of duties when she remembered she had a Jack now. Mattock didn't know Truro like he'd known Redruth, but he was used to dealing with humans: he could easily buy all the provisions their people needed. Though it would go a lot faster if he'd let Ivy teach him to travel by magic, instead of tramping an hour through the countryside each way . . .

"Anyway," said Thorn, breaking into her thoughts, "if you've got any advice for Broch, he could certainly use it. If he makes an egg of himself and gets locked up by the humans for his trouble, it won't be much good to any of us."

"It's good to know my wife has such confidence in me," said Broch dryly from the front room, and the sofa creaked as he got up. "It's not that difficult, Thorn. I'll just ask Timothy."

"*Not* Timothy." Thorn's voice was sharp. "He'll ask questions. And probably guess the answers, too."

Broch appeared in the doorway, his dark hair even more rumpled than usual. "Rob, then."

"Rob hates Martin. He won't help him—or you either, once he gets a sight of that treasure." Thorn folded her arms. "Besides, what human's going to do business with him? He looks even more like a ruffian than you do."

"What about that woman who used to be a faery?" Ivy asked. "The one you called Knife?"

Thorn turned pale and then very red. "Absolutely not," she said. "And don't *you* go blabbing to her either."

"About what?" Ivy asked, surprised. She'd only met Peri McCormick briefly, but she'd seemed like a decent person.

"Anything," Thorn snapped, and stormed out.

Broch waited until the study door slammed behind her, then sighed. "I apologize," he said. "But my wife doesn't want Knife to know she's having a baby. Or any of our fellow Oakenfolk, either."

Was that why they'd come to Cornwall? Ivy had wondered why the faeries seemed so determined to throw in their lot with her, especially when she had so little to offer in return. She'd guessed they were staying to keep an eye on Martin, and Valerian obviously hoped they'd be able to make peace with the piskeys as well. But neither of those things explained Thorn's odd behavior.

"Why?" Ivy asked. "Did they not want the two of you to marry?"

Broch shook his head. "Most of our people would not care, and the few who did would be only too pleased for Thorn's liking. But Knife is barren, and Thorn cannot bear to hurt her by revealing that she is not."

Finally, an explanation that made sense. But for Thorn to leave the Oak and flee all the way to Cornwall . . .

"So," Ivy ventured, "she must love her very much."

Broch gave a half-smile. "With all her tough, stubborn heart. So I ask you to be patient with my wife. She can't hide the truth from Knife forever, and deep down she knows it. But for now, she is determined to try."

When Ivy stopped by the barn the next morning, all was peaceful. Thrift and two of the other children sprawled across Dodger's back, brushing him. Copper and the old uncles were playing dice in one corner, while Yarrow carded wool for Teasel and the other women to spin. The younger men all seemed to be out patrolling or hunting, except Hew and Feldspar who were guarding the door—though Feldspar's lazy posture and the casual way Hew leaned on his thunder-axe made clear they weren't expecting trouble.

It was as though Matt had given all the piskeys a dose of his own calm, steady nature. Ivy had never fully appreciated how important a good Jack was to their people, until now. She nodded to her fellow piskeys and went outside to look for him.

She found Mattock trudging across the pasture, with the collar of his coat turned up and his cap pulled low over his rusty hair. His face lit when he saw her, and Ivy felt a flicker of guilt, but she suppressed it. She'd been honest with him about her feelings, and she couldn't do anything about his.

"I need your help," she said, and explained about the provisions. "I can give you the money, if you don't mind where it came from."

Mattock sighed. "I do mind, but I don't see we've got much choice. All right."

"Then let me teach you how to leap. I know Mica doesn't like it, but—"

"I don't give two bits of slag for what Mica thinks," Mattock said firmly. "But it's not how we do things, Ivy."

"It's not faery magic," she insisted. "The droll-tales say piskeys used to do it, too. We've just forgotten."

"With good reason, maybe. Ivy, you can't keep pushing our people to change, not when we've had to sacrifice so much already. You need to be patient."

Ivy folded her arms. "That would be fine, if I was only trying to spare you a bit of walking. But what happens when Gossan attacks, and our people can't get away because they all followed your example?"

That hit home. He looked troubled, and Ivy pressed on. "You have power now, Matt. If you take the lead, they'll do what you do. And we're not asking them to change for nothing. We're trying to keep them safe, and isn't that more important than keeping them comfortable?"

Mattock rubbed a hand over his face. "How do you do that?"

"What?"

"You see something you want, and you refuse to give up until you've got it. You don't stop to doubt or ask questions, you just keep pushing until all the obstacles fall down." He grimaced. "You and Mica aren't as different as you think."

That stung, but she couldn't let it daunt her. This was too important. "Tell me I'm wrong, then. Our people call me Joan because they don't have anyone better to follow, but they made you the Jack because they believe in you. Give me one good reason you can't do this, and I'll listen."

"You're not wrong!" His voice rose loud enough to shock her, and cracked. He reddened and continued more quietly, "I hate it. But you're not wrong."

"Well, in that case—"

"But one day you will be, Ivy." Mattock's eyes held hers, accusing. "You'll push too hard, and our people will break. And I don't want to have to pick up the pieces when that happens."

"You will, though," she insisted, shaken but trying not to show it. "Because you're my Jack."

She didn't realize how that had sounded until hope flared in Mattock's eyes. He stepped closer, reaching for her hand.

"Ivy!"

It was Cicely, waving madly out the kitchen window. Ivy turned, glad for the interruption and embarrassed at herself for needing it. "What is it?"

"Phone for you," said her sister, holding it up. "It's Molly."

"You sound out of breath," Molly said when Ivy answered. "Made you run, did I?"

Her voice was cheerful, curious, and utterly human. Grateful for the distraction, Ivy leaned back against the kitchen wall, cradling the phone. "Yes, but it's all right. How are you?"

"Dying of homework. I have three massive projects, and

they're all due next week." Molly gave a soulful sigh. "Can I run away and join the piskeys?"

"Only if I can run away to theater school," said Ivy, trying to keep her voice light. "You wouldn't believe what's been happening here."

"I might, if you tell me. How's Martin?"

Ivy hesitated, watching Cicely help herself to bread and butter. Then she walked down the corridor to her bedroom and shut the door behind her. "That's the most unbelievable part," she whispered, and told Molly about the barrow.

The other girl gave a tuneless whistle. "Thirty kids! That's brilliant, but he must be going mad. How's he going to look after them all?"

It was a pleasure to finally talk to someone who not only knew Martin, but liked and cared about him. "I don't know," Ivy said. "I don't think he's had a lot of experience with children. But the older ones will probably help."

"And you'll help too, I'm sure." Molly sounded wistful. "I wish I could."

That was twice now she'd had hinted at running away. "Is something wrong, Molly? Do you not like the school?"

"I *love* it," said Molly fervently. "It's just . . . I'm supposed to go to Dad and Marigold's wedding party this weekend. And I'm happy for them, I really am. But I can't help thinking about Mum and wondering . . ." She broke off with a wet laugh. "Sorry. I know she was awful. But she was still my mum."

"It's all right," Ivy told her quietly. "I understand."

"I wish you and Cicely were coming, but she says you're too busy looking after your people. It sounds like you and Martin both have your hands full."

It was tempting to confess all her struggles, but Ivy restrained herself. Molly might be a good listener, but she was only fourteen, and it wasn't right to fill her head with worries she could do nothing about.

Yet there was one thing the human girl might be able to help with. "Molly, do you know of any shops that buy old treasure? Coins, jewelry, that kind of thing?"

"In Cornwall, you mean?"

"No, in London," Ivy said, and went on to explain what Thorn had told her. "Martin used to sell to a dealer named Thom Pendennis, but he's closed up shop now, so . . ."

"*Ivy*," Molly broke in, sounding fond and exasperated at once. "I know magical folk aren't very imaginative, but honestly! Do you have any idea what my dad does?"

She knew David Menadue did a lot of traveling, but she'd never paid attention to the details. "Something to do with pictures?"

"He works for a documentary film company," Molly said. "And he knows loads of people. I'm sure he can help Broch find somewhere to sell that treasure, and probably make up a brilliant story about where it came from. Do you want me to ring him now, or ask him on the weekend?"

When she finally hung up the phone, Ivy's spirits felt lighter. David Menadue would surely be glad to help Broch, especially since he owed the faery man for saving Marigold's life. She glanced about to make sure Cicely wasn't in earshot, then knocked at the door of the study and told the faeries the good news.

"Hm," said Thorn. "That'll do, I suppose." But she looked more pleased than her tone let on, and Broch seemed gratified as well. Ivy left them to talk it over and went to fetch her coat.

"Where are you going?"

Ivy clutched the coat stand, heart hammering. She'd thought Cicely was in the barn. "Just . . . out for a bit."

"Are you going to see Martin?"

"Cicely!"

"Are you?"

Well, she could hardly do it now. "No," Ivy said, flat with the effort of hiding her disappointment. "I'm just going to fly."

Cicely's eyes welled. She thumped down into the armchair and hid her face in her hands.

"What is it?" Ivy asked, but the younger girl only shook her head. Suppressing impatience, Ivy patted her shoulder. "You can tell me. It's all right."

"Why should I?" Cicely's head jerked up, cheeks blotchy with anger and tears. "You never tell me anything. You haven't taught me how to fly like you do, either—"

"Cicely, you already have perfectly good wings of your own." Or at least at piskey size she did, though between the house and riding Dodger, she spent most of her time in human shape these days. "And I taught you how to leap, didn't I?"

"What difference does that make? You won't let me go anywhere by myself, and nobody wants to go with me." Her voice wobbled. "Not even M-Mica."

Ivy's heart softened. When they all lived together in the Delve, Mica had been Cicely's hero and champion. But like Ivy, he was too busy to pay much attention to their little sister these days. "I'm sorry," Ivy told her more gently. "But it's not forever, it's just for now. Things will get better."

Her sister pulled away. There was a hectic color in her cheeks, and she didn't look at Ivy when she spoke. "I heard. About you and Matt."

"Yes?" Ivy asked cautiously.

"You don't deserve him!" Cicely burst out. "He's been in love with you practically forever, and everybody wants him to be your Jack except you! And you haven't even told him you can't make fire!"

Oh. Oh *no.* "I am going to tell him," Ivy said hastily. "I just haven't had the chance. Cicely, it's not like you think—I didn't mean to trick you or Matt or anyone, it just happened—"

"Does he know about you and Martin? Are you going to tell him that too?"

Ivy was speechless.

"I'm not stupid, you know. It's so *obvious* how you feel about him. And I know we owe Martin a lot, and I don't want him dead, but Mica's right, he's *nothing* compared to Mattock, and I don't understand you at all!"

I'm not the only one who's obvious, thought Ivy sadly. *How could I not have seen it before?* "I do care about Matt, but . . . not the way you do. And I can't change that."

"You haven't even tried!" Cicely flung herself out of the chair, glaring at Ivy. "But you'd better. Because Matt doesn't deserve to be treated like this. And if you don't tell him the truth . . ." She took a deep breath. "Then I will. I'll tell *everyone.*"

Ivy's stomach turned over. "Cicely, no. Matt knows how I feel, he even knows about Martin, I'm not trying to hide any of it!"

Her sister gave a little, hysterical laugh. "You think that makes it *better?*" She moved for the door.

"Stop!" Ivy jumped up, desperation flooding her. She grabbed Cicely's arm. "I'm not going to see Martin, all right? I—I'll let him go and keep my distance from now on."

She'd never wanted to make this sacrifice, and it felt like her soul was dying. But Ivy knew it was the only way. If the truth came out like this, it wouldn't just destroy the piskeys' confidence in Ivy, it would make Matt look like a fool as well.

And then they'll go back to the Delve and die with Betony, because they think they've got no other choice.

"I won't see him again," Ivy repeated, willing Cicely to believe it. Willing herself to mean it, with every broken piece of her heart. "I'll stay here with you and Mattock and our people."

"And you'll tell Matt everything? Right now?"

Ivy's eyes burned, and her throat felt like she'd swallowed a rock sideways. But she nodded.

Cicely chewed her lip, watching Ivy. Then she stepped back from the door. "Go on, then," she said. "Prove it."

10

W hen Ivy came out Mattock was still in the yard, waiting for her. Like a true piskey, he didn't give up easily.

"I'm sorry," she told him, but he shook his head.

"Don't be. We do need to learn new tricks if we're going to beat Betony and Gossan, and as your Jack I ought to be helping you, not holding you back." He straightened up, determined. "Teach me to leap. And I'll teach the others for you."

Ivy's chest felt like it was being crushed by a millstone, and she had to blink back tears. But his words only confirmed the choice she'd made already. "You're a good man, Matt," she said. "And more patient than I deserve. I . . ." The words scorched her throat, but she had to speak them. "I need to tell you a secret. Something I should have told you long ago."

"No, you don't." His big hands folded around hers, like a gentle embrace. "Remember what I said before? Whatever happens, I'm on your side. You don't need to prove anything to me."

"But you ought to know I can't—"

"Make fire?" He spoke softly, meeting her wide green eyes with his blue ones. "I know."

Ivy dropped her gaze, flustered, as Mattock kept talking. "I mean, I didn't at first, obviously. But I could tell you were afraid, especially after Yarrow came and told us about Betony. Then Mica told me he'd put petrol on the wakefire, and that's why I hit him. Because I knew you'd never want to trick your people that way."

So he hadn't just guessed or found out. He'd *understood*, and he'd fought his best friend to defend her. Ivy stood still, barely breathing, as Matt raised her hands and pressed them to his heart. "But you're still the true Joan, Ivy. I believe that. Even if you can't make fire now, you will when you really need to."

The same way she'd learned to become a swift, then a falcon. Maybe he was right. "Then . . . you don't think I should tell the others?"

"Not right away. Let's wait until things quiet down a bit. And when we do tell them, we'll do it together." He leaned closer. "I'll make sure Mica owns up to what he did, too."

That was some comfort. Ivy spread her fingers, feeling the steady beat of his pulse. "I don't understand what Mica wants. I don't understand him at all."

"It's not that complicated. He wants you to be the Joan, and he wants you to marry me. That's all he's ever wanted."

Her head jerked up, incredulous. She'd known the second part, but the first?

"Ivy, he's always thought there was something special about you. He just didn't want to say anything until he was sure."

Her brother believed in her that much? The thought was bewildering. He knew Ivy couldn't make fire, no matter how hard she tried; that was why he'd poured petrol on the wood before the Lighting, so the other piskeys wouldn't be disappointed too. He'd lectured her, argued with her, pushed her to choose Matt with no care for her feelings whatsoever . . .

Or maybe he'd been trying to help her, in his own high-handed way. Maybe he still was.

"But *I'm* sure," Mattock said huskily. "I've always been sure about you."

Ivy stared at his shirt buttons, hot with shame. Cicely was right: Matt deserved so much more than the few crumbs of trust she'd been giving him. But how could she tell him about her promise to Cicely without raising false hopes? "I'm sorry," she said at last. "I haven't been very kind to you."

"You've only been honest, and there's nothing wrong with that. But . . ." He squeezed her hands a little. "You know you can't be with Martin and lead our people at the same time. Don't you?"

Once more he'd guessed the truth without her having to tell him. Feeling more wretched than ever, Ivy nodded.

"And by now he must know that, too. If he loves you as much as I love you, he'll understand."

She gave a ragged laugh. "Easy for you to say."

"I'd still say it if I were the spriggan, and he was the piskey standing here. You belong with your own people, Ivy. You'll never be happy until we're safe, and you're the only one who can save us."

The only one. The weight of it felt so enormous, she could hardly believe it. But if Ivy didn't think she could save her people, where would she find the courage to try?

And if she and Matt couldn't depend on each other completely, how would they succeed?

"Please." His hand cupped Ivy's chin, feather-light. "I don't blame you for loving Martin. But you have to let him go."

His gentleness broke her. She buried her face in Mattock's chest, muffling a sob. His arms folded around her, hugging her close . . .

"Hey, boys!" Feldspar shouted from the barn door. "Have a geek at this! Six weeks, she said, but I'd say we've got ourselves a betrothal!"

Mattock stiffened and let go of Ivy. "I didn't think," he murmured. "Sorry."

"It doesn't matter," Ivy told him. She still felt shaky and lightheaded, but there was no more point delaying the inevitable. "Let them think what they like."

Ivy tried to write to Martin that night, but she'd never been good at putting words on paper, and after a few feeble, barely coherent efforts she gave up. He had no reason to worry about her absence yet, so she'd wait until she found the right way to tell him goodbye.

Meanwhile Ivy did her best to smile when her people congratulated her and bear patiently when they talked about her betrothal. Matt had warned that there'd be no feast until they were all safe from Betony, and nudged the more excitable piskeys to focus on preparing for battle instead—but even so, the atmosphere in the barn was notably cheerier than before.

Over the next two days it became even more obvious, if no less painful for Ivy, that she'd made the right decision by choosing Matt. Once she'd taught him how to travel by magic, he quickly convinced the other piskeys to follow his example. Even Mica gave in at last, though he insisted it was a coward's trick and he'd never use it unless forced to. They all practiced leaping to the landmark Matt had chosen—a lightning-hollowed tree trunk on the far side of the wood, big enough to hide most of them if they pressed together. They were still determined to fight rather than flee, but at least they'd have somewhere to escape if things went badly.

Mattock also sorted the piskeys into work groups, making sure each of them had at least one daily task that would make them feel important, and appointed the old uncles and aunties to settle minor squabbles among the young ones. He invited Broch to tell stories to the children, including a few tales from his own Welsh homeland that Ivy's folk had never heard before, and coaxed Thorn into teaching carpentry, wood carving, and archery to all who wanted to learn. Ivy's heart warmed at the sight of the piskeys crowding around the faery couple, and when Matt caught her eye and smiled, it only took a little effort to smile back.

"You're doing so well," Ivy said, as he walked across the barn to join her. "I don't know how we managed without you."

Mattock's ears turned pink, but he kept his face straight. "It's no more than Gossan used to do in the Delve. However he's changed, he was a good Jack once."

True, but Gossan would never have allowed a faery to talk to his people, let alone teach them. She was about to say as much when Matt spoke up again.

"But I think you should talk to Yarrow. She's having a hard time settling in."

Ivy followed his gaze to the healer, who stood apart from the other women with her moth-wings flattened stiffly behind her. Her eyes were no longer haunted, but she seemed ill at ease, and it wasn't hard to guess why. In the Delve Yarrow had spent long hours making and dispensing medicines for her ailing patients, but there was no sickness here and no need for salves and bandages—not when Broch could heal any minor injury with a touch. The other women did their best to keep Yarrow occupied, but she was clearly unhappy to find her traditional role filled by a stranger.

"I'll try," said Ivy, "but I'm not sure how to—" She broke off in surprise as Mica strolled up to Yarrow. He said something that made her relax and smile, and the two of them walked out of the barn together.

"Never mind," said Mattock wryly.

"What's that about?" Ivy asked. Apart from the ordeal they'd shared in the wood, it was hard to imagine what interest her hotheaded brother could have in Yarrow. She was older, grave to the point of severity, and plain compared to Jenny and the few other piskey-girls he'd admired.

"He's been taking her out for walks, trying to get her used to the surface. I think he's decided that since he found her, it's his duty to look after her." Matt shrugged. "Whatever keeps him busy."

"Are you and he still . . . ?"

"I wouldn't exactly say all's forgiven, or forgotten. But he's happy enough now he's got what he wants. As usual."

Ivy could only wish her sister's problems could be solved so easily. Cicely was still moping about the house, barely talking to anyone.

"But what about you, Ivy?" Mattock's voice lowered. "How are you feeling?"

She couldn't remember the last time another piskey had asked her that question, but Ivy could only answer with a pained shrug. Last night she'd lain awake for hours thinking about Martin, wishing she could see him one last time. When she finally fell asleep she'd dreamed she was back in the Delve, fighting Betony at the edge of the Great Shaft, and when she woke she could still feel the burning print of her aunt's fingers around her neck.

Matt didn't press her. He simply opened his arms, and Ivy walked into them. She clung to him, desperate for comfort, until she felt his lips brush her hair.

Revulsion filled her, followed by a crushing weight of shame. Somehow she had to get over her feelings for Martin— she and Mattock were as good as betrothed now, after all. But though Ivy longed to be held, she couldn't bear the thought of Matt kissing her. It took every ounce of her will not to push him away.

A throat cleared behind them, and abruptly Matt released her. Gem stood in the doorway with a nervous expression and cap in hand. "Sorry, m'lord Jack, but you did say . . ."

"All right," Matt cut him off, with unusual sharpness. "I'll be there in a moment." He paused, eyes narrowed in thought, then turned to Ivy. "You need to get away for a bit, I can tell. Why don't you fly for a few hours? I'll look after things here."

Ivy blinked. She hadn't dared leave the farmstead since Cicely confronted her, and she'd never expected that Matt would offer her the chance now. Had he sensed her discomfort, before Gem came? Was this his way of apologizing to her? "Are you sure?"

"Perfectly. Take as much time as you need."

He smiled at her, and Ivy's misgivings vanished. She might not be ready to love Matt, but at least she could always count on him to be kind. She stretched up to plant a grateful kiss on his cheek, then swooped out of the barn as a peregrine, barred wings stroking the sky.

Her instincts pulled westward, urging her toward the Delve, but that was risky. The barrow lay in that direction too, and if Cicely saw her, she'd think Ivy had broken her promise. So she turned east, soaring over the outskirts of Truro and between its cathedral spires, then on to the rugged heathland of Bodmin Moor.

It felt glorious to stretch her wings, and for the first couple of hours Ivy relished the peace and quiet of flying alone. She visited the carn where she and Martin had found their first spriggan trove, then the fogou where they'd camped below, silently bidding farewell to all their shared memories—and though her heart ached, she also felt better for it. She'd never forget Martin; she didn't even want to. But for the first time since her promise to Cicely, she thought she might be able to find the words to say goodbye.

She was perched atop a radio tower, watching the

late-afternoon traffic on the roadway far below, when a
troubling thought nagged at her mind. What had Gem been
about to tell Mattock, before she left? And why had he looked
so uncomfortable about it?

Perhaps he'd felt awkward disturbing them, but it wasn't
like Gem to be shy about such things. It wasn't like Mattock
to speak so curtly to a friend, either. At the time Ivy had put
it down to frustration, but now she wondered if there'd been
something more going on there—some nuance she'd missed in
her discomfort with the situation and her eagerness to escape.
Had Gem been bringing bad news, and Matt hadn't wanted Ivy
to hear it? Was that why he'd been so quick to send her away?

If so, they'd be having words when Ivy got back to the
farmstead. She had no doubt of Mattock's loyalty or his good
intentions, but he had no right to hide the truth from his own
Joan, no matter how young she might be. Ivy swooped down
from the tower and changed to piskey-shape, then conjured a
mental image of the Menadue farm and willed herself into it.

Her feet had barely formed on the cobbles when a flare of
green light dazzled her, and a sizzling crack rang in her ears.
Ivy staggered as the ground lurched, blinked the brightness
from her eyes—and gasped.

Three knockers in mining helmets and iron breastplates
were attacking the barn, thunder-axes flashing as they struck.
They hadn't come alone, either. In the distance, a troop of
Delve hunters fanned out across the darkened pasture, ready
to capture any piskey who tried to escape.

Orange light flickered on the far side of the barn, and fresh
panic stabbed at Ivy. Heart skittering, she turned invisible,
glancing wildly in all directions. But there was no sign
of Betony.

Where were Mattock and the other men? Why weren't they
defending the barn? Surely they hadn't just abandoned it: she
could hear a horse whinnying inside, and shrill piskey voices

clamoring out in terror. The wards hadn't failed yet, but by the grim determination on the knockers' faces, they wouldn't stop hammering until they did. Swallowing fear, Ivy dropped her invisibility spell and leaped into the barn.

Smoke billowed around her, and heat rippled from the rafters. The roof was on fire. "Get out of here!" Ivy choked, stumbling down the corridor. "All of you, before—"

"Shh!" hissed Quartz, nearly hysterical with excitement. "It's only me and Elvar." He cupped his hands to his mouth and let out a convincingly girlish wail, then declared in a gruff voice, "Stop that, woman!"

Elvar gave a loud horsy neigh, grabbed the back door of the barn and rattled it. "Help, help!" he shouted.

"That's enough," ordered Ivy, sharp with relief. She felt sick to think of losing the barn, but the walls were shaking, and the wards wouldn't hold much longer. "Go! Now!"

The boys tipped their caps to her and vanished. Wiping her stinging eyes, Ivy ran from one box stall to another. They were all empty, even Dodger's.

So her people hadn't been caught unprepared. They'd seen Gossan's soldiers coming and left Quartz and Elvar to keep them distracted while the other piskeys leaped away. But the flames racing overhead struck a deeper fear into Ivy. Betony had returned, as dangerous as ever—and Ivy had no way to stop her.

"Come out, cowards!" a harsh voice shouted through the wall. "This is your last chance!"

Come out for what? There weren't enough dungeons in the Delve to hold all of Ivy's followers, even if Betony chose to show that much mercy. Ivy grabbed a straw bale and heaved it over the crack, shoving Dodger's feed bucket, the hayfork, and other loose objects around it to make a clumsy barricade. Then she leaped to the house, where her wild-eyed little sister was struggling into her coat.

"We have to go," Ivy panted. "Once they find the barn empty, they'll come here next. Where are Thorn and Broch?"

"They left, but Dodger—"

"He's safe, don't worry. Just go!"

Cicely gave a little whimper and disappeared. Ivy snatched a rucksack from the cupboard, stuffed it with all the food it would hold, and leaped after her.

She landed hard by the broken tree, almost dropping the pack. Firm hands steadied her, and a warm voice said, "There you are, maid. Don't fret yourself, we're all safe."

Ivy blinked, disoriented. Then her night-vision focused and she recognized Teasel, Fern, and the other women, with the children clinging to their skirts. Thorn marched about in the near distance, bow in hand.

"Where's Dodger?" Cicely burst out, and dashed around the tree to look for him. But there was no sign of the pony.

"Where are Mattock and the others?" Ivy demanded. No matter where she looked, there wasn't a single male piskey in sight. Not even old uncle Agate, who could barely stand up without his cane.

Teasel put a calming hand on her shoulder. "Mattock's in charge, so never you worry. Let the men do their part, and we'll do ours."

Ivy gave a short, disbelieving laugh. "And what's that? Sit here waiting until it's all over?" But even as she spoke she regretted it. Teasel bristled, her eyes flashing.

"Someone has to guard the baggage," the older woman said, "and keep fresh weapons handy. Someone has to protect the little ones and tend the wounded if it comes to that. But if Gossan and his folk should find us . . ." She drew herself up proudly. "You'll see how we can fight, my Joan."

"I'm sorry," Ivy said. "You're right. But I can't stay here." She turned to Cicely, who was still wringing her hands and looking for Dodger. "Don't worry, Ciss. I'll find him." Then she changed to falcon-shape and flew away.

As she flapped above the trees, Ivy was seething. How *dare* Matt trick her into flying off when he knew Gossan was coming? Whether she could make fire or not, a Joan's place was with her people. But Mattock hadn't told her his plan, so Ivy had no idea how to find her own soldiers right now, let alone help them.

Yet Matt hadn't been the only one to betray her. Gem must have been in on the plot too, or he'd have reported his news straight away instead of waiting to tell Matt in private. Did they have so little faith in Ivy that they thought they'd be better off without her?

Breaking free of the wood, Ivy swooped uphill to the farmstead. Apart from the crack in one wall, the barn was still standing, and even the fire in the roof had gone out. But when Ivy glided closer, an invisible force rebuffed her. She back-winged, screeching, and tried a different angle. But the barn was unreachable, and the house too. She couldn't even leap there anymore.

That had to be Betony's doing. Any fool with a torch could have lit up the barn, but only the Joan could cast a barrier so strong. How her aunt must have sneered at Ivy's efforts to protect the farmstead! She'd dismantled her wards so easily that Ivy hadn't even sensed it. And now she could only flap in circles, while her people fought for a home they'd already lost.

Yet they still had their lives to fight for, and Ivy refused to give up yet. She wheeled and shot eastward, her falcon's eyes scanning the ground.

There! At the edge of the wood two small figures were clashing—Feldspar with his hunter's knife against one of Gossan's knockers, whose heavy thunder-axe put him at a disadvantage. As Ivy neared them, Feldspar ducked the other man's swing and shouldered him off-balance. The knocker toppled, and Feldspar wrenched the pickaxe from his hands.

Meanwhile Quartz dashed across the rocky pasture, making rude gestures at the piskeys pounding after him. He'd been the fastest runner in the Delve, and though the men jabbed their spears at the boy, they couldn't touch him.

But though they were slow and clumsy, the Delve warriors were better protected than Ivy's. Every one of them wore a stout breastplate and helmet from the treasure cavern—armor crafted for their war against the faeries a century ago. So when Hew burst from the trees and smashed his thunder-axe into one of the enemy knockers, his opponent barely staggered before hefting his own pick and swinging at him.

Hew blocked it, but the force of the blow sent him reeling. He stumbled and fell back as the enemy loomed over him, ready to strike.

With a shriek Ivy dove at the knocker's face, talons out and wings beating. He dropped his weapon, clapping both hands to his eyes. Ivy landed on the grass in her own shape, helped Hew to his feet, and together they raced for the cover of the wood.

"Where's Mattock?" she asked him. "And the others?"

"All—over," Hew panted. "Got them to—chase us, so we could—split 'em up, keep 'em busy. Give him—a chance."

Ivy was about to ask who he meant, but a shrill whinny distracted her. Dodger came plunging down the path toward them with Gem, Pick, and Elvar clinging to his saddle. He reared in front of Ivy, teeth bared and mane flying, then dropped to his hooves and blew out a gusty breath.

"Up and on, uncle!" Gem called as the men reached to help Hew onto the pony. "Let's away!" He didn't even notice Ivy until she shot up to human size and grabbed Dodger's bridle.

"Wait! Tell me what's going on."

Gem looked thunderstruck. "You shouldn't be here, my Joan!"

"If I'm your Joan," Ivy retorted, "I should be fighting beside you, not kept in the dark. Where's Mattock?"

"We can't tell yo—oof!" Elvar gasped as Pick stuck an elbow in his stomach. He gave his father a wounded look and fell silent.

If Matt had ordered them not to say where he'd gone, it could mean only one thing. Ivy flung herself into falcon-shape and shot off as fast as her wings could carry her.

She only prayed she wouldn't get to him too late.

The wood ended at the outskirts of the village, giving way to the shallow dip of a brook and a patch of moorland beyond. As Ivy burst from the trees, a stone came whizzing at her; she banked, but it passed close enough to ruffle her feathers. Some enemy hunter had a sling, and he'd known to watch for her. But in seconds Ivy was out of range, and her falcon-gaze locked onto two small, glowing figures grappling below.

Mattock and Gossan.

Metal glinted to one side, nearly hidden in the heather: Matt's hunting knife. Gossan must have knocked it from his hand, and he'd grabbed the older Jack's wrist to stop him using his own weapon. They staggered back and forth, powerful arm and shoulder muscles straining as they fought. Matt was taller, but Gossan was broader, and though they shoved and twisted, neither could break the deadlock.

Ivy circled the dueling ground, wracked with helplessness. They fought so closely, she couldn't dive at Gossan without blinding Matt as well—and the distraction could prove fatal, if the older man recovered first. All she could do for the moment was watch and wait.

Where was Betony? She'd set the barn alight to drive out

Ivy and her followers, and raised wards to keep them from coming back. But Ivy had yet to see her anywhere.

Still, a peregrine's night-vision could spot details that even a piskey's couldn't. Ivy scanned the glowing trails of animal spoor that dotted the landscape, watched a rabbit dash for its burrow and mice scurrying away from the tread of invisible feet . . .

Her instincts jangled, bird and piskey alike. Betony paced the heath a stone's throw from Gossan and Mattock, and Ivy could feel those cold eyes on her even if she couldn't see them. If she flew too close to the battling Jacks, her aunt would fell her with a single firebolt.

But she couldn't fly off and leave Mattock. Mustering all her courage, Ivy dropped from the sky and landed by the brook in piskey-shape. If Betony threw fire at her, at least she'd have water to douse it with. She swept her gaze over the spot where she knew her aunt was standing and raised her chin in defiance.

The darkness shirred as Betony made herself visible. She'd lost weight since their last confrontation, and her skin looked waxy and sallow; there were deep creases around her mouth and eyes, and even the patterns on her moth-wings seemed less vibrant. But she still had the strong-boned beauty that made Ivy feel plain and feeble by contrast, and she'd lost none of her haughtiness or her effortless air of command.

"Your so-called Joan is here, Mattock," she announced, crisp as the night breeze. "How brave of her to come and watch you die."

Matt, still wrestling with Gossan, didn't answer her directly. But his eyes flicked to Ivy's, and his clenched jaw opened in a roar. With a burst of strength he shoved the older Jack away and dove for his fallen knife.

Ivy tensed with anxiety as Mattock rolled over, leaping up just as Gossan slashed the air where he had been. The two Jacks circled each other, boots crunching on the stony path, and when Gossan lunged again, Mattock was ready for him. He swept his knife down and their blades connected— with a flash of green light and a shockwave that made them both stagger.

But a hunter's knife was plain steel, not magical. How could that be?

Matt's eyes went round with astonishment. "You filthy cheat," he breathed, but Gossan only shrugged. He shifted his grip—

And his knife transformed to a thunder-axe.

Matt ducked Gossan's first swing and leaped away from the second. But the path was rocky, and his boots skidded out from under him. He stumbled and fell, dropping the knife, and Gossan brought the pickaxe down on his outstretched hand.

Mattock screamed.

Ivy shrieked at the same moment, a raw chord of grief and horror. She leaped over the brook and flung herself in front of Matt's crumpled body, crying, "Stop! Stop hurting him!"

Gossan hesitated, his thunder-axe poised to strike. Then slowly he lowered it and stepped back. Ivy knelt beside Mattock, gripping his shoulder. "It's all right," she choked. "I'm here."

Mattock whispered her name, but it was more groan than word. His hand lay bleeding on the gravel, fingers crushed beyond recognition. Gritting his teeth, he tried to sit up—then his eyes rolled and he collapsed to the ground, unconscious.

"The Jack's down!" a shout rang out in the distance. "Protect the Joan!"

Gossan whirled, raising his thunder-axe, as Dodger galloped from the trees with a cluster of piskey warriors on his back. Feldspar leaped off to tackle the sling-wielding guard, and the two of them tumbled away as Dodger came to

a snorting halt. The other piskeys poured off the pony like a
rockslide and rushed toward Ivy.

"Stop!" Betony commanded. "One step closer, and you'll
regret it."

Ivy's followers ground to a halt, gripping their weapons
and eyeing the Joan warily. Gossan murmured, "Careful,
love," but Betony ignored him. She stalked to Ivy, who knelt
with Matt's head in her lap, and grabbed her by the hair.

"You stupid, ignorant child," she hissed, as Ivy cried out
in pain. "What do you know of being a leader? You have no
power to protect yourself, let alone the fools who follow you.
You're as weak and pathetic as your mother." Then she shoved
Ivy's head away and clapped her hands together.

Light kindled between Betony's palms, swelling into a
crackling sphere of fire. Ivy flinched away from its heat, but
she wouldn't let go of Mattock. His eyes were closed, but his
pulse still throbbed against her fingers. If she could muster the
strength to leap, and take him away with her . . .

Yet she couldn't leave Gem and the others to fight Betony
alone. She only hoped they'd remember that they could
leap, too.

"You see?" said Betony, lifting the fireball for the men
to see. "This is the power of a true Joan, not some trickery
with petrol and matches. You have despised your heritage
and dishonored your families to follow a powerless, half-
faery child."

Petrol and matches. The words struck like cold darts
into Ivy. How did her aunt know what Mica had done at the
wakefire? Had one of her followers betrayed her?

"That's dross!" yelled Quartz, his young voice hoarse with
outrage. "We all saw Ivy do it! You're the—" But Hew gripped
his shoulder and spoke over him.

"There's more of us than you here, and you can't fight the

lot of us at once. Stand back and let Ivy go, or you'll be the one to regret it."

Desperately Ivy pressed her trembling hands together. If she didn't make fire now, she never would. But though her whole body shook with the effort, her fingers stayed numb. She couldn't conjure a single spark.

Betony pursed her lips as though considering, then thrust one flaming hand at Ivy. Heat scorched her cheek, and with a cry Ivy jerked away. "Lay down your weapons and surrender," the Joan said coolly, "or I'll burn her to ashes."

The men paled and shuffled backward. Ivy bowed her head, sick with helplessness and shame. Yet they could still survive this, if her people trusted her even a little. Would they give Ivy the chance to save herself and Mattock? Or had they lost even that much hope?

"You know what to do, boys," said Hew grimly. "Ivy-maid, we haven't forgotten all you taught us. Don't you forget, either."

Relief swept over Ivy. One quick thought, and they'd all be safe with the other piskeys. Where they'd go after that was anyone's guess, but at least her people would be free.

"Dad!" Elvar's voice wobbled with panic. "I can't do it!"

Ivy's eyes flew open. The boy's outline blurred, but he wasn't disappearing. Nor were any of the others, though they stood with clenched fists and faces screwed up in concentration.

She'd seen this before, when the faery who called herself Gillian Menadue had tried to leap out of the Delve. Ivy had supposed it was something in the surrounding rock that had stopped her, like the iron piskeys used so freely. But why was it happening here, aboveground?

"Fools," said Betony in a pitying tone. "You know nothing of a true Joan's power. My presence is a ward against all such faery tricks." She opened her hands and flames ran down her arms like water, enveloping her body in a corona of fire. "There is no escape. Surrender, or your so-called Joan will die!"

The piskey-men exchanged looks, their shoulders sagging. Then one by one, they laid their weapons down.

"No," Ivy whispered, her eyes welling with tears, as Gossan's soldiers swarmed out of the wood to seize the piskeys. Eight of her most loyal followers, every one of them a husband or father or son to the women waiting at the broken tree, and there was nothing she could do to save them. Or herself.

"A wise decision," Betony told the men. "You have saved your false Joan and crippled Jack, for what little joy that may bring you." She nodded at Gossan. "Take them back to the Delve."

"Wait," blurted Ivy. "You promised to spare my life, but what about theirs? Swear you won't hurt them!"

Betony shrugged, and the fire around her body winked out. "I will make no such promise," she said, "least of all to you. If you truly cared for your followers you would never have deceived them or put their lives in danger."

With a last contemptuous glance she turned away, then paused and spoke over her shoulder. "You have seven days to repent of your treachery and bring *all* my people back to the Delve. If you do not..." She swept her arm toward the prisoners. "These men will be executed."

By the time Betony, Gossan, and the others left, it was fully dark, and a thin, icy rain was falling. Ivy huddled close to Mattock, trying to share her warmth with him until she could leap again.

He'd stirred once, but only to mumble something inaudible before sinking back into unconsciousness. His brow felt clammy and sweat darkened his russet hair. Ivy rubbed her face on her coat sleeve, struggling to make sense of what had just happened.

It wasn't hard to guess why Betony had left Matt behind: he was unconscious and too heavy to carry back to the Delve. But why hadn't she killed Ivy when she had the chance? Or at least taken her captive with the others?

Because I'm no threat to her, Ivy thought bitterly. *I can't make fire, so challenging her would be suicide. She's captured all our best fighters except Mica, and he . . .*

The possibility sickened her, but she had to face it. Mica surely would have been here if he'd had any choice in the matter, so he was probably wounded or dead. And the old uncles, like Agate and Copper, were likely dead too.

She'd failed the men who'd followed her and betrayed their trust in the worst possible way. All Ivy could do now was bring the grim news to their families, who had every reason to hate her for it. So why would Betony arrest her? Shutting Ivy up in some quiet cell would be a kindness, compared to the reckoning she was about to face.

But she couldn't avoid it any longer, or Matt would die. Struggling upright, Ivy grabbed him under the armpits and willed them both to the broken tree.

It was the hardest leap she'd ever taken. Her magic felt thick as pouring treacle, and the journey as slow. But when the fog cleared, she was surrounded by anxious piskeys.

"Mattock!" Fern rushed to him—then froze, horrified, at the sight of her son's mangled hand. "Broch!" she shrieked.

The crowd parted, and the faery man strode through, bending over Mattock and kindling a glow-spell for better light. "What happened?" he asked Ivy, as Thorn came puffing up to join them.

"Gossan had a thunder-axe," Ivy said.

Broch knelt, probing Mattock's hand with his fingertips.

When he sat back, his lean face was troubled. "His injury is severe. We need to get him warm."

"The house?" asked Thorn, but Ivy shook her head.

"Betony put a ward around it and the barn. It'll be days before we can get through."

"So we're trapped here?" demanded Daisy, clutching Thrift. "But it's freezing! What about the children?"

Broch raised his brows at Ivy, as though she knew the answer. But how could she? Apart from the farmstead, there was only one place she could think of . . .

Oh, no.

"We can't do that," she pleaded with him. "It's too risky."

"Perhaps," Broch replied. "But for Mattock's sake, I would take that risk. If he stays here, he will die."

Ivy bit her lip, fear and longing warring inside her. Then she said hoarsely, "Go."

Broch laid his hand on Matt's forehead, and the piskey shrank to the size of a mouse. In a flash Broch changed to rook-shape, snatched up the tiny form, and flapped away.

Distraught, Fern started to follow, but Thorn caught her. "Broch will take care of him," she said firmly. "And we've got other things to worry about right now." She planted her hands on her hips and gazed around at the women. "Right. Gather your things and let's go."

"What about our men?" Teasel demanded. "We can't just march off without—"

A snort interrupted her, and they all turned to find Dodger trotting up the bridle path. Cicely sat astride his shoulders, red-faced and defiant, while behind her clung Mica and Copper, with two piskey uncles dozing between them.

"Mica!" Ivy rushed over. "Where have you been?"

"Following Matt's orders like a gormless fool, that's where." Her brother helped the older men down from the pony, then slid off and dropped to the ground. "Agate and Pyrite couldn't keep up, so he told me and Copper to stick with them and make sure you and Cicely were safe." His lip curled. "Should have known he was just trying to get me out of the way."

"But what about Quartz?" Moss peered anxiously down the darkened path. "He went with Hew and the others. Where are they?"

Mica opened his mouth, but Cicely spoke first. "We looked everywhere, but we couldn't find them." She gazed down at Ivy from the horse's back, cold-eyed as a giantess. "Do *you* know where they are?"

Ivy was exhausted, and she couldn't stop shivering. She wanted nothing more than to creep into a dark hole and cry. But the women were all looking at her, expecting an answer, and they deserved to know the truth. No matter how much they might hate her for it.

"They were captured," Ivy said thickly. "Betony took them back to the Delve."

By the time they found shelter in a derelict shed, it was past midnight. Thorn gathered wood and lit a fire with grim efficiency, while the other piskeys wrapped themselves in blankets and curled up to sleep. But the roof was half missing, and the floor littered with rusty metal and broken concrete. It was not a comfortable place to stay.

Ivy sat apart from the others, hugging her knees. When she told them what had happened to Mattock and the other men, the piskey-women had wept and clung to one another for comfort. But since then they'd been silent, and no one would look at her. Not even Mica and Cicely.

She felt so weary her bones ached, but there was no use

trying to sleep. Her mind kept churning over the events of that night, wondering what she could have done to change them. But no matter how Ivy tried to imagine a different outcome, it always turned out the same. Betony was too powerful and Gossan had grown too ruthless for her to stop them.

Still, she'd never forget the shock on Quartz's face, or the looks of dismay from the older men, when Betony spoke of petrol and matches. If they'd counted on Ivy defeating her aunt in some spectacular duel of fire, they knew better now.

Yet they'd still surrendered, to save Ivy's life. She buried her head in her arms, wishing she could crumble into dust and blow away.

Delirious with grief, she'd lost track of time when a hand touched her arm. She jolted upright to find Broch standing in front of her, regarding her soberly.

"Mattock's awake," he said. "He's asking for you."

In the dead of night the hole beneath the hillside looked forbidding, the fallen trees like great spiders eager to devour her. But the door opened instantly to Ivy's touch, bathing her in comforting golden light. She climbed the stairs with Broch close behind her and stepped into the spriggan barrow.

Only a few days ago it had been a place of ancient mystery, walls lost in shadow and floor shrouded in sand. Now glow-spells bobbed cheerily about the ceiling, shedding light into every crevice, and the stones were scrubbed clean: even the egg-shaped divots that once cradled the sleeping children had vanished. Instead, thick rugs piled with blankets lay scattered about, and a boy sat in the middle of each like a gawky hatchling in its nest. When they saw Ivy, they all jumped up and bowed.

"Please don't," begged Ivy. But the spriggan boys only looked puzzled, so she hurried on.

Mattock lay on a pallet in one of the side chambers, his bandaged hand resting on his chest. The mud on his hair and clothes had vanished, no doubt thanks to Martin's cleaning spells, and when he saw Ivy his face brightened.

"No, don't," she urged, as he struggled to sit up. She

dropped to her knees beside him and gripped his good hand. "I'm so sorry, Matt."

"You did all you could. Don't blame yourself." He glanced about the chamber. "Where are we?"

Ivy cast a questioning look at Broch, but the faery man only shrugged. It seemed he was leaving it up to her. "It's a place I found with Martin a while ago," she said. "How do you feel?"

Matt shifted restlessly. "The pain's better, but I can't move my fingers."

Ivy bowed her head, grieving for him. Broch had warned her that Mattock's finger bones had been shattered, practically to dust in places, and the nerves and blood vessels too damaged for even magic to repair. He'd made Matt comfortable for the moment, but the fingers would have to be amputated, and he'd never grip anything with his right hand again.

"Ivy?" Matt's voice broke into her thoughts.

"I'm glad you're alive," she replied, forcing a smile. "I was afraid for you."

"Broch told me what happened to Hew and the others. I'm sorry."

"Matt, you've nothing to be sorry for. I'm the one who made a mess of everything."

"But I kept you in the dark, and I shouldn't have. I should have told you as soon as I knew Gossan and Betony were coming. I just . . ." He swallowed. "I couldn't stop thinking about Jenny."

Ivy sank back on her heels, feeling numb. "You told Gem, didn't you? That I couldn't make fire."

"And Hew. But nobody else, I swear! And they understood, once I explained what happened at the Lighting. They didn't blame you, Ivy. They just wanted to help."

He was talking faster now, almost babbling with agitation. His cheeks were pale, and his forehead glistened with sweat. Broch moved quickly to Matt, laying a hand on his brow. "He has a fever. We need to act quickly, before the infection spreads."

Ivy knew what that meant, and it nauseated her. But they had no choice. "Matt," she said gently. "Broch can't heal your fingers. They have to go."

His eyes went wide as a frightened child's. "Ivy?"

"I know, but I'll be here. Thorn's looking after our people, they're safe. I won't leave you." She brushed back his hair. "Please, Matt. It's the only way."

Mattock took a deep breath. Then he gave a shaky nod.

Broch gripped Matt's shoulder until the piskey went limp, then got up and strode to the inner door. "I've put him to sleep," he called. "It's time."

The door opened, and Martin walked in. His gaze met Ivy's, his mouth quirked—and she hugged herself tight, because it felt like her heart was trying to burst from her chest and fly to him. She backed away, struggling to master her feelings.

She'd told Cicely she would give Martin up, and a few hours ago she'd thought herself ready to do it. But how could Ivy forget the bond they'd forged between them? They'd broken tradition and defied prejudice to work together, heal each other, and share thoughts too intimate for words. No matter how much she owed Matt or how hard she might try to love him, her heart and soul would always belong to Martin.

She even sensed what he was feeling right now, though his face showed no sign of emotion. As he drew the knife from his belt and passed a hand over the blade to spell it clean, he was fighting a rush of hateful memories, remembering the lives he'd taken for the Empress. Watching Broch unwrap Mattock's injured hand sickened him, and it was taking all his courage not to drop the knife and bolt.

Yet he didn't flinch, or even look away, until Broch said, "Ivy, I need an anchor."

She'd been there when Broch healed her mother, so she

knew what he wanted. Deep healing could be dangerous without someone to remind the healer where his own magic ended and his patient's began. With an effort Ivy pulled herself upright and put her hand on Broch's shoulder.

"I'm ready," she said.

Ivy couldn't watch the surgery—it was too awful. She kept her eyes shut, grateful for the spell of silence that kept her from having to hear what Broch and Martin were doing. But Broch healed Matt's wound without a trace of scarring; he even managed to save the thumb, since the thunder-axe had only grazed it. When he finished it looked as though Mattock had been born without those fingers, much as Ivy had been born without wings.

"Let him sleep until morning," said Broch, sounding dull with weariness. "I'll come back and see him then." He made a feeble effort to get up, but Martin stopped him.

"If you try to leap now, you'll end up in the ocean. *You* sleep. Thorn will be all right."

Broch didn't protest. He dragged a blanket off the nearby pile, rolled himself up in it, and closed his eyes. Martin watched him a moment, then turned to Ivy.

"Are you all right? That was . . . unpleasant."

She couldn't speak to him, not with Matt lying there. She could only stare at her shoes until Martin took her arm and drew her out to the main cavern.

The spriggan boys sat up, eager for news, but Martin waved a dismissive hand. "Go to sleep, little groundlings," he said, and all the hovering lights went out.

There was a chorus of disappointed groans, but to Ivy's surprise the boys obeyed. Martin led her across to another storeroom, and shut the door behind them.

"Now," he said, taking a seat on one of the boxes. "Unpack your heart with words, as Hamlet would say. What's happened?"

Ivy hesitated. How could she burden him with her troubles, when he'd already taken such a huge risk for her sake? Mattock hadn't seen Martin or the spriggan children, and Ivy hoped to keep it that way, but he'd surely be full of questions about the barrow when he got better. He'd want to know why Ivy had kept it a secret, and how could she satisfy him except by telling him the truth?

"There's too much," Ivy said helplessly, sinking down beside Martin. "I don't know where to start."

"Well," said Martin, leaning back, "begin at the beginning, then. All I know is that Broch showed up at the door tonight with your half-dead fiancé and begged me to let him in."

"So you know about the—" She couldn't even bring herself to say it. "How?"

"I pried it out of Broch, but it wasn't all that surprising. I'd guessed your people would want a Jack to go with their Joan, and I knew you'd feel duty-bound to oblige them." He folded his arms. "He's a good-looking fellow as piskeys go, and clearly cross-eyed with love for you, so why not?"

He spoke mildly, but there was a tiny, wicked curl at the corner of his mouth, and Ivy smacked him. "You're why not, and you know it," she flared—then her face heated as she realized he'd tricked her into giving herself away. If she'd thought she could convince him her feelings had changed, it was too late now.

Martin's smile deepened. He slid off the box and crouched in front of Ivy, gazing up into her face. "I do know it," he said. "Which is why I can't feel anything but sorry for Mattock. Or for you either, so . . ." He took her hands. "You may as well tell me everything."

In halting words Ivy began to explain all that had happened since they'd last seen each other. But there were so many details, and she was so tired, that by the time she finished it felt like she'd been talking for hours.

"So all that's left now are women and children, Mica, and a handful of old uncles who can barely stand up to fight. I've got seven days to save my people from Betony. And I don't know what to do."

She finished in a whisper, her eyes lowered. They were sitting on the floor now, with Ivy's back against Martin's chest and his legs framing hers; his arms circled her waist, and he was pressing little meditative kisses into her hair. Somehow he'd coaxed her into his arms while she was talking, but he hadn't interrupted her; even now he was quiet, his breathing slow with thought.

Ivy waited until she couldn't bear the suspense any longer, then twisted to look at him. "Well?"

"I need to think," Martin said. "And you need to sleep." He brushed his thumb across her cheekbone, leaned forward— and stopped as she shied away. "Still feeling guilty about Mattock, I see."

"Don't you?"

Martin cocked his head to one side, considering. "I don't feel *that* sorry for him. He made his own choices, Ivy. You didn't force him to fight Gossan, and you certainly didn't force him to lose." He rose, offering a hand to her. "And keeping your distance from me isn't going to bring his fingers back."

Ivy gripped his wrist and let him pull her to her feet. "No, but it might make him feel less miserable about losing them. I should go."

"Your people will be asleep by now." he told her. "There's nothing you can do for them tonight." He walked to the door and opened it. "Come. You can sleep in the girls' chamber. And by morning, with any luck, Mattock will be well enough to go with you."

"My lady?"

Ivy stirred and rubbed her eyes, too disoriented to know where she was or how she'd got there. Then it came back to her and she sat up, looking around.

Last night the chamber had been dark, the air thick with drowsy silence. She'd collapsed onto the rug Martin spread out for her, too tired to even cover herself with the blanket, and fell instantly into dreamless sleep. But now glow-spells floated about the ceiling, bathing the room in multicolored light. And she was surrounded by spriggan girls, all gazing at her.

Several of them shared Martin's pale skin, sharp features, and wiry appearance, and their hair was mostly light like his as well. But a few of the younger ones were nearly as brown as piskeys, while two had a faery-like delicacy that made Ivy wonder who their mothers had been.

"What is it?" Ivy asked, rubbing sleep from her eyes.

The oldest girl bowed, her red-gold hair parting like a waterfall over her shoulders. "Breakfast, my lady," she said, holding out a wooden bowl.

I'm not your lady, Ivy wanted to protest. She didn't deserve to lead her own people, let alone anyone else's. But she didn't like to make Martin seem foolish by contradicting him, so she gave a wan smile and took the bowl.

Immediately all the other girls jumped up and ran to the main chamber, returning with bowls of their own. It seemed they'd all been waiting for Ivy to eat first—and by the way they dug in with their silver spoons, they were hungry.

The porridge was thick and grainy but sweetened with honey to help it go down. Ivy managed to finish most of it, but the frank stares of the spriggan girls made her self-conscious. Did they think her ugly, with her cropped curls and missing wings?

"I'll take that, my lady," said the oldest, as Ivy set the bowl aside. "Did it not please you? Would you like something else?"

"Not at all," Ivy assured her. "It was a fine breakfast, I'm just full. And please . . . call me Ivy."

The girls traded uncertain looks. Then the oldest said cautiously, "Ivy."

Well, at least she hadn't offended them. "Do you have names? Or do you have to earn them, like the boys?"

One of the smaller girls giggled, and her neighbor shushed her. The oldest gave the two of them a quelling glance, then turned back to Ivy. "Our mothers named us," she said. "I am called Jewel."

"Opal," offered the second oldest, and the others chimed in, "Topaz . . . Diamond . . . Ruby . . ." all the way down to the youngest, Pearl.

Which made sense, now Ivy thought about it: spriggan women not only kept their family's treasure, they were treated like treasures themselves. Highly prized and closely guarded, they spent their married lives invisible to all but their own husbands, so no one could see the wealth they wore and be tempted to steal it—or them—away.

Still, most of these girls' names would have been boys' names in the Delve. Could that be why piskey legend claimed that spriggans had no women of their own?

"I'm glad to meet you," Ivy said. "And grateful you've made me so welcome. It can't be easy for you having a stranger here, especially one like me."

"My mam was a piskey," said Topaz, with a lift of her brown chin. "Ruby's mam, too."

Ruby nodded. "But the knocker-men came and took them

away." Her eyes grew dark with memory. "I cried and cried, and I could hear mam crying too. But she never came back."

So their mothers must have been taken by the spriggans only to be recaptured years later by the piskeys, equally against their will. No wonder Ivy's people and Martin's had hated each other.

"The Gray Man's son told us how he was captured by the piskeys," Jewel said. "He said he would have died in the false Joan's dungeon, if you hadn't come to lead him out. So we trust you. Because you saved him, and he saved us."

The other girls nodded eagerly, faces shining with admiration. "I'm honored," Ivy managed to say, though her heart felt bruised. If any harm came to these children because of her, she'd never forgive herself.

"Are you there, Ivy?" Broch's voice drifted through the doorway, and with a gasp the spriggan girls vanished. She could still hear their shallow breathing, but every one had turned invisible, and the air around them vibrated with dread.

"Don't be afraid," Ivy said quickly. "He's a friend."

There was a collective exhale, and a few of the girls winked back into visibility, though the rest remained hazy, like nervous ghosts. Ivy got up and followed Broch to the main chamber. "What is it?"

The faery man looked grim. "Mattock's awake, but his fever's returned, and I had to heal his hand again this morning. I've never seen anything like it."

"I have," said Martin, rising to join them. "The first time I healed Ivy, the spell unraveled and I had to do it again. She had a fever, too."

"That's true," Ivy remarked. "I thought it must be something to do with the poison in the Delve."

"But the second time he healed you, it worked?"

Ivy nodded.

Broch scrubbed a hand through his hair, making it messier

than ever. "Then I must be doing something wrong, or there's more to his injury than we thought. Could Gossan or Betony have put a curse on him?"

Martin started toward the sickroom, but Ivy caught his arm. "You can't. If Matt sees you—"

"He'll know I'm here. But since he doesn't know where *here* is, does it matter?" He pulled away, and reluctantly Ivy followed.

Mattock lay ashen and sweating on his pallet, head tossing from side to side. His injured hand was swollen, and though his eyelids fluttered, he barely seemed to notice when they came in. But when Martin bent over him, he made a croaking sound and jerked away.

"It's all right," Ivy said quickly. "He's here to help. Will you let him?"

Mattock's bloodshot eyes slid to hers, searching. Then he gave a little grimace and nodded.

Martin took Ivy's hand, then reached out to Mattock. The piskey's jaw clenched, but he held still as Martin closed his eyes in concentration. "His blood's poisoned," he said distractedly. "And it's spreading fast. But I think . . ."

His grip on Ivy's tightened as green light spread from his outstretched hand, rippling down the length of Mattock's body. It hovered over him, pulsing gently, then sank into him like water into pumice stone.

Matt groaned and Broch started forward, but Ivy waved him back. "Not yet." She'd cried out the first time Martin had healed her, too: she'd been so close to death he'd had to practically bully her back to life, and it hurt. But that was a small price to pay for living.

Bilious mist rose from Matt's skin, snaking in all directions. Martin dropped Ivy's hand and flung up both his own, lifting the cloud like a blanket and whisking it away. The air cleared, and Mattock relaxed at once. "It's gone," he mumbled. "How . . . ?"

Broch stooped to check his temperature, then his pulse. "How indeed," he said, with a sidelong glance at Martin. "But rest a little longer. We need to be sure the healing will take."

Mattock struggled up onto his elbows. "I'm hungry."

"I'll get you some porridge," Martin said. He sounded casual, but Ivy could see the weariness in his shoulders.

"Wait."

Ivy held her breath. Matt was studying his injured hand, turning it back and forth as though seeing it for the first time. He flexed the thumb, rubbing it across the place where his fingers had been. Then he looked up, resolute.

"You saved my life. I owe you a great debt." His gaze slid to Martin. "All of you."

Martin paused in the doorway, one hand braced against the arch of stones. "You're welcome," he said quietly, and went out.

13

"It's extraordinary." Broch strode into the main chamber, sidestepping the two boys squabbling over the last helping of porridge. "I knew something was wrong with him, I just couldn't see how to make it right. But you cured Mattock completely. How?"

Martin deftly plucked the ladle from one spriggan boy and the pot from the other, then handed both to a third and scrawnier boy who looked both startled and delighted by his good fortune. "I don't know what to tell you. Perhaps I've just got a knack for healing piskeys."

"That doesn't make sense," said Ivy. "Broch's been healing my people for weeks."

"Only injuries," Broch countered. "Not illnesses. Or infections, either."

He had a point. Faeries could be wounded but almost never took ill, so there was no need for their healers to learn about such things. Yet Martin had cured Ivy by pure instinct, and now he'd healed Matt the same way. Could it be his spriggan magic, bringing good luck instead of bad for a change?

"Still," Broch continued, "it would be wise to let Mattock rest a few hours before sending him back to the others. He'll need all his strength to lead them now. As will you, Ivy."

Ivy knew he meant it kindly, but his words felt like a mockery. How could she lead her people when they had nowhere to go? And how could Matt protect them with only one hand? Right now he couldn't even wield a knife, let alone a thunder-axe. And they only had six days left to rescue Hew and the others.

She could feel Martin's eyes on her, knew that he sensed her turmoil. But he was waiting for the small boy to finish his porridge, and he didn't speak.

"I must get back to Thorn," Broch said. "Are you coming, Ivy?"

"Soon," Ivy promised him, and with a nod the faery man walked out.

"Right," said Martin briskly. "Caliban, Tybalt, you're on wash-up." He handled the pot and ladle back to the boys who'd been arguing; they made sour faces but began collecting the dirty bowls at once. "Hamlet and Horatio, sweep the cavern. The rest of you, roll up your beds. Then we'll talk."

The boys seemed not to mind their Shakespearean nicknames, because they all jumped to obey. "You're good at this," Ivy murmured, but Martin only smiled.

"I used to work at a hostel in London. It's not so different."

Perhaps, but it wasn't Martin's housekeeping skills that had impressed her. "I meant being a leader."

"Only because they're still young and ignorant enough to be in awe of me. I'm sure it'll wear off." He took Ivy's arm. "But we have things to discuss, before you go back to the others."

He was leading her back to the room where they'd left Mattock. "Wait," said Ivy, but Martin's grip stayed firm.

"I know what I'm doing," he said. "Or at least I hope so. Let's talk to your Jack and find out."

When Ivy left the barrow, she felt dizzy with apprehension. She'd been taken aback when Martin told them his plan, and so had Mattock; they'd both protested that it was too much to accept, and far too great a risk.

Yet he'd been adamant, so what could they do but give in? Even the faint hope Martin offered was better than no hope at all. Steeling herself, Ivy leaped back to her fellow piskeys.

As soon as she materialized, Fern jumped up and rushed to her. "Where's Mattock? Is he all right?"

Her hair was straggling out of its topknot, her eyes bagged with lack of sleep. Ivy took off her coat and draped it around Fern's shoulders. "He's well, and you'll see him soon," she promised, leading Matt's mother back toward the fire.

The other piskeys huddled around the flames, looking equally dirty and exhausted, while Mica turned a rabbit on a makeshift spit and winced as the smoke got in his eyes. Broch sat next to Thorn in the corner, one arm protectively around her; by her dazed expression, she'd been up all night. Outside the shed Cicely stood at human size, petting Dodger's neck and whispering to him. But she didn't look up, even when Ivy cleared her throat to speak.

"I know this is hard," she began. Her heart was thumping and her mouth felt dry, but she had to stay calm or she'd never get the words out. "We were ready to fight like true piskeys, but we weren't prepared for treachery, and that's how Gossan and Betony defeated us. It wasn't because Mattock and the other men weren't strong enough. It was because they were too honorable to stoop to such cruel, deceitful tricks."

A few of the women looked up, nodding. But Copper

and the other men sat with jaws clenched and arms folded, watching the rabbit roasting slowly over the fire.

"But we have something our enemies don't," Ivy continued. "We have allies. Other magical folk with their own strengths to offer, who want peace as much as we do." She gestured to Thorn and Broch. "And we could make even more new friends if we're willing to ask for help, instead of thinking we can fight Betony all by ourselves."

"Mam?" whispered Thrift, but Daisy hushed her. Mica shifted restlessly on his haunches, and Daffodil, Copper's wife, gave a feeble cough. But nobody spoke.

"I banished one of those friends," Ivy went on, "because you were too afraid to trust him. But he's chosen not to hold that against us. He helped Broch heal Mattock—"

Fern's head jerked up, eyes red and disbelieving.

"—and now he's offering us a place to live. A safe, warm place that no one else knows about, where we can stay for the next few days while we decide what to do."

"Is that so." Mica sat back, his lip curling. "How lucky for us. And what kind of payment does your *friend* want in return?"

"Only kindness," Ivy told him. "He wants us to swear we won't hurt him, or . . . or anyone under his protection. And that we won't tell other piskeys about this secret place, or show them where to find it, unless he agrees."

It was a huge gamble, telling Ivy's followers about the barrow. But as Martin had pointed out, it was their best chance to prove that spriggans weren't the selfish, greedy monsters of piskey legend. And that wouldn't just help the piskeys, it would help Martin's people too.

Mica gave a bitter laugh. "Let's be honest," he said, standing up. "You talk about *friends*, but what you're really asking is for us to put ourselves at the mercy of a spriggan. Or if you cared to tell the whole truth, instead of just the part you think we're ready for . . ."

She knew that look in her brother's eyes, and it never meant anything good. "Mica—"

"You want to march us straight to the lair of *your* spriggan lover and a horde of other spriggans as well!"

The bottom dropped out of Ivy's stomach. She stumbled back as the piskeys leaped to their feet, staring at her in accusation. "*Other* spriggans? You said he was the last of his kind!"

Ivy's thoughts raced, tripping over one another in panic. How had Mica known about the children? The only person she'd told was Molly, and she'd never betray Ivy that way. "I . . . I thought he was," she stammered. "And so did he. We didn't find the others until—"

Mica cut her off with a gesture. "We've heard enough. No more excuses." He turned to the others. "Now you know why she wouldn't make up her mind about Mattock. Her heart's not with us, it's with that spriggan. And now he wants to lure us into his trap too."

Daisy and Clover clutched their children protectively, while Teasel turned the spit Mica had forgotten, her mouth a troubled line. Only Fern kept her gaze on Ivy, but it was so full of bewildered hurt that Ivy couldn't bear it. Hot with shame, she looked away.

"Our men are trapped in the Delve now," Mica said harshly, "because Ivy couldn't stop Betony when she had the chance. Now she wants us to go hide in some filthy spriggan's den and abandon them?" He shook his head. "I won't do it. And neither should you."

"That's right!" Copper thumped the floor with the haft of his thunder-axe. "We're piskeys, not rabbits. We oughter stand up and fight!"

"I never said we'd abandon them!" Ivy was trembling, but

she was also furious. What was her brother doing? Matt had sworn Mica believed in her, but there was no sign of that now. "I only said we needed time to rest and think!"

"We don't *have* time," Mica retorted. "And we've done too much thinking already. We need to take action now, or eight good men will end up swinging from Betony's gallows. And your spriggan boy can't help us, no matter what pretty lies he's told you."

He spun back toward the other piskeys, spreading his arms. "Do I have to say it? Ivy's my sister and I've done my best to support her, but she's not fit to be Joan. And even if Matt's not addled by spriggan charms like she is, he can't fight Gossan with one hand. So I say we stop waiting for Ivy to prove she knows what it means to be a piskey, and look to someone who's already proved it." He gestured to the back of the circle. "Yarrow."

The young healer rose, stepping past the fire. Her cheeks were pale, but she met Ivy's eyes without flinching. "I never wanted this," she said quietly. "Neither did Mica. But you've left us no choice."

"So you're offering to be his Joan?" demanded Ivy, incredulous. "What good will that do? You can't stand up to Betony either. You can't even make fire!"

"Not yet," Yarrow said, a tremor in her voice, "but neither can you. And the whole Delve knows it."

Her words fell on Ivy like a thunder-axe. She stared at the healer, too aghast to speak.

"A true wakefire is kindled by magic, and that's what they hoped for when they came to your Lighting. But all you gave them was a burning pile of wood, and as soon as they went back underground, they knew it." Yarrow's chin came up. "Our people believed in you, but you've done nothing but deceive them. You're no more fit to be Joan than I am."

Ivy could feel the other piskeys' eyes on her, knew they

were waiting for an answer. But what could she say? Even if she told them what Mica had done to the wakefire, she was still guilty of letting them think she'd lit it by magic.

"You're right," Ivy said at last. "I'm sorry." Then she walked to the other end of the ruined shed and sat down, defeated.

"So," said Mica, triumphant. "You've heard it all, and you know what your choices are. Who's with me and Yarrow?"

The piskeys hesitated, shuffling their feet. Nobody answered until a determined young voice said, "I am," and Cicely walked through the doorway, changing to piskey size as she went.

No, no, no, Ivy's heart wailed. All at once it was painfully clear how Mica had found out about the spriggans. It wouldn't be the first time Cicely had fooled Ivy by turning invisible, and it wouldn't have been hard for her to eavesdrop on Ivy's conversation with Molly . . . or her private talks with Thorn and Broch, either.

Ivy had been so caught up in her own troubles, she hadn't paid much attention to Cicely. But Mica had.

The other piskeys turned to one another, whispering. Little by little their voices rose, until they were all talking loudly at once:

"—the children—"

"—too dangerous—"

"I'm no coward, *you're* the—"

"—bewitched her, plain as plain—"

"—put his head in the noose yourself!"

But soon the noise died down as one piskey after another moved away, lining up behind Mica. Putting their last hopes in him, and not in Ivy.

Ivy pressed her forehead to her knees, heartsick. She knew Mica too well to think he could hold their people together, even with Yarrow's help. Even if they managed to get into the Delve without being caught, they'd never come out again. But there was nothing she could do.

"So," Mica said brusquely, "we're done. Let's go."

Gravel crunched as her brother and his followers marched off, and Dodger clopped placidly after them. Dreading what she was about to find, Ivy looked up.

Fern still sat by the fire, which was no surprise: she was desperate to see Mattock again, spriggans or no spriggans. But she wasn't alone. Daisy and Clover with their little ones, the old aunties, Moss and even Teasel—nearly all the women and children had stayed except for Cicely and Copper's wife Daffodil, whose cough still echoed faintly in the distance.

Numb with disbelief, Ivy climbed to her feet. She wanted to ask the women why they'd stayed, but she was afraid to test the fragile, precious trust they'd placed in her. The long walk to the barrow would be trial enough.

"I promise you," she told them fervently, "I'll do everything I can to get your men back from Betony. And I know Matt will, too."

There was an uncomfortable pause. Then Thrift's small voice said, "Mam, I'm hungry."

Mica and his followers had taken the roasted rabbit, and with no hunters left, Ivy couldn't replace it. She hurried to the pile of baggage in the corner, searching for the pack she'd brought from the cottage. But the food she'd packed into it was gone, and she found nothing but a handful of dirty wrappers.

Across the shed Thorn sighed and lifted her head from Broch's shoulder. "Give us an hour or so," she said gruffly. "We'll see what we can do."

After a late breakfast of roasted squirrel and an icy wash in the brook, Ivy and her small band of followers set off. It would have been easy for her and Broch to leap to the barrow, but neither Thorn nor any of the others had been there yet, so they had no choice but to take the long way.

Fortunately, the women didn't object to turning human size for the journey, and both Daisy and Moss had a knack for invisibility charms that would keep them doubly safe. Broch carried Thrift piskey-back and Clover's two boys trotted after him, while Ivy followed with the rest and Thorn marched doggedly in the rear.

Neither of the faeries had spoken out when Mica challenged her, but Ivy didn't blame them: she knew as well as they did that it would only have made matters worse. She had no doubt of their loyalty, in any case. They'd proven themselves staunch as any Cornish piskey . . . and though it hurt to recall it, truer than Ivy's own brother and sister.

They plodded along all day, skirting human towns and roadways, following Ivy's inborn direction-sense on the slow westward march. In the afternoon it began to rain, but the drizzle was mercifully light, and the brisk walk helped keep them warm. Still, the aunties were breathing heavily and the children stumbling with exhaustion by the time they crested the last hill and found Martin waiting for them at the bottom.

Ivy longed to hurtle down the slope into his arms. But her followers had chosen to believe she'd made this choice wisely, not dazzled by some spriggan love-charm, and she wouldn't give them any reason to doubt it. She led them down to the fallen trees, and stepped up to Martin.

"You've offered us refuge," she said formally, "and we're grateful. My people and I vow to do no harm to you or to those under your protection, and never reveal the secret of this place to anyone, even our own flesh and blood." She turned to the women behind her. "Do you all swear to keep this promise?"

"Ayes, we swear," said Teasel, and a soft chorus of voices

agreed. Martin studied them, expressionless, then turned and led them into the hill.

When they came up the stairs, Mattock was waiting, and Fern burst into tears of relief. She hugged him tight, scolding him—then caught sight of his half hand and fell into stunned silence.

"I know, Mother," Mattock said. "It's a change, and it'll take getting used to. But it's not the end."

Fern smiled wanly, but she still looked shaken, and Ivy knew what she and the other women were thinking. A Jack who couldn't lead his people into battle was useless as a Joan who couldn't wield fire.

As Matt greeted the rest of the piskeys and handed them blankets to get warm, Ivy realized the rest of the chamber was empty. Had the spriggan children hidden out of shyness? Or had Martin ordered them to stay away?

Ivy would have asked him, he'd disappeared as well. So she helped Mattock get all the piskeys settled, then found a spot at the back of the cavern and sat down with a weary sigh.

She must have dozed off, because the next thing she knew a warm bowl was being pressed into her hands, and the smell of fish teased her nostrils. Hazily Ivy looked around to find the cavern full of the spriggan children, serving supper.

The smallest ones were the boldest: they thrust out their baskets of crusty bread with pride and scampered off to get more. The older children moved more warily, gripping their bowls of fish stew with both hands and avoiding the piskeys' eyes. And Dagger looked positively disgusted: he shoved the bowl at Mattock so hard it slopped over, and stalked off without even offering him a spoon.

But it was good stew, thick and savory. The fish was fresh, the bread only a little stale. When all the piskeys had eaten, the spriggan children silently collected the bowls and took them away. Teasel coughed and sniffed, and when Ivy got up in concern to check on her, she found the older woman weeping.

"I thought they'd be monsters," she whispered. "Like the old tales said. I only came because I was afeard for Daisy and Clover and their little ones." Her fingers plucked at her muddy skirts. "I knew if Hew was here, he'd fight all the spriggans in the world to save them, and he'd want me to fight too. But . . ." She met Ivy's eyes with her red, brimming ones. "They're only children."

Ivy put a hand over Teasel's. There was no need to say anything more. They sat side by side in the twilit warmth of the cavern, until the older woman's skin-glow faded and she drooped against Ivy's shoulder, fast asleep.

14

Ivy paced the storeroom, teeth worrying at her lower lip. Martin lounged on a pile of flour sacks in the corner, eating an apple left over from breakfast, while Mattock stood awkwardly by the door, waiting for Ivy to explain why she'd called for them.

"This is a disaster," Ivy burst out. "I'm not blaming you, Martin—you and the children have been wonderful. But I can't ask all these piskey-women to stay here without trying to do *something* to save their men. And we've only got five days before Betony executes them." She gestured helplessly. "What am I going to do?"

"Well, you can't stop her all by yourself," said Martin, making the core vanish with a twirl of his fingers. "I'd do my best to help if it were just me, but . . ."

"Of course," said Ivy. "You have to protect the children." And how much help could Martin give her anyway? Even if he could find the courage to go back into the Delve, he'd be no more a match for Gossan than she was for Betony. "I just need advice. If you have any."

Martin sat up, fingers drumming on his crossed leg. "Well," he said after a moment, "there are only two options I can think of. One is to find a spell that will stop Betony's fire. The other is to raise an army."

"An army of what?" Ivy asked in frustration. "Birds? Animals? You've seen my followers, Martin. I can't ask old aunties and mothers with little children to fight Betony."

Martin raised his brows at her. "Ivy, I know you grew up in the Delve, and you still think of yourself as a piskey. But your father died months ago, your mother left, and your brother and sister turned against you. And with only one exception I know of"—he nodded politely at Mattock—"you've done far more for your people than they've ever done for you. Why are you asking *yourself* to fight Betony?"

Ivy felt like a fist had clenched around her heart. She looked desperately at Mattock. But his eyes were lowered, and he didn't seem to have any more answer than she did.

"You're right about my family," Ivy said at last. "And my people aren't perfect, either. But if I start thinking about how much they owe me, or what they do and don't deserve—" She shook her head. "That may be how faeries do things, but it's not the piskey way. And I don't want it to be mine, either."

Martin narrowed his eyes, and for a moment Ivy feared she'd insulted him. But then he leaned back with a shrug. "*It boots not to resist both wind and tide,*" he quoted. "As usual, you'll do whatever you think is right. No matter what anyone else thinks."

"It's not just that." Ivy dropped onto a barrel, head in hands. "Those men gave themselves up to save me. How can I walk away and leave them to die?"

"A noble sentiment," said Martin. "But I don't think you'll be honoring their sacrifice if you run back to the Delve and get yourself killed as well." He looked at Mattock. "Shouldn't you be trying to talk sense into her? Isn't that what the Jack's supposed to do?"

"I—" Mattock began, but the creak of the door interrupted

him. Thorn came marching into the storeroom, towing her husband behind her.

With all that had happened lately Ivy had forgotten Broch's promise to sell Martin's treasure, but clearly neither of them had. Where Martin had found a full suit of modern clothing, Ivy couldn't guess. But in a tailored jacket and dark trousers, with hair trimmed to match the neatness of his beard, Broch looked almost human.

"Do any of you know how to tie one of these?" Thorn demanded, waving a crumpled silk necktie. "Broch's got to be in London by midday, and I'm ready to chuck the blighted thing into the fire."

Shaking his head in amusement, Martin unfolded himself and rose. He whisked the tie from Thorn's hand and spelled it smooth with a gesture, then draped it around his own neck and knotted it loosely with a few deft twists. "*What a deformed thief this fashion is,*" he quipped, handing it back to her. "But that should do it."

That made two Shakespeare quotes in as many minutes. Martin was too good an actor to betray it, but he clearly had strong feelings about something.

"Hmph," said Thorn, as she looped the tie around Broch's neck and tugged it into place. "Well, I'm no expert like Wink, but it looks all right." She eyed him sidelong. "How long is this business going to take?"

"If all goes well, I'll be back by tomorrow. If not . . ." Broch gave an apologetic shrug. "It might be another day. Or more."

Thorn made a face at that, but she didn't argue. David Menadue had agreed to help Broch and even give him a place to stay, so there was no need for her to worry.

"I'll get the treasure," said Martin, and slipped out to the main cavern. Mattock sat quietly a moment, not looking at Ivy, then got up and left without saying a word.

Maybe he was trying to think of a plan—or at least Ivy

hoped so. Because much as attempting to rescue her men frightened her, telling their families she'd given up would be worse. She studied the barrel, picking at a splinter, until a series of jingling footsteps told her Martin had returned.

"Here you go," he said, swinging a leather pack off his arm and handing it to Broch, who staggered and nearly dropped it. He cast Martin a startled look.

"Too heavy?" Martin asked mildly.

"Almost, but I'll get used to it." Broch turned to Ivy. "Any message for your mother?"

She'd probably rung the house at least once and wondered why no one answered. "Tell her I'm fine," Ivy said. "And that Cicely's . . ." She hesitated. "Helping Mica. And I hope to see her soon."

Broch hefted the pack and went out. Thorn followed, leaving Ivy and Martin alone.

"That evasion was positively faery-like," said Martin, pressing a hand to his heart. "You've come so far. I'm proud."

Ivy gritted her teeth in exasperation. Martin had visited the main cavern only once last night, to say a few quiet words to Mattock. But his gaze had held Ivy's all the while, and she'd felt his longing as keenly as her own. Yet now they finally had a moment together, he seemed to be pushing her away. "Are you *trying* to irritate me?" she asked. "This isn't a joke, Martin."

His expression sobered. "No. But Ivy, you need to think—"

A child's shriek rang out from the main cavern, followed by pattering footsteps and the sound of hysterical weeping. Anxious, Ivy started toward it, only to stop short as Mattock strode through the doorway, dragging a wildly kicking Dagger behind him.

"Let go, you piskey oaf!" the spriggan boy snarled. "Get your dirty paws off me!"

Martin's jaw tightened. "Let him go, Matt."

Mattock dropped the boy and stepped back, folding his

arms. "He tried to grab the treasure from Broch," he said flatly. "And when Thorn gave him a clout on the ear for his trouble, he blawed up like a quilkin and scared Thrift out of her wits."

Martin cast a bemused look at Ivy. "Blawed up . . . ?"

"Puffed up like a frog," Ivy told him. "Whatever that's supposed to—" She bit off a startled oath as Dagger's face swelled to monstrosity, his thin body erupting into the stumpy, misshapen form that spriggans used to frighten enemies away. She'd seen it in one of Martin's childhood memories, but she'd never expected to witness it with her own eyes.

Martin's hand whipped out, seizing Dagger by the ear, and the boy yelped and deflated. *"Like the toad, ugly and venomous,"* Martin said coldly. "What do you think you're doing, you wretched little imp?"

"You're no spriggan!" the boy spat, eyes filling with angry tears. "The Gray Man would be shamed o' you. Filling up our barrow with knocker folk and giving away our treasure—"

"I'm shocked to hear you disapprove," Martin said drily. "You've been so subtle about it." He whisked a handkerchief from his pocket and tossed it to the boy, then turned to Ivy and Mattock. "If you'll excuse us, we have business to settle." Without waiting for an answer, he put a firm hand on Dagger's shoulder and steered him through the inner door.

Mattock turned to leave, but Ivy blocked him. "Don't you have *any* idea how to help the others? Think about Quartz, and Elvar—they're just boys! There has to be some way we can get them back from Betony." She pushed her hands through her curls, gripping them in frustration. "Think, Matt! I can't do this without my Jack."

Mattock flinched like she'd whipped him. "I'm not the Jack you need," he said, his voice low and rough. "I'm nobody's Jack now. And I can't help you. No matter how I wish I could."

Then he pushed past Ivy and walked out, leaving her alone.

Ivy lay on her bedroll, staring at the ceiling of the main cavern. Not that there was anything to look at: with all the glow-spells extinguished, the barrow was black as any mineshaft. But she couldn't sleep.

It wasn't that the rest of the day had gone poorly—quite the opposite. Apart from Dagger's outburst, there'd been no squabbles between the piskeys and the spriggans at all. And though Martin's elusiveness frustrated her, she understood now why he was doing it. He knew how fearful her people were of spriggan tricks, and he didn't want to give them any reason to doubt Ivy's judgment.

Yet in his subtle way, Martin had made a powerful impact on the piskeys. When they followed Ivy to the barrow they'd expected a grudging welcome at best, followed by an interrogation—or worse, bewitchment. But Martin had retreated, and sent the children to serve the piskeys dinner instead.

The choice had been calculated, but there'd been nothing dishonest about it. He'd let all his charges behave according to their nature, from Pearl's shy eagerness to Dagger's resentment, knowing Ivy's people would see that honesty and be reassured by it in a way no pretense could do. Without a word he'd disarmed the piskeys' fears and left them doubting everything they thought they knew about spriggans.

But Clover's youngest son had sobbed himself to sleep tonight, missing his father, and Daisy's eyes still welled up at every mention of Gem. Ivy's followers might be safe here, but they'd never be happy.

Ivy had lain awake for what felt like hours when the door

to the adjoining room opened and a sliver of light shot out. Fern appeared in the doorway, beckoning furtively, and with a soft rustle three more women got up and padded to join her, as though they'd been waiting for her signal.

None of them had said anything to Ivy about a meeting. If the other women were plotting behind her back, she had better know about it. Turning invisible, Ivy jumped up and sprinted after them, slipping through just before the door shut.

What she found on the other side, to her surprise, was a cozy nest of sacks and blankets on the floor, and Fern pulling the cork from a wine jug. She sniffed it, took a tentative sip and then a bigger one before passing the jug to Teasel and sitting down next to her. "Well," she declared, leaning back, "this is more like it."

"Proper job, that wine is," said Teasel, wiping her mouth. "Where'd you find it?"

"Oh, I've been poking about," Fern told her. "Mattock showed me practically the whole place, when that spriggan fellow and his boys were out fishing. It's not the Delve to be sure, but it's a fine big barrow, and there's a whole crate of wine jugs in one of the storerooms. I thought with so many children about, who'd miss it?"

They fell into a comfortable silence while the jug made its way around the circle. At last Moss cleared her throat. "So, Teasel, what's on your mind? I like a drop as much as any piskey, but you've not called us here for that, I'm sure."

The older woman sat up, smoothing her skirts briskly. "Ayes, you're right. Truth is, I've been thinking of Ivy. I've been watching her and the spriggan since we got here, but I don't see much sign of her being bewitched, do you? And it puts me in mind of a story the aunties used to tell in secret, when I was a young maid—"

"Ah, you mean 'The Spriggan Lover.'" Old Bramble

grinned, eyes twinkling wickedly. "I got a right wallop when my mam caught me listening to that one!"

Fern pursed her lips disapprovingly, but she didn't look surprised, and neither did Moss. Whatever the story was, it seemed to be well known by the older women.

"The thing is," Teasel continued, "we thought 'twas only folly, imagining love could make a monster into a man. And the droll-tellers made so much of spriggans being all wicked, telling us we daren't go out on the surface for fear of them, we never dreamed it could be otherwise. But what if it weren't just an old aunties' tale? What if it really happened, long ago?"

"There's no happy ending to that story," Fern said darkly. "At least as it was told me. The piskey-girl's brothers caught the spriggan and flung him down a mineshaft, and she died of a broken heart."

"But they had a grand love first," Moss murmured, then caught Fern's glare and took a hasty swig of wine.

"And that's the point, isn't it?" Teasel said. "Not how it ended, but that such a thing could happen. And might not have ended badly either, if her folk hadn't been so hard against it."

"You've not made your point yet, by the look of you." Fern took the jug from Moss, her jaw set. "Out with it, then. I'm not afraid of plain talking."

Teasel gave her a sympathetic look. "Your Mattock's a fine boy, Fern. We'd have been glad to crown him our Jack, if Gossan hadn't served him so badly. But for all they've been tiptoeing around each other, it's clear Ivy's in love with that spriggan, and he with her. So maybe . . ." Her gaze travelled the circle. "Maybe we should stop holding her to a promise her heart can't keep."

Fern bristled. "So you think Matt's not fit to be her husband? And some—some pinch-faced slip of a spriggan is?"

"I'm not talking of what ought to be," Teasel said gently. "Only how things are. And wouldn't it be better for Matt to find a wife who can love him with all her heart, instead of waiting on Ivy to make him a corner in hers?"

That silenced Fern. She ran her thumb around the lip of the jug, her mouth lined with unhappiness.

"The thing is," Teasel continued, "we've all been looking to Ivy to save us, and no one can say she hasn't tried. If it weren't for her we'd never have known about the Delve being poisoned, let alone have a chance to come out of it. But Betony's got our men, so we have to go back and face her. And if she's got fire and Ivy doesn't . . . there's only one way that story's going to end."

"Like Jenny's did," said Moss huskily, and the other women looked grave.

"Betony doesn't want Ivy, anyhow," Bramble pointed out. "She banished her, like she did her mother."

"That's right," Teasel said. "It's us she wants." She motioned for the wine jug, and reluctantly Fern gave it back.

"So what you're saying is we wait another day or two and then take ourselves back to the Delve, us and Daisy and Clover and Matt and all, and leave Ivy with her spriggan fellow."

"Ayes." Hew's wife wiped her mouth and set the jug aside. "That's what I'm saying. But someone's got to break it to Ivy and make sure she doesn't chase after us and throw her life away. We wanted a new Joan so badly, we talked ourselves into thinking she could save us. But now we know she can't, it's high time we stopped asking her to try."

Ivy shut her eyes, hot tears streaking her cheeks. There was nothing behind their conspiracy but kindness, but it hurt to be reminded how cruelly she'd disappointed these women, and how little faith they had left in her now.

Still, they were offering Ivy a way out, and part of her longed to take it. But how could she be happy staying with Martin while her people sickened and died under Betony's rule? If she did nothing, she'd soon be the last of the piskeys—and this time there'd be no prophecy and no magic to save her people from extinction.

She couldn't let that happen. There had to be another way.

Please, help me, she prayed silently. *I'm alone and helpless, and I don't know what to do.* Then she bowed her head and sat motionless until the older women finished off the jug of wine and went away.

But though Ivy waited, no answer came, and a coil of bitterness tightened around her heart. Maybe there was no higher being who cared about piskeys anymore, if there ever had been. Maybe the Shaper or the Great Gardener or whoever it was had given up on Ivy's people when they wiped out the spriggans, and now they were on their own.

But as she tossed atop her bedroll, desperate to sleep, she suddenly remembered what Martin had said that morning.

One is to find a spell that will stop Betony's fire.

The other is to raise an army.

Ivy sat up, wide awake. Then she kindled her skin-glow and scrambled out of bed to find Thorn.

"No," Thorn said crossly. "Absolutely not."

She'd refused to answer last night, no matter how Ivy pleaded: she'd pulled the blankets over her head and curled up like a furious snail until Ivy gave up and went away. So she'd coaxed Thorn outside for a walk after breakfast, but the faery woman still wasn't cooperating. "I'm not taking you to the Oak. If you want to see Queen Valerian, ask Broch when he gets back."

"I can't wait that long," Ivy protested. "He could be gone for days. Anyway, isn't this why the queen sent you and Broch to Cornwall—to make peace between your people and mine? I know you don't want anyone to find out about the baby, but doesn't duty come first?"

The wind whipped Thorn's hair into her eyes, and she swiped it back with a scowl. "Your idea of *peace* seems to involve a lot of fighting. And you're standing on a thin twig with your talk of *duty*, too."

Yet she hadn't turned back to the barrow, even though the breeze was chilly and they could both see their breath. Determined, Ivy pressed on. "There might not have to be a battle, if Queen Valerian can teach me more magic. She's the queen of all the faeries, isn't she? So she must be at least as powerful as my aunt is. Are you *sure* she can't make fire?"

Thorn made an impatient gesture, and the grass between them burst into flames. Ivy jumped back, then realized it was only illusion: the fire looked real, but it wasn't burning anything at all. She stooped to touch it and felt no pain, only a gentle heat.

"Glamour," Thorn said. "That's all. It doesn't even warm you really, it's just a trick of the mind." She waved her hand again, and the illusion vanished. "If I can do that, of course the queen can. But I can't see how it's going to help you."

Ivy pointed at the grass, concentrating. But no matter how hard she wished nothing happened, so at last she let her hand drop. Besides, Thorn was right. What good would mere pretend fire be against the woman who'd burned Jenny and Shale to death?

"But your queen's power isn't *all* glamour," Ivy said. "There has to be some spell she knows that can help me stop Betony and save Hew and the others."

Thorn shrugged. "There's spell-fire, I suppose, but it doesn't really burn either, just shocks you a bit. Unless you're using dark magic."

Gillian Menadue had used dark magic to create the Claybane, and a few old piskey tales mentioned dark spells in passing. But Ivy still wasn't sure she understood. "What's the difference?"

"Dark magic's what you use to seriously hurt someone, or change them against their will. I don't know how it's done, and I don't want to, but it's what the Empress did. That's why everyone was so afraid of her."

"I see," said Ivy slowly. It didn't surprise her to find out her aunt was using dark magic, but it made her wonder how Betony had learned it. "So this spell-fire you were talking about . . . could you show me?"

Thorn shook her head. "Can't do it myself, let alone teach you."

"Fine," said Ivy, suppressing her impatience, "but maybe Queen Valerian could. And how will I know, if I can't get in to see her? I can't just march up to the Oak and demand an audience, can I?"

"Not with all those dratted wards, you can't." Thorn thumped her fist into her palm. "Wither and gall! Why does *everything* have to happen to me upside down and backward?"

"We could make ourselves invisible," Ivy said, trying not to sound overeager. She could tell Thorn was softening, but she feared to press her luck too far. "I'm sure the wards won't keep *you* out, whether the other Oakenfolk can see you or not. We'll go straight to the queen and leave as soon as I've talked to her. No one will ever know."

"For a little poplar, you've got a lot of fluff," Thorn grumbled, but then she sighed. "Oh, all right."

Ivy could have hugged the faery woman for sheer relief, but she'd tested Thorn's patience enough already. She clasped her arm gratefully instead and ran back to the barrow to tell Martin.

When she came up the stairs, however, there was no sign of him. Only Daisy, dragging her wriggling daughter out of the treasure chamber. "Thrift! What have I told you?"

The little piskey wailed and struggled, and the tarnished circlet she'd been wearing clattered to the floor. Pearl, the youngest of the spriggan girls, picked it up and clasped it to her chest, watching her playmate sorrowfully.

Ivy wished Daisy would just let the two of them play together, but she had no time to sort that out now. She checked the food storeroom, then searched all the other chambers, finding several children and a couple of dozing aunties in the process. But Martin and the older spriggan boys were missing, and by the looks of it, Mattock had gone with them.

They were probably out fishing or hunting, which meant they wouldn't be back for hours. Ivy hurried back to the main cavern to find Fern.

"When you see Matt," Ivy asked her, "could you give him a message for Martin? Thorn and I are going to the Oak, and we'll be back as soon as we can." Not waiting for an answer, she headed for the stairs.

"The Oak?" Mattock's mother sounded puzzled. "What do you think you'll find there?"

Ivy glanced back at her, smiling. "Hope."

Ivy had traveled to the Oakenwyld twice now: the first time to beg the faeries to save her mother's life, the second to repay them by leading them to Martin. But she'd never guessed there was a hidden entrance until Thorn tugged her beneath the rose hedge and she nearly fell into it. Flustered, Ivy followed the faery woman into an earthy-smelling tunnel, then down an adjoining corridor to the heart of the Oak.

The vast atrium at the tree's center no longer awed Ivy as it once had, but it was a long way to the top, and there was no staircase. High above, faery girls spread their dragonfly wings and flitted from one floor to another, while the male faeries took bird-shape to do likewise. Light slanted through the windows, bathing the hollow trunk in light—and leaving no shadows for Ivy to hide in. Thorn could fly while keeping invisible, but Ivy couldn't. And as Thorn had warned her, none of the Oakenfolk could become either a swift or a peregrine, so if any of the faeries spotted Ivy they'd know she was a stranger at once.

Well, she'd just have to move fast, then. Slipping past the

faeries wandering in and out of the kitchens, library and other chambers at ground level, Ivy waited restlessly until the atrium above her stood empty. Then she dropped her invisibility spell, took swift-shape, and shot to the topmost level.

"Ow!" said an irritable voice, as Ivy landed and changed back. "You're on my foot!"

Well, at least she didn't have to wonder where Thorn had got to. Hastily Ivy stepped off and followed the grumbling faery through the arch to the queen's chambers.

They'd only taken a few steps when Thorn stopped short, and Ivy nearly ran into her. "Blight," the faery woman swore. "There's a council meeting."

Ivy was about to ask how she knew, since all the doors ahead of them were closed. But then she heard muffled sounds floating out from a door on the right.

Thorn whirled to escape, but Ivy grabbed her just as she turned invisible. "You can't go yet!" she pleaded. "You have to take me to the queen!"

She must have spoken louder than she thought, because the door to the council room creaked open, and a short red-headed faery peered out. It was Periwinkle, the queen's attendant— and one of the few Oakenfolk who knew Thorn's secret.

"Wink!" Ivy whispered urgently. "It's me, Ivy, and I've brought Thorn. We need to see Queen Valerian in private."

The faery's face brightened, and she hurried toward them. Thorn wilted, then shook Ivy off and turned visible as Wink grabbed both their arms.

"Don't worry, I'll hide you," she promised. "This way."

She led them to a serene, modestly furnished room, whose windows faced the nearby human house. Thorn thumped onto the sofa, her back to the view, while Wink led Ivy to one of the armchairs.

"I'll tell the queen," she said. "And don't worry, Thorn. I won't tell anyone else you're here."

Thorn wrapped an arm defensively across her belly. "You'd better not. Especially Timothy."

Wink gave Thorn a reassuring smile and trotted off, shutting the door behind her. Ivy sat forward, about to ask Thorn what was wrong with Timothy in particular, but then she remembered—the boy was human, and Knife's cousin by marriage. Some faery might have turned him small so he could visit the Oak, but what would he be doing in a council meeting?

It was tempting to ask, but the mulish expression on Thorn's face warned Ivy against it. So she forced herself to sit back and wait until her anticipation turned to nervousness, then anxiety. Why hadn't the queen come yet? Hadn't Wink told her it was important? Or did she not care about making a treaty with Ivy's people anymore?

Unable to bear it any longer, Ivy was about to get up when the door opened and Queen Valerian walked in. Simply dressed in a slate-colored robe, her hair crowned by a plain circlet and hanging loose down her back, she carried herself with a poise that Ivy would have envied if she weren't so close to resenting it. Valerian certainly didn't look as though she'd been in any hurry to get there, though Wink was quivering with excitement as she followed her mistress in.

"The queen wants to talk to Ivy alone," she told Thorn. "You can come to my chamber, she's dismissed the council so it's safe, I'll make you some tea—oh, it's *wonderful* to see you!"

Thorn got up stiffly, frowning at Valerian. "Don't you want my report?"

"I had one yesterday, from Broch," said the queen. "He stopped by on his way to London. Be at peace, Thorn. Your presence alone tells me that this is no small matter, and Ivy can tell me the rest."

Reluctantly Thorn followed Wink out, while the queen watched with a faint, tender smile. Then she turned to Ivy and said, "Are you thirsty? May I pour you some tea or berry wine?"

"That's . . . kind of you, but no," said Ivy, taken aback. Surely Wink or some other attendant ought to do that, not the faery queen herself. "Your Majesty, I'm sorry to interrupt your council, but I need your help."

Valerian sat down, regarding her seriously. "What is your need, Ivy of the Delve?"

At once Ivy poured out her story. Judging by the queen's expression, little of it surprised her, but she said nothing, even when Ivy was done.

"I've tried everything I could think of," Ivy said, "but I realize now that I can't do this on my own. You're my only hope." She clasped her hands together, imploring. "Is there *anything* you can show me, or give me, to help me save my people?"

Valerian considered this, her eyes thoughtful. Finally she said, "If I did, what would you offer in return?"

Warmth spread through Ivy. If the queen was willing to bargain, this gamble might work after all. "You want peace between our peoples," she said quickly. "So do I. If you help, we'll make a treaty with you. We'll swear not to attack you or any faery under your protection for as long as you rule, if you promise to do the same for us." She drew a deep breath. "And we'll allow the faeries back into Cornwall."

She'd rehearsed the speech as she lay awake last night, waiting for morning. Her people wouldn't be happy to see the faeries return, not when their ancestors had fought so hard to get rid of them. But once they realized what Queen Valerian had done for them, they'd come around. They had to.

"You say 'we,'" said the queen. "Have you discussed this with your followers?"

Ivy flushed. "Not yet."

She'd meant to tell Martin and Mattock before she left, but

she couldn't find them. And she couldn't risk telling Teasel and the other women in case they tried to stop her . . .

Or worse, got their hopes up, only to be disappointed all over again.

"So you speak to me as one queen to another," said Valerian. "You believe it is your right to decide what is best for your people, whether they agree or not."

Ivy shifted in her chair, uncomfortable. Did she have to put it that way? It made her sound like Betony. "I think they will agree," she said carefully, "when they see how much healthier and better off they are. I—I never wanted to be Joan, or at least I didn't think so, but . . . I don't know how else to help them."

The faery queen gave her a sympathetic look. "Leadership is a heavy burden," she said. "Especially for one so young. And I can tell you have felt that weight keenly since your people left the Delve to join you. You have seen the ignorance of your subjects, their shortsightedness and resistance to change, their petty squabbles and misguided notions, and you have learned to guard your own counsel, as queens often must."

Valerian rose and walked to the cupboard, taking out a bottle and two delicate, old-fashioned goblets. She poured the wine and crossed the floor to hand a cup to Ivy. "But tell me. What do you think changed your aunt from the good Joan she once was to the tyrant she is now?"

Ivy sank back in the armchair, staring into her cup. At last she said, "She's always been strict, but she used to hear people out before she judged and treat them fairly. And now she doesn't listen to anyone." She shrugged helplessly. "I don't know. Maybe it's the poison affecting her."

"Perhaps," said Valerian. "But no one else has been driven mad by the poison, have they?"

No, they hadn't. Not even Marigold, who'd been the first to feel its deadly effects, or Ivy's father Flint, who'd endured the worst of it down in the diggings. They'd grown ill and even depressed, but not ruthless like Betony.

"Yet there is a poison that twists the mind," the queen continued, taking her seat again, "and none of us is immune to it, not even the mightiest or most wise." Her gaze held Ivy's. "Fear."

Ivy nearly laughed. With all the power she wielded, and a Jack strong enough to kill anyone who escaped her fire, what could Betony be afraid of?

"You may think me foolish," said Valerian, "but I pity your aunt. She knows how to manage all the business of the Delve, but not how to cultivate her people. She can force the piskeys to obey her, but she cannot command their love. And the thought of change, especially the change you would bring, is abhorrent to her. Because to allow her people to leave the Delve, she would have to admit that she was wrong and you were right." She gave a sad smile. "She is sick with fear, Ivy. Fear of losing her people and not being strong enough to save them."

The words thudded like stones into Ivy. She'd never thought she and Betony had anything in common, until now.

"But . . . I don't know how to help her," Ivy said unevenly. "She won't believe the poison is real, even with all the evidence in front of her, and she won't let our people go. So what choice do I have? I can't let her kill everyone I love, just because I'm afraid of becoming like her!"

Queen Valerian's face softened. "No. That too would be a choice made from fear, not wisdom. But though she has done great evil and you are right to oppose her, your aunt was once a woman like you. And might be so again, if she can find the courage to repent." She sipped her wine and gazed out the window pensively.

Ivy raised her own cup and drank, her thoughts tumbling about in confusion. Was the faery queen going to give her the help she needed, or not? She'd expected her to talk terms, not philosophy.

"I cannot teach you to conjure fire as Betony does," said Valerian at last. "But I can show you this." She rose and moved to Ivy, a ball of light coalescing on her palm. "Take it from me, if you can."

This must be the spell-fire Thorn had mentioned. Hesitantly Ivy cupped her hand to the globe, feeling its sizzling energy against her skin. It rolled off the queen's fingers onto hers, and Ivy's heart leaped—but as soon as Valerian withdrew her hand, the glow winked out.

"Again," said the faery queen, drawing up a chair next to her. "Focus, and try to keep it alight."

Ivy concentrated, trying to feel the queen's power flowing into the spell and make her own power match it. But though she tried until sweat prickled her hairline, the magic always vanished as soon as Valerian let go.

"I can't!" Ivy burst out, slapping the arm of the chair. "I don't know what's wrong with me!"

The queen laid a comforting hand on her shoulder. "Don't blame yourself," she said. "Many faeries find spell-fire difficult or impossible. And I know little of piskey magic, so I may not be the best teacher for you."

Perhaps, but if the queen of the faeries couldn't teach her, who could? "Are there any other spells I could use?" Ivy asked, without much hope.

"If you were fighting a different enemy, perhaps. But the fire your Joan wields burns hotter than any I have ever known. And if your own mother could spend six years fighting in the Empress's army, yet still be too weak to resist her . . ." She spread her hands. "I dare not give you false hope, Ivy. Even spell-fire would be a feeble weapon against Betony's dark magic, and I know no spell that will keep her from killing you."

Ivy bit her lip. Deep down she'd known it would come to

this, however fervently she'd hoped otherwise. "Then . . . will you give me an army?"

The queen gazed at Ivy with pity. Then, sadly, she shook her head.

"Please," Ivy blurted in mounting panic, "it's our only chance. Your people fought the Empress, they're better trained than any piskey in the Delve—"

"Yet they are faeries," said the queen, "and under my protection. Much as I wish for peace, I will not buy it that way. The cost is too high."

She'd known faeries could drive hard bargains, but Ivy had only one thing left to offer. "We'll pay whatever you want," she said hoarsely. "My ancestors could find gemstones and precious metals anywhere—they made beautiful things, like you've never seen. Your soldiers can take as much treasure as they like from the Delve, and every year we'll send more. *Please.*"

"Ivy." Valerian spoke softly, but her voice was firm. "You are not the first to offer me wealth in exchange for soldiers. Martin promised me all his father's hoard if I would bring my army into Cornwall, depose your aunt, and crown you in her place. But my people suffered too much at the hands of the Empress for me to force them into another battle, especially one they have no stake in. What prize can you offer that is worth even one drop of faery blood?"

Ivy clutched her wine cup, shaken. So Martin had tried to make the same bargain when he was here? He'd really been willing to give up everything he owned, for her?

"And my help would cost you more than you realize," the queen continued. "If I lent you my army, it would be my power you wielded, not your own. You might claim to have freed your people, but would they believe it? Would they not see you as a puppet Joan under my control?"

It was true, Ivy realized, heart sinking. With an army of

faeries she might defeat Betony and Gossan, but her rule over the Delve would be short-lived. Her people would never fully trust her, and the moment some other piskey-woman proved she could make fire, they'd lose no time in overthrowing Ivy and setting up a new Joan in her place. Then all hope of peace between the piskeys and the faeries—let alone the spriggans—would be lost.

"Then I'll step down," Ivy said, heavy with defeat. "As soon as Betony's out of the way. I'll let my people choose anyone they want to lead them, and I won't interfere. But if you don't help us . . ." Her throat closed up, grief choking her. She finished in a whisper, "Then the piskeys of Kernow will die."

"Even the stars will not last forever," said Valerian. "But whether the end has come for your people, I cannot say. And neither can you, though their need is great and all your hopes seem fruitless." She laid her hand over Ivy's. "There are powers greater than magic or strength of arms. And if you know you have nothing, you have more than you know."

She meant it as comfort, no doubt, but it sounded like so much rubble to Ivy. Fighting bitterness, she pushed herself to her feet.

"I'm sorry to have disturbed you, Your Majesty. I'll go now."

16

There was no use staying in the Oak any longer. If Queen Valerian wouldn't help Ivy, certainly no one else would. Feeling hollow, Ivy walked down the hallway, trying to remember which of the doors was Wink's.

"Thorn!" she called, hoping the faery woman could hear. "It's time to—oh!"

The door across from Ivy had opened, but it wasn't Wink looking at her. It was Linden, the queen's youngest attendant. And behind her, alert and curious, sat two others: Rhosmari, Broch's fellow countrywoman from the Green Isles . . . and the human boy Timothy.

Silently Ivy berated herself. She'd thought they'd all left when the queen dismissed her council. "Never mind," she said hastily, trying to pull the door shut, but Timothy had already leaped to his feet.

"I knew it! She's here, isn't she?" He pushed past Linden, dodging Ivy's attempt to block him, and set off down the hallway. "Thorn!"

A muffled oath came from the door nearest the landing—Thorn remembering she couldn't leap away, no doubt. Ivy raced after Timothy and flung herself in front of him. "Don't go in."

The human boy wasn't much older than Ivy, but he was a head taller, and it would have been easy for him to push her aside. Yet he stopped. "Why not?"

"Because . . ." Ivy cast about for an answer that would satisfy him. "She doesn't want to talk to anyone. And we have to leave right away."

Timothy looked crestfallen. "Really? That's too bad. I was hoping to find out how she was doing, so I could tell Peri—I mean Knife. She's been worried."

"She's fine," Ivy assured him. "Please tell Knife there's nothing to worry about."

"If you say so." Timothy heaved a sigh, then added more loudly, "Take care, Thorn. I'll see you."

That wasn't so hard, Ivy thought with relief, as the human boy turned away. But then a wicked smile curled his mouth, and before Ivy could stop him he lunged past and flung the door open. "Boo!"

Thorn stood silhouetted against the light of the windows, while Wink struggled to help her into her jacket. For an instant both faeries froze, gaping at Timothy. Then Thorn thrust her arm down the remaining sleeve, strode forward, and drove her fist into the boy's stomach.

He doubled over, wheezing, as Thorn glared at him. "Meddlesome brat," she growled. Then she flung her coat closed, though it didn't quite meet over her belly, and stamped off to the landing.

A pained silence followed, while Timothy staggered about clutching his stomach. Then Rhosmari exclaimed, "Ivy!" and rushed to greet her with a warmth that took her by surprise. "I'm so glad to see you. How is Martin?"

"Ouch," said Timothy plaintively, but Rhosmari shook her head at him.

"You should know better than to cross Thorn by now. And

pretending to be jealous of Martin won't make me feel any more sorry for you."

Ivy liked the Welsh girl, all the more since she'd seen Martin's memories of the time they'd spent traveling together. And both Linden and Wink had been kind when Ivy first came to the Oak. But Ivy couldn't bear to talk to them any longer.

"I–I can't," she stammered, backing away to the landing. "I'm sorry." Then she changed to a swift, and fled.

"Blighted boy can't keep his nose out of anything," Thorn fumed when Ivy caught up to her in the hedge tunnel. "And the queen doesn't even try to stop him—you don't think he noticed, do you?"

He might not have, if Thorn hadn't reacted so spectacularly. But there was no point in saying that now. "I don't know."

"Should never have come here in the first place." Thorn kicked a pebble out of the way and stamped on. "Fat lot of good it did either of us."

Ivy was startled. "How did you know?"

"You look like you asked Queen Valerian for an egg and she gave you a squashed hedgehog, that's how," said Thorn. "But there's nothing to be done about it, so back we go."

It took them only a short time to return, but the journey was far from easy. They had to do it in stages, resting between each leap, and every place they stopped it was raining. By the time they reached the barrow, Ivy was hungry, wet to the skin, and sorry she'd ever heard of the Oak or Queen Valerian.

Wearily Ivy followed Thorn up the steps, and nearly bumped into her when the faery woman halted. "Odd thing about this place," she said, wrinkling her nose.

"What?" Ivy asked.

"It doesn't stink. With no windows anywhere it ought to, but even cooking smells don't hang about for long."

She was right. The spell that had held the barrow in stasis was broken, so Martin and the children should have been suffocating long before Ivy brought a pack of dirty, sweaty piskeys to join them. Yet the air held no trace of staleness. "There must be vents hidden somewhere," Ivy said, but Thorn snorted.

"They must be budding good ones, then. The Oak's full of windows, and even in springtime it doesn't smell as fresh as this place." She stepped into the main chamber, and Ivy followed her—only to stop short, amazed.

After just two days of spriggan hospitality, the wall of prejudice between the piskeys and Martin's people had crumbled. Thrift and Pearl were playing happily together, and the skinniest of the spriggan boys—Martin called him Falstaff, though no one else understood the joke—was tossing a ball with Clover's two young sons. Even Jewel's shy admiration of the piskey-women's shawls had born fruit: now Teasel sat with her by the back wall, teaching her how to knit.

"Mam told me you went to visit the faeries," said Mattock, coming over to Ivy. "What happened?"

"Nothing."

Matt studied her, taking in her dripping curls and slumped shoulders. Then he picked up a blanket and wrapped it around her. "All right," he said, steering Ivy into the adjoining chamber and shutting the door. "Now. Tell me."

Ivy sank down on one of the boxes. "I talked to Queen Valerian, but she wouldn't help me stop Betony. She couldn't even teach me a single spell." She pulled the blanket closer, shivering. "So I came back. That's all."

Mattock blew out his breath. "Well, nobody can say you

didn't try. But I think . . ." He scratched the back of his neck self-consciously. "Ivy, you have to stop."

She'd known this was coming, but it didn't make it easier. Ivy bowed her head, waiting for the pick to fall.

"I like him," Matt burst out, surprising her. "Martin, I mean. He cured me of that fever, and I thought that was the end of it. But while I was waiting for you to bring the others, he showed me around the barrow and introduced me to all the children. We've talked a fair bit now, and he's been teaching me to fight left-handed."

Was that what they'd been doing? Ivy had noticed Mattock didn't seem to be around much, but she'd assumed he was out walking to build up his strength or gathering wood for the cookfire. She'd never guessed he was sparring with Martin.

"Anyway, I understand what you see in him, Ivy. He's a good man."

Knowing about Martin, it was hard not to smile at that. But Matt was so earnest, she didn't want to seem like she was mocking him. "In his own way," she agreed, not quite steadily.

"He told me how he met you," Mattock went on, turning his cap in his hands, "before he even knew he was a spriggan. He said he would have died if you hadn't saved him from that cell we put him in." He looked at the floor. "He didn't say it, Ivy, but I could see it in his face. He thought you were the most beautiful thing he'd ever seen."

That wasn't how Ivy remembered it. She'd never seen daylight before she met Martin, and a lifetime of breathing the Delve's poison had left her pale, scrawny, and humiliatingly wingless. She'd been filthy from climbing the Great Shaft, her curls tangled and limp with sweat. There'd been nothing beautiful about her.

"He's a bit dramatic," she said. "You may have noticed."

Mattock made an exasperated noise. "Ivy, will you stop being difficult? This is hard enough as it is."

She reddened. "Sorry."

"The point is, you and he have been through a lot together. And I think–" He swallowed. "If anyone deserves a happy ending, it's you. So I think you should stay here. With him."

"And leave you and the others to die? There's nothing happy about that ending." Ivy shook her head. "I can't do that."

Mattock tossed his cap aside and knelt in front of her, laying his good hand over her clenched ones. "What have our folk ever given you, Ivy? The whole time you were growing up they never thought you'd amount to anything. You were just poor Marigold's sickly daughter." His grip tightened. "When you went missing from the Delve, they didn't even send out a search party."

"Stop," Ivy said tightly. "Stop trying to turn me against them."

"I'm only telling the truth. Our people never gave a pebble for you, until you came back to save us from the Claybane. Even when you stood up to Betony, they were too cowardly to stand up for you in return. They only left to get away from the poison, and because they hoped you'd find them a new home without them having to dig one." He gave a short laugh. "And you've been half killing yourself to please them ever since."

Ivy wanted to deny it, but how could she? It was true that she'd never felt appreciated, or even fully accepted, in the Delve. Her winglessness made her an outsider, and she'd always been too faery-like to blend in as Mica and Cicely did. And once Marigold went missing, Ivy had been so busy trying to fill her mother's shoes that she'd had no time to carve space of her own.

Maybe that was why she'd been so anxious to prove herself when the piskeys turned up on her doorstep. To show they'd been wrong to overlook her, that she was worth more than they'd ever guessed. Her heart had soared with every sign of her people's approval, while the slightest rebuke sent her plummeting into despair. But no matter how hard Ivy worked or how much she sacrificed, it was never enough. And perhaps it never would be.

"You tried to be the Joan we needed," Matt continued softly. "No one could have tried harder. But you don't have the power to fight Betony, and the next time you cross her, she'll kill you."

Ivy gazed down at his big, calloused hand on hers. Then she said, equally quiet, "I know."

"Then you know why I have to say this." He sat back, squaring his shoulders. "We're going back to the Delve."

"Matt, no!"

"It's the only way to save our men, and you know it. If Betony spares us, maybe we'll find another chance to escape. But . . ." He stood up. "You won't be coming with us. That's final."

Tears burned Ivy's eyes. "You can't do this."

"I can and I will." He moved to the door. "Because I still love you, Ivy. And I'd rather know you're alive, even without me, than have to watch you die."

"It's a little high-handed," said Martin thoughtfully, "but I can't argue with the sentiment. I wouldn't want to see your aunt burn you to death, either."

From the moment Mattock had left Ivy in the storeroom, he and the piskey-women had stopped talking to her. They'd even excluded Thorn, who had called them a lot of rock-headed fly-wits and stomped off for a walk to relieve her feelings—which, Ivy knew, meant she'd become fond of the piskeys and was deeply worried about them.

"I don't even know what their plan is," Ivy said, wiping

her eyes. They were sitting together on the hillside above the barrow, watching the spriggan boys chasing one another across the heath below. "He wouldn't even tell me that."

"What plan? Matt's no fool: he knows he can't ask those women to fight Betony. Not without putting their children in danger, and probably getting their husbands and sons executed as well." Martin picked a bit of gravel off the rock between them and flicked it down the slope. "All they can do is surrender and hope your aunt comes to her senses before it's too late."

Which was possible, but scant comfort to Ivy. How many more piskeys would die before Betony admitted she'd been wrong about the poison? How much suffering would it take to convince her that holding her people captive was no way to keep them safe?

"I hate this." Ivy dug her fingers into her crossed arms. "I hate that I can't make fire. I hate that I can't do anything to stop her. I hate that I'm so—" Her throat tightened with the old, helpless grief of it, the shame she'd battled all her life. "Weak."

Martin reached out and stroked her hair. "You," he said gently, "are a better woman, and a better leader, than Betony will ever be. They're going back to her because they've got no choice, but they'll never love her as they love you."

Ivy gave a shaky laugh. "After all I've done to disappoint them? I don't think so."

"I know so. Do you think Hew and those other piskeys who surrendered were cowards? They could have fought and maybe even escaped." He traced the shape of her ear, over the pointed tip and down to the soft curve of lobe beneath. "They gave themselves up to save you."

Just like the women and Matt were doing now. "It's not right," Ivy said thickly. "I'm not worth it."

"Ivy." He dropped his hand and laced his fingers through

hers. "You can't put a price on love, or deserve it. You have to take it as a gift or not at all."

"It doesn't feel like a gift," she whispered. "It feels like a terrible burden."

"I know. But it will pass. You're not being selfish by letting your people go, Ivy. It's what they want."

Her resistance crumbled, drowned by the aching need for comfort. She leaned against Martin and he tugged her close, pressing a kiss to her temple.

"Ew!" yelled a boy's voice from below. "Disgusting!"

Martin let go of Ivy, exasperated. "No, Benedick, your boots are disgusting. And for that remark, you can clean everyone else's as well." He stood up, brushing dirt from his trousers, as the spriggan boy groaned and flopped over the fallen tree in anguish. "The rest of you, inside. It's lesson time."

"Lessons?" asked Ivy. "What are you teaching them?"

"Shape-changing, mostly," Martin said. "They come by it naturally, as you've seen, but they haven't got much of a repertoire. They're a bit like your people, afraid to try anything new. But I'm showing them how to take bird-shape. And they've taught me a few tricks, too."

"Really?"

Martin turned to face Ivy, holding her gaze. Little by little his features altered, bones squaring and jaw broadening, eyes changing from gray to summer blue. Ivy watched, mesmerized, until his pale hair began to redden and she realized with a jolt who he was mimicking. "Martin, no. Stop."

"I made it green again, didn't I?" He shifted back to his own shape. "Dratted color-blindness."

She'd forgotten about that, but it was hardly the problem. "No, it was red. Just don't."

The corner of his mouth twitched. "I thought you might like it. Best of both worlds, as the humans say."

Ivy knew he was teasing, but the thought of Martin with

Mattock's face nauseated her. She shook her head. "He likes you, you know," she said after a moment. "In spite of everything."

"I like your Matt, too." He turned toward the barrow, a lean silhouette against the cloud-rumpled sky. "If I get myself inconveniently killed at some point, you might consider giving him another chance."

"*Martin*," said Ivy between her teeth, but he only laughed and vanished.

She was still sitting on the hillside when Thorn returned from her walk and sat next to her, red-cheeked with cold and exertion. "So that's the end, I suppose," she said.

Ivy rested her chin on her knees, feeling emptier than ever. It wasn't just her own people she'd let down, it was Thorn and Broch, too.

"It's too bad," Thorn went on. "This Cornwall of yours is all right. Not a lot of big trees, and all that wind and rain's a mite tedious. But it's a no-nonsense kind of place. Sturdy. Good roots." Her hand strayed to her belly, rubbing the growing roundness there. "I thought he might like it."

"How do you know it's a boy?"

"That's what the queen said." Thorn shrugged. "She knows these things."

But she hadn't known how to stop Betony, or at least she hadn't been willing to try. Now that the first shock of disappointment had faded, Ivy didn't blame Valerian for that: she wouldn't have sent an army of piskeys to fight the Empress and defend the Oak, either. But it was hard not to feel like the faery queen had given up on her. "Do you think she's disappointed about the treaty?"

"Couldn't say." Thorn leaned back on her elbows, squinting at the clouds. "Not much surprises her, though. Maybe that's why she didn't argue when I told her I wanted to leave. Maybe she knew I'd be back in a few weeks anyway."

Ivy was quiet, studying a patch of lichen between her feet. Only when Thorn began to rub her nose furiously did she realize that the faery woman was crying.

"I hate this," she snapped. "I don't *want* to go back to the Oak. If it weren't for the dratted baby, I'd—I'd march off and fight that blighted aunt of yours myself."

Ivy knew pregnancy made women emotional, but it sounded as though Thorn really meant it. "I'd rather you didn't," she said. "But you don't have to leave, unless you want to. I'm sure Martin won't mind."

Thorn humphed. "Doesn't matter. I can't go anywhere until—" She sat up sharply. "What's that?"

A long wail echoed from inside the hill, then broke into hiccuping sobs of despair. Daisy marched out of the barrow with her daughter in her arms, while Clover and her two sons followed.

"I'm *not* going!" Thrift pummeled her mother's shoulders. "I want to stay with Pearl!"

"Be quiet!" Daisy told her. "And don't you dare say a word about spriggans from now on! Do you want to get us all killed?" She gave Thrift a little shake and set her down, then grabbed her again as the little girl tried to bolt.

"Don't worry," said Mattock, climbing out of the barrow to join them. "I can put a silencing spell on her until we're in the Delve." He waved his hand at Thrift.

"No!" she shrieked. "No, n—" But though her mouth kept moving, no sound came out. She collapsed to the ground at Daisy's feet, weeping.

The light from the door flickered, and Pearl stepped out. She slipped past the piskey-women, knelt, and patted Thrift's shoulder. "I lost my mam," she whispered. "You've still got yours."

Thrift threw her arms around the little spriggan girl,

hugging her fervently. Then she got up and clung to her mother's skirts.

"All ready?" Mattock looked around at the cluster of women and children, who nodded and linked hands. He put his half hand on Teasel's shoulder and gazed up at Ivy.

"Good luck," he said, and all the piskeys vanished. Only Pearl was left, standing forlorn at the foot of the hill.

17

"Take one, my—I mean, Ivy." Jewel nudged her with the platter. "You've not had a bite all day."

Ivy raised her head blearily. After Matt and the others left she'd lost track of what time it was, or even where she was. But she must have followed Pearl back into the barrow, because she was sitting against the wall of the treasure chamber, and someone had draped a blanket around her.

"Pasties?" Ivy murmured, reaching for one. The pastry was poorly crimped and a little black around the edges, but they smelled good. She rolled the meat pie from hand to hand until it cooled enough not to burn her fingers, then bit into it as Jewel watched hopefully.

"Did I use enough salt and pepper?" she asked. "Teasel was going to show me, but . . . she left."

"You did very well," Ivy told her, and with a smile Jewel moved on to serve the other girls sitting around the cavern. All of them were surrounded by piles of half-polished jewelry and loose gemstones: they seemed to have made it their business to clean the whole hoard, and by the looks of it there was enough to keep them busy for weeks. But their faces were somber, and it was clear they felt almost as sorry to lose the piskeys as Ivy did.

"Pearl," called Ivy, and the little girl shuffled over. Her expression was tragic, her mouth trembling, and she slumped next to Ivy like an abandoned doll. "I'm sorry about Thrift, but you were very brave and kind to help her. Here." She pressed the rest of her pasty into Pearl's hands. "You should eat something, too."

The spriggan girl took a bite, chewed and swallowed with a visible effort. Then she dropped the pasty and curled up with her head in Ivy's lap.

Ivy stroked Pearl's silky hair, feeling helpless. She was so young—they all were. And though like Martin they'd survived against all odds, they'd lost their families, their clans, and the world they'd grown up in to do it. No wonder these girls had been drawn to the motherly piskey-women and Pearl had embraced Thrift like her own sister. They must be terribly lonely.

Soon Pearl's thin shoulders drooped, and her body grew heavy with sleep. Ivy eased out from under her, leaving her pillowed on the blanket, and went out to the main cavern to find Martin.

He was sitting cross-legged in a circle of spriggan boys, watching them play a complicated game with sticks, stones, and a small knife. But when he saw Ivy, he got up at once. "Broch came back a little while ago," he said. "He and Thorn have gone off for a . . . private conversation."

His tone was innocent, but his smile and the way he hooked his fingers like quote marks said otherwise. "I'm sure talking will be involved at some point," said Ivy tartly. "And will you stop trying to provoke me? I know you'd rather see me annoyed than miserable, but I don't want to be angry at you."

"Then let me offer you a more pleasant distraction. Shall we fly to St. Ives? It isn't far, and I'm sure Jewel and Dagger can manage for a few hours without us."

Ivy had never been to that town before, but it must be the

closest place to buy more food and supplies for the barrow. Perhaps helping Martin would make her feel more useful. "All right," she said, and went to fetch her coat.

It was a rare cloudless evening in Cornwall, the first stars glittering like ice crystals on the deep blue dome of the sky. Martin launched off as a barn owl, and Ivy followed him as a peregrine. The cool air revived her, and the wind rippled pleasantly beneath her wings as they soared over rambling pastures and gorse-stippled hills toward the sea. She was almost sorry when the scattered lights below clustered into a splash of brilliance, and Martin swooped lower to guide her into St. Ives.

She expected him to land at the supermarket, but he ignored the sprawl of modern buildings on the outskirts and headed for the close-packed shops of the town center. They landed by the wall of the parish church, changed to human shape, and Martin turned to Ivy.

"Do you trust me?" he asked.

"For what?"

"You'll find out, if you're patient. I have a plan."

Knowing Martin, that could mean anything from the theatrical to the mildly criminal. But curiosity won out, so Ivy followed him down to the harbor. The sea breeze tugged at her curls, and she shivered as the damp air seeped through her winter coat. But Martin set a brisk pace, and as they walked the curving road along the shoreline Ivy soon warmed up again.

"This will do, I think," said Martin, stopping at a ramshackle cluster of old buildings covered in slates and white plaster. Mystified, Ivy followed him across the cobbled forecourt to the door, where he rapped and waited until a harried-looking man came to let them in.

Warm light washed over them, along with a clamor of human voices and the smells of roast potatoes and beer. "Table for two, please," said Martin. "Upstairs, if there's room."

"Wait," said Ivy. "I thought we—" But Martin raised his eyebrows, and she remembered she'd promised to trust him. She fell silent as they crossed the crowded pub to the stairs.

They climbed up to a room framed by creamy walls and low, dark timbers, with fewer tables—and humans—than the pub below. Martin led her to a seat, ordered dinner with airy confidence, and sat back looking satisfied as the server hurried away.

"I've been staring at the menu outside this place for weeks," he said. "I hope you're as hungry as I am."

Ivy hadn't been hungry at all before they left the barrow, and she wasn't sure she was now. But if Martin had been looking forward to this meal, she wouldn't spoil it for him. "I'll do my best."

"No, don't. Do what you *want* for once, Ivy. The world won't fall to pieces, and neither will I."

Ivy exhaled, tension easing from her shoulders. "All right."

But when the platter of mixed seafood, greens, and hot buttered potatoes arrived, Ivy's appetite rekindled at once. Her share was as generous as Martin's, but by the time she finished there was nothing on her plate but empty shells.

It was dark when they left the restaurant, but Martin showed no sign of hurry. He took Ivy's hand, and strolled with her through the quiet, lamplit streets. They passed shuttered shops and art galleries, cafes and inns, all packed so close that if Ivy hadn't looked up, she might have thought they were walking through a tunnel. In a strange way, it reminded her of the Delve.

Homesickness welled up in Ivy, and with it the old shame and grief of failure. Yet she forced her mind back to the present. It might be too late to save her own people, but she could still help Martin protect his.

When they reached the next corner Martin turned, leading Ivy down a narrow lane to a footpath. The shops receded and the beach spread out before them, glimmering like a golden torc. On the moon-silvered waves a few small boats bobbed at anchor, and far in the distance a plane glided westward, flashing its ruby lights.

"I know a lot has happened since I came back," Martin said, slipping his free hand into his coat pocket. "And between your people and mine, we've not had much time together. But I'm done waiting for the perfect chance to do this, so I'm doing it now." He turned to Ivy, gray eyes searching. "A few months ago I offered you something without knowing what it meant. Now I do know, I'd like to offer it to you again."

She knew what it was, even before the stone touched her palm. An emerald necklace, old but beautifully crafted, with a filigree setting and a cunningly twisted chain. Ivy gazed at it, her heart in her throat. The thought of accepting made her dizzy.

Martin laid his hand over hers, covering the stone. "You're not your people's Joan anymore, and there's nothing I can do about that. But you can still be queen of the spriggans, if you want."

Could she? Ivy had never thought of Martin as a king before. But the children had knelt to him when they awoke, and though they no longer cowered in his presence, they still obeyed him. Even Dagger had never refused a direct order from Martin, no matter how much he sulked as he carried it out.

And the spriggans liked her, the girls especially. They didn't care about Ivy's winglessness, or look down on her for being thin and small. They didn't see her as Flint's daughter or Marigold's, Mica's little sister or Cicely's big one. They didn't expect her to be anyone but herself.

Martin's fingers curled around Ivy's, his thumb stroking her wrist. "You told me once that the Joan is called *Wad* or torch in the old language, because she's the light for her people.

The one who drives back the darkness, and shows them the way. Well . . . that's what you did for me, when you found me in Betony's dungeon." He raised his free hand, brushing a windblown curl from her face. "*My* Joan."

There was no point reminding him she couldn't make fire, or defeat Betony in single combat. He knew that, and everything else about her. But he'd chosen to believe in her anyway.

Ivy turned Martin's hand over and pressed the pendant into it. She lowered her eyes as she spoke:

"Would you put it on me, please?"

In piskey tradition, a boy offered his sweetheart a necklace he'd crafted and waited anxiously to see if she'd wear it. But among spriggans, the necklace was the first piece a spriggan bride would wear of her husband's hoard, and it was his privilege to fasten it.

Martin's quick intake of breath told her he understood. With reverent care he draped the chain about Ivy's neck and clasped it, then caught her face between his hands and kissed her fiercely.

They were both trembling when they parted, and not from cold. "I love you," Ivy whispered. "And I'll be honored to marry you, when the time comes. But I can't stay invisible like your mother did. Even if I had the power, I couldn't live that way."

"And I couldn't bear to make you," said Martin, smiling down at her. "So by all means, let's cause a scandal. If nothing else, it will give Dagger something new to take offense at." He touched the pendant lightly where it lay against her heart. "This is all I ever need you to wear, Ivy. You're my treasure."

She leaned against him, tucking herself into the circle of his arms. "And you're mine."

It took two leaps to get all the provisions they'd bought back to the barrow, but as Ivy helped Martin carry the first load up the stairs she felt stronger and more alive than she had in weeks. She'd tucked her betrothal necklace inside her sweater, and a thrill went through her every time the pendant brushed her skin.

"It feels wrong to be happy," she'd told Martin as they left the supermarket, but he'd shaken his head at her.

"How would it be any better if you weren't? The only person who wants you miserable is Betony. If you can't stop her taking your people, you can at least deny her that."

So she'd resolved to stop brooding, at least for now, and consider how to help the spriggan children adjust to their new life. Could she teach the girls to change shape as Martin had taught the boys? That would give them one more way to protect themselves from enemies, and see more of the world than they ever could on foot. She could teach them to leap too, once they'd travelled enough . . .

"Have they all gone to bed?" Martin sounded puzzled, breaking into Ivy's thoughts. She'd assumed the door at the top of the stair was closed, but it wasn't: the whole barrow was dark.

"You must have worn them out with all those lessons," she replied, stepping into the chamber and dropping her bags next to his. Her skin-glow lit up several boys curled in their nests of blankets, but none of them stirred.

"Well, in that case, I'll have to do it more often." He stooped to give Ivy a lingering kiss, then headed back down the stairs for the second load.

Moving quietly so as not to wake the children, Ivy carried the supplies to the storeroom and set out the ingredients they'd need for breakfast. It was comforting to do such a simple, homely task, with no worries about where her people's next meal would be coming from or where they'd sleep tonight.

"Ivy." Martin spoke tersely through the doorway. "We have a problem."

Perplexed, she walked out of the storeroom to find him pacing the main chamber, kindling one glow-spell after another until the whole room blazed with light. The younger boys sat up, rubbing their eyes and yawning, but the older ones looked nervous, and some of the huddled shapes didn't move. Martin stalked to the nearest hump, and kicked it with a ruthlessness that shocked Ivy until she saw why. Under the blanket lay a rolled-up rug and an oat sack, instead of a boy.

"How long ago did they leave?" Martin demanded, rounding on Horatio.

The boy hugged his blanket, eyes huge and guilty. "A-about an hour ago."

There were four boys missing from the cavern: Dagger, Caliban, Tybalt, and Benedick. Ivy exchanged a worried glance with Martin. "Do you know where they went?"

Horatio gulped. "No." But his eyes strayed to the door of the treasure chamber, and fear chilled Ivy as she realized the boys might not be the only ones with something to hide. Willing her skin-glow to full brightness, she ran to the room where the girls slept.

To her relief, they were all awake and visible, with no fake sleepers in sight. But they looked even more distraught than Horatio, and as Ivy's gaze travelled from Jewel's tense posture to Ruby's swollen eyes, she realized with a shock what was wrong.

"Pearl," she said. "Where did she go?"

Jewel stepped forward, ashen. "It's my fault, my lady. I should have watched her more closely, but I never thought . . ."

Ivy whirled to Martin. "She's gone after Thrift."

"Of course she has," he said wearily. "And let me guess—Dagger and the other boys went to look for her. Did *no one* think of asking Thorn and Broch to help, instead of haring off in all directions like a pack of tomfools?"

Jewel hung her head but didn't reply. Probably she'd hoped the boys would find Pearl and bring her back before any of the grown-ups found out.

Still, what could have possessed Pearl to think she could follow Thrift in the first place? She'd never been to the Delve before, so she'd have to make the journey on foot, alone, in the cold and dark. It would be terrifying—and how would she know the way?

"Get Pearl's blanket," Martin told the girls, "or something else that belongs to her. If we don't find her with the others, we can use it to track her down."

He took Ivy's hand, and they hurried out of the barrow. Standing in the moonlight, they cast one finding-spell after another, and in moments they'd located all the missing boys and ordered them back home.

But even with Pearl's comb to focus on, Martin couldn't find her. In ermine-shape he could track her scent as far as the fallen trees, but after that he and Ivy found no trace of the little girl anywhere.

"It doesn't make sense," Martin said, scratching the back of his head. It was such a Mattock-like gesture that it hurt, and Ivy had to look away. "She's too young to travel by magic, let alone go somewhere she's never been before. She *can't* have leaped to the Delve."

"But she could have gone underground," Ivy pointed out. "If she sneaked down a dry adit or holed up in a carn for the night, that would explain why we can't find her."

Martin looked bleak, and she knew what he was thinking: *Or she's dead.* But Ivy refused to give up so easily. She changed back to falcon-shape and flapped off to continue the search.

Hours later, they'd checked every mine tunnel and rock pile within walking distance. But they still hadn't found a trace of Pearl. They leaped back to the barrow defeated, and Ivy stumbled to the treasure room and fell into exhausted sleep.

It seemed only moments before a tap on the arm roused her, and Ivy rolled over to find Jewel kneeling at her side. The other bed-mats lay empty, and the smell of frying sausages drifted in from the outer chamber. Surely it couldn't be morning already?

"I'm sorry to wake you," Jewel said. "But I've found out something about Pearl."

Ivy sat up, instantly awake. "What is it?"

Jewel glanced over her shoulder. "She was too shy to speak of it last night," she said, "and now she fears you'll be angry with her. But when Thrift was here, Ruby overheard her telling Pearl about the Delve and showing her an illusion of the place you call the Engine House. And just before the piskeys left, Thrift gave Pearl one of her hair ribbons, and Pearl gave her a coin from our hoard."

Could that be enough? Most magical folk would never dream of willing themselves to a place they'd never set foot, even with a token to guide them. But a young girl heedless of the danger, with no thought except finding her playmate again . . .

Ivy flung back the covers and leaped up to find Martin.

18

"If Pearl's gone to the Delve," Martin said, pacing the floor of the storeroom, "then we've got no choice. We have to get her back before anyone finds her."

Ivy bit her lip, knowing he was right. If Betony found the spriggan girl, she'd consider it an act of war.

"What makes you think they haven't found her already?" demanded Thorn. She'd been cross all morning, but Ivy knew that was only a mask for her guilty feelings: Jewel had rapped timidly on the faeries' door last night, and Thorn had barked at her to go away. "If the wards Betony put around the Delve are anything like the ones on the house and barn, there's no way a spriggan could get in without her knowing it."

"She could if Thrift was with her," Ivy said. "The wards keep out enemies, not guests."

Broch stroked his beard thoughtfully. "So you think the girls planned this between them? It wasn't just Pearl's idea?"

"I'm certain of it." Ruby had told Ivy that her clan and Pearl's were kinfolk, and that in more peaceful times they'd often walked past the Delve on their way to visit one another. That explained how the spriggan girl could leap there, especially with an image of the present-day Engine House to guide her. "That's why they exchanged gifts."

"So they could track each other," Thorn said, with grudging admiration. "They're clever little nits, I'll give them that. Pity they've landed us all in such a bees' nest. So what's the plan?"

"I'm going to the Delve," Ivy said quickly, before Martin could speak. "I know where Daisy and Thrift's cavern is, and if Pearl isn't there I can think of a few other places to look. But I have to go alone."

Thorn frowned. "What for? I can make myself invisible just as well as you can. And I've no fear of tunnels, or the dark either."

Ivy's heart warmed. Finding the faery woman so loyal, even now, made up for all of Queen Valerian's reluctance. "I'm sure you're right. But the air in the Delve's too bad now, especially for faeries. You'd be coughing in minutes, and it could hurt your baby as well."

"Blight." Thorn wrinkled her nose. "Hadn't thought of that. But if the air's too bad for me, what about you? You're half faery yourself, and—no offense—a lot twiggier than I am."

"It doesn't matter. I've got no choice." Neither Broch nor Martin could get into the Delve without Ivy, let alone navigate its maze of unfamiliar tunnels. If they blundered into the wrong cavern, they'd be captured and likely executed at once.

"Well, you're not going alone," Martin said. "I'm going with you."

"You can't," Ivy protested. "You hate being underground."

"No, what I can't stand is being trapped in the dark. Which is a fairly reasonable sort of trauma to have, if you ask me."

"But . . ." Flustered, Ivy cast about for another objection. "What about the children? If anything happens to us—"

"Then Dagger and Jewel will look after them. They're older than I was when Helm sent me through the portal, and I survived." He turned to Thorn and Broch. "Though they'll need help, if you're willing to give it."

"It's more if they're willing to accept it," said Broch. "Dagger doesn't think much of outsiders, from what I've seen."

"I'll deal with him," Martin said. "But in any case, we'll need you two to keep watch for us on the surface." His eyes turned bleak. "And tell the others what happened, if we don't make it out again."

The others. Such a simple phrase to describe all the people who cared for Ivy and Martin and would grieve to lose them. Like Marigold, who'd trusted Ivy to keep Cicely safe and had no idea that both her daughters were in such danger. And Molly would be shattered if she found out that not only was her best friend dead, but the young man she called her "faery godfather" as well.

"No," said Ivy, with sudden passion. "We can't just go barging into the Delve and hope for the best. There has to be another way."

"You'd rather plot some kind of devious strategy?" asked Martin. "That's new."

For Ivy, it would be—just as risking his life to save one little girl was something Martin would never have done in the past. But that wasn't what she had in mind.

"Not me," she said. "You. You're good at that sort of thing."

"Which is her diplomatic way of saying I'm a weasel," said Martin to Broch and Thorn. "You see why I love her."

Thorn snorted, and Ivy's cheeks flared hot. "No, I'm just saying that we only have one chance at this. So we need to do it right."

"A distraction could be useful," Broch pointed out. "We might be able to provide one, if your brother doesn't."

Ivy was about to ask what he meant, and then it hit her. Mica and his followers were trying to get into the Delve as well. If they burst in at the wrong moment it would be a disaster, but if they could time it right . . .

"I'll try to find him," she said. "He probably won't tell me what he's up to, but at least we'll know where he is."

"I wouldn't tell him our plans, either," said Martin. "The more he knows, the more trouble it'll make when he's caught. Better to get help we can count on." He turned to Broch. "We need more faeries."

"I already tried that," said Ivy. "It didn't work."

Thorn nodded grimly. "I don't know what's got into the queen, but she wouldn't budge."

"She has the Sight," Martin pointed out. "She may have seen something that convinced her not to intervene."

"Well, hopefully it wasn't our fiery deaths," Thorn said. "But she's not going to send us an army, no matter how much we beg for it."

"We're not asking for an army," Martin replied. "Even one or two could make a difference. Broch?"

"I . . . could try. But—" He broke off as Thorn held up a warning hand, her eyes fixed on the door.

Martin nodded, as though Thorn had spoken. Then he flung the door wide and pounced like a striking mink, seizing the eavesdropper by the collar. *"The fox barks not when he would steal the lamb,"* he quoted. "If you want to spy on people, Dagger, you'd better learn not to hiss like a pantomime villain while you're doing it."

Thorn glared at the spriggan boy, who blanched. But as soon as Martin let go, Dagger turned on him. "The faeries never gave a farthing for us, so why go begging to them now? You think we're not good enough to help?"

Martin regarded him sternly. "As usual, my callow youth, you have a positive genius for missing the point. This is not about you."

"Then who is it about? Pearl's a spriggan, one of us. We should be marching off to save her ourselves, not crawling to some—some fool of a faery queen!"

Martin went still, his eyes a cold blank. When he spoke, his voice was deadly. "In all my murders, treasons and detested sins, boy, I have never struck a child. But you are sorely tempting me. Get out of my sight."

Dagger stared at him, swallowing. Then he backed away and scuttled out the door.

"I thought you said you were going to deal with him," said Thorn, and Ivy tensed. But Martin only looked rueful.

"He spent half his life being thrashed, kicked and starved by his old foster-chieftain, and now he thinks I'm weak for not treating him the same. He'd stab me in the back if he could, just to prove he didn't suffer for nothing. But the only way to satisfy him is to live up to his worst expectations, and I'm not going to do that."

Thorn's brows shot up. "You *have* changed. When Valerian pardoned you I thought she was giving you too much credit, but I'm beginning to think she was right." She tipped her head to one side, studying him. "So did you swear her a blood oath, then?"

Martin gave a short laugh. "Of course not." His face sobered. "But I might as well have. In all the years I served the Empress, she never touched me except to cause me pain. But when I came before Queen Valerian as a prisoner and she saw the iron burns on my wrists, she brought a salve she had made and put it on me herself. So . . ." He spread his hands. "I chose to trust her then, and I trust her now. Whether she gives us what we ask or not."

"I'll go, then, if you wish it," said Broch. "But if help comes, it won't come quickly. None of the other Oakenfolk have been to Cornwall, so we'll have to fly."

Which would take until nightfall, or even later—and with every hour they delayed, Pearl would be in more danger. Ivy cast an anxious look at Martin, who met it with a resigned one. "There's no time, then," he said. "We'll just have to work with what we've got."

"I'll look for Mica," said Ivy, and Martin caught her hand and kissed it.

"Be careful," he said. "And good luck."

Coming from a spriggan, that was more than mere wishful thinking. Or at least Ivy hoped so, because she'd need all the help she could get. "Shaper guide you," she replied, and Martin looked startled, then touched. He bowed to her, and went out.

"Shaper?" Thorn asked skeptically, but Ivy didn't answer. She only knew it was the sort of thing Helm, Dagger's sire and Martin's old protector, used to say—an old spriggan blessing, long forgotten by the world. But if there were even a chance that some unseen power was watching over the Small People of Cornwall, Ivy prayed it would show them some mercy now.

Ivy glided over the winter-dulled countryside as a peregrine, rain beading on her feathers as she scanned the fields and hillsides for signs of Mica and his company. Every few miles she landed and cast a finding-spell, hoping for the bright flare inside her mind that would tell her magical folk were nearby. But though she searched as close to the Delve as she dared, she found no trace of a piskey camp.

That didn't prove much, though. Cicely had a gift for illusions and invisibility spells, and though Mica could be reckless, he was too skilled a hunter to leave an obvious trail. If they worked together, they could hide themselves right under Ivy's wingtip, and she'd never know it. All she could do was keep flying in circles and hope they'd take the hint.

But if Mica spotted Ivy that morning, he wasn't responding.

Had he dusted her off his boots for good, or had he gone underground already? Were his followers still trying to break into the Delve and free the trapped piskey-men, or had they been captured as well?

There seemed no way to find out, and she'd wasted enough time already. Resigned, Ivy wheeled back toward the Menadue farmstead. Betony's wards probably hadn't faded enough yet for Ivy to get inside, but if the worst happened, she didn't want to disappear without leaving her mother and Molly a note to say goodbye.

By the time Ivy reached the farm, the clouds had thinned and the sky was a flat pearl-gray. She circled the barn at a cautious distance, then swooped, bracing herself for impact. But her wings met no resistance, and she landed easily in the cobblestone yard.

Puzzled, Ivy changed shape and sent out a tentative thought to test the wards. They hadn't just weakened: they were gone, dissolved so completely that she couldn't feel a trace of Betony's power.

Bemused, Ivy turned toward the house, where a glimmer of light shone through the kitchen curtains. Had she forgotten to turn off the switch before she left, or was someone inside? Could Marigold have grown anxious when no one answered her phone calls, and dashed here to find out what was happening?

There was only one way to be sure. Ivy concentrated and leaped inside the house.

"Hello?" she called, glancing around the sitting room. "Is anyone here?"

For a moment there was no sound but the slow tick of the mantel clock. Then came a sniff, a hiccup, and a small, glowing figure stepped out from behind the coat stand.

"*Cicely,*" breathed Ivy, and her little sister's face crumpled. She flung herself into Ivy's arms and burst into tears.

Ivy guided her to the sofa and sat down with her, rubbing her back soothingly. But Cicely sobbed so hard it was like trying to still an earthquake.

"Mica s-sent me away," she gasped out, when she could speak. "I w-wanted to fight, but he wouldn't l-let me, he threw me onto Dodger's back and told him to r-run."

And Mica's gift with animals was strong, even for a piskey's, so Dodger would have obeyed no matter how hard Cicely tried to stop him. "Fight?" Ivy asked. "You mean Gossan found you?"

Cicely nodded miserably. "We were camping in the wood near the Delve. Mica wanted to tunnel in through one of the old adits, but the uncles kept getting tired so it wasn't going fast enough. And we couldn't find anywhere dry to sleep, so Daffodil got sicker and sicker, and finally Yarrow said she'd die without medicine and she was going into the Delve to get some."

Mica wouldn't have liked that one bit, and he'd doubtless let Yarrow know it. But the healer could be just as stubborn as he was in her own quiet way, especially when a patient's life was involved. "Go on," Ivy said.

"She told us she'd be careful, but we waited all night and she didn't come back. Then Daffodil d-died—"

She broke off, shuddering, and Ivy bowed her head in grief for the poor old auntie. If Copper hadn't been so set on following Mica, his wife would still be alive.

"I'm so sorry, Cicely." Ivy stroked her sister's hair. "So you buried her, and then?"

"Copper went wild, he was pounding the rocks with his thunder-axe and calling down curses on Mica, and we tried to calm him down but we couldn't, so Gossan and his men found us. And I d-don't know what happened then, because by the time I got back they were . . ." She pressed her lips together and shook her head, too distraught to finish the sentence.

Ivy's heart gave a painful thump. "You mean captured?" *Please,* she begged silently. *Please don't let them be dead.*

Cicely nodded, and Ivy let out her breath. So Mica and his followers were alive. Though if Betony found out that he and Yarrow had tried to set themselves up as Jack and Joan, they might not stay that way for long.

"I've been here since last night," Cicely mumbled. "I was so tired of being dirty and hungry. It took me hours to get past Betony's wards, and when I heard someone outside I panicked because I thought she was coming to get me. But it was you."

"You did the right thing," Ivy told her. "You got away safe, and that's what Mica wanted."

"I don't care what Mica wants," blurted Cicely, bolting upright. "He's stupid! I hate him!"

It was tempting to agree, but Ivy knew better. "He can be stupid sometimes," she said gently. "But he was trying to do the right thing, even if he went about it the wrong way. You couldn't have helped him, Cicely. If you'd stayed, Gossan would have caught you too."

Cicely hung her head. Then she said in a small voice, "I'm sorry I spied on you. Mica asked me to make sure you didn't hurt Matt, and I—"

"I know." Ivy squeezed her, reassuring. It would always hurt to remember how her sister had betrayed her. But Cicely looked so ashamed already that there was no need to hammer that spike in. "You wanted to be useful to somebody." And Ivy had been so caught up trying to be useful herself that she'd ignored Cicely until it was too late. "Anyway, we can't change the past, so let's not dwell on it. I'm just glad you're safe."

"I don't want to be safe." Cicely screwed up her face. "I want to *help.*"

"With what?" Ivy asked, hiding her dismay. Had Cicely guessed what she and Martin were planning? But how could she?

"You're going to the Delve, aren't you? That's why you stopped here." She snatched the letter out of Ivy's coat pocket and waved it accusingly. "This is for Mum and Molly, I'll bet. And you want me to give it to them if you don't come back."

Ivy gave an inward sigh. Cicely knew her too well. "The best gift I can give Mum now is you. So yes, that is what I'm asking. And if you really want to make it up to me for siding with Mica, you'll do it."

Cicely scrubbed her eyes. "I don't want Mum," she said thickly. "She was gone so long I barely remembered her, and now she might as well be human. *You're* the one who's always looked after me, and if you don't come back I'll—" Her head came up, defiant. "I'll march into the Delve and fight Betony myself."

"Cicely!"

"You don't think I mean it, but I do. I'll tell her exactly what I think of her. And I don't even care if she burns me up. I'd rather die than be a coward."

This was getting out of hand. "What about Dodger?" Ivy challenged. "Are you just going to leave him to starve?"

"I'll turn him loose. Somebody will find him." Her small mouth was set with determination. "You know I'm good at turning invisible. We can sneak into the Delve tonight and rescue Mica and the others before Betony even knows we're there."

Ivy pinched the bridge of her nose and sighed. She dreaded bringing Cicely into this, but Martin *had* said they needed more help. "All right. You can come."

Cicely brightened. "Really?"

"Yes. But you have to promise to stay close, and do everything I tell you. No arguing or sneaking about. If I tell you to run, you run, and don't come back for me or Mica or anybody. You'll find Thorn and Broch and tell them what happened, and then you'll come straight here and call Mum to come and get you."

"But what if—"

"No, Cicely. If you want me to trust you with something this important, you have to trust me too. That's the bargain."

Cicely toyed with the end of her braid. Then she said, "Fine. I'll do everything you say. I swear."

"Good." Ivy got to her feet. "I'll go tell Martin and the faeries."

"Wait," pleaded Cicely. "Come and see Dodger first. He's missed you."

Ivy doubted that, but it was clear that Cicely wanted a little more time with her. And this could be the last private moment they had together, before the end. She took her sister's hand, and together they leaped to the barn.

The bay pony snorted a greeting as they landed, and Ivy reached to stroke him. But as he lipped her fingers, her eyes strayed to the crack in the wall, where the knockers had forced their way in. Had it really been only a few days ago? It felt like a lifetime. Stepping back to make room for Cicely, Ivy glanced upward—and froze.

"Good boy, Dodger," Cicely murmured, rubbing his neck. "You're glad to see Ivy, aren't you?"

Ivy barely heard her: she stood like a pottery statue, staring at the roof of the barn. In a vivid flash she remembered how it had blazed on the night of the battle, the searing heat that had stung her eyes and the smoke that had filled the air. And the sight of those beams where Betony's fire had once burned sent a shiver through Ivy, from her crown to the soles of her feet.

"What is it?" Cicely asked, but Ivy couldn't answer. The thought that had sprung to her mind was too overwhelming. If their plan to rescue Pearl failed, and she was forced to confront Betony . . .

"Ivy?" Cicely tugged at her. "Are you all right?"

She tore her eyes from the roof and met her sister's worried brown ones. "It's fine," she said hoarsley. "I was just thinking."

"**S**he's posted guards at the entrance to the Earthenbore," Cicely whispered, creeping under the gorse bushes to rejoin Ivy, Martin, and the two faeries crouching there. "We'll have to get past them first."

The sun had set long ago, and at this late hour the piskeys of the Delve would usually be sleeping. But clearly Betony was taking no chances. Ivy turned to the others. "Two guards at least, and probably more inside. What do you think?"

"Don't look at us," said Thorn sourly. "This is as far as we go, remember?"

She wasn't complaining, really: they'd all agreed to this plan. But it still chafed the faery woman that she and Broch weren't going with them. "I know," said Ivy, putting a hand on Thorn's shoulder. "I still value your advice, though."

Broch flicked Martin a questioning glance. "Put them to sleep?"

"We'd have to touch them to do it," Martin said. "And they'd likely wake up and sound the alarm before we got out again." He plucked a pebble from the ground, tossing it lightly. "I have a better idea."

Thorn grabbed his wrist. "Don't you *dare*."

Her fierceness would have shocked Ivy, if she hadn't known

the reason behind it. The last time Thorn had seen Martin toying with a pebble, he'd transformed it to a dagger and killed the Empress.

"Not quite sure of me yet, I see." Martin pried off Thorn's grip and rose, his eyes on the guarded entrance. "But sometimes a stone is just a stone." With a snap of his forearm he sent the pebble flying past the piskey-men to rustle the gorse nearby.

The guards spun toward the noise, and Martin caught Cicely's hand. "Hide me," he told her. "The rest of you, wait here." And before Ivy could protest, the two of them vanished.

"Show-off," muttered Thorn, shaking her fingers. "He'd better not muck this up."

Ivy scanned the hillside, but even her piskey night-vision couldn't track Martin and Cicely. She held her breath, waiting for the guards to crumple or flee. But they stayed motionless, and when Martin flashed into view at the mouth of the tunnel and beckoned, Ivy realized why.

"He's stopped time around them," she told Thorn and Broch. "We can walk past and they'll never know we were there." She took the faeries' hands, sobered by the knowledge that she might never see them again. "I'll send Cicely back to you as soon as I can. And if we aren't out by morning—"

"None of that nonsense," said Thorn brusquely. "We'll do our part. Just go."

Broch nodded, his eyes grave. "And may Rhys and the Great Gardener be with you."

Ivy pressed their hands gratefully, then slipped out from the thicket and ran to join Martin and Cicely. Together they slipped past the frozen guards and down the baked-clay passage into the Delve.

"I can't believe you can stop time," breathed Cicely as they crept along, holding hands so they wouldn't lose each other in the darkness. "I've never heard of *anyone* who could do that."

"Well, I've also cast a spell of silence," said Martin, "so you don't have to whisper. But keep your ears open."

He spoke casually, but Ivy could feel the tension in his body. The farther they walked from the entrance, the harder it was for him to hold the time-spell. "You can let go now," she said. "They can't see us anyway."

"Good point." He exhaled, relaxing. Then his hand slid up Ivy's arm, and she stifled a gasp as his lips brushed the hollow of her jaw. "Missed," he said regretfully. "Shall I try again?"

"Are you *kissing* her?" demanded Cicely. "That's dis—"

An abrupt silence followed, as her hand in Ivy's went still. "Did you just time-freeze my sister?" Ivy asked as Martin tugged her toward him, but the only answer was the slow curve of his mouth on hers.

"I'd have done this earlier," he murmured, "but you didn't give me a chance. I'd like to think this won't be the last time, but if it is, let's make it a good one."

The practical part of Ivy wanted to push him away and scold him for being so frivolous. But if the worst happened and Betony scorched her to ashes, at least let her heart burn with something sweeter than regret. "For someone who can stop time, you have a terrible sense of it," she whispered, and Martin made a startled noise against her throat.

"Ivy, my queen, my heart's love, was that a *joke*?"

"'*O single-soled jest,*'" Ivy began, but Martin stopped her lips with his before she could finish. She should have known better than to quote *Romeo and Juliet* at a time like this. They both knew too well how that story ended.

When he let her go Ivy was breathless, but her skin tingled and her blood surged with sparkling energy. She felt stronger than she had for days, and the shaky feeling that had gripped her since the barn subsided. Despite his quicksilver tongue and unpredictable impulses, Martin could be steady as bedrock when she needed him, and it wasn't so hard to be brave when they were together.

She brushed back his silky hair and pressed her brow to his, inhaling the faint fir-needle fragrance of his skin—which must be from his faery mother's side, because as Thorn had pointed out, spriggans didn't smell like anything at all. It was cruelly hard to let go of him, wondering if they'd ever be this close again. But time had only stopped for Cicely, and they couldn't afford to waste any more of it.

"—gusting," Cicely finished in the same aggrieved tone, and Ivy smiled.

"Don't worry, it's over now. Let's go."

It had been three months since Ivy set foot in the Delve, and nearly twice as long for Cicely. But they'd grown up in these tunnels and knew every turning by heart. Treading slowly for Martin's sake, cloaked with invisibility and silence, they crept to the end of the Earthenbore and down the Hunter's Stair to the Narrows.

They'd nearly reached the first junction when they heard the distant, familiar clump of miners' boots hitting stone. Two knockers were tramping up the tunnel toward them.

"More trouble than it's worth," one grumbled, as they rounded a bend in the corridor and their skin-glows lit up the walls. "Can't even get any digging done with that lot in the way."

"And they're no use to anyone either," said the other. "We're spread thin enough as it is without—" He stopped, spluttered, and broke into a hacking cough.

Cicely tugged Ivy's hand. "Quick," she whispered, "while we've got the chance."

The intersection was only a few paces away, and with luck they'd make it before the coughing guard spotted their shadows. Ivy tugged Martin's hand and the three of them dashed forward, past the men's flickering glow and into the side tunnel.

They made it just in time. The knocker straightened, clearing his throat, and the two men set off again. Pressed to the wall, Ivy waited until their glows faded. Then she tapped Cicely, and they all moved on.

Martin hadn't spoken since their kiss in the Earthenbore, and now he stumbled after Ivy in a parody of his usual grace. His palm felt clammy, and his hand clutched hers painfully tight. Despite all his assurances, he *was* afraid, but they'd gone too far to take him back to the surface now.

"We're almost there," Ivy said, hoping to comfort him. "This tunnel we're going through is called the Upper Rise, and it's one of my favorites. When the day-lamps are lit, it's the brightest place in the whole Delve, and it's covered with mosaic tiles in every color you can imagine. Remember when I was leading you out the first time, and you saw the gemstones sparkling in the walls? It's just as beautiful. Only this tunnel has pictures of plants and animals, so the children can learn about them." She paused, wistful with memory. "I wish you could see it. I wish I could show you the whole Delve."

Martin didn't speak, but his grip eased. He raised Ivy's hand gratefully to his lips, and they continued on.

A few moments later Cicely halted, sputtering out a cough. The deeper they went into the mine, the more poisonous the air became. But it surprised Ivy that her sturdy little sister was the first to feel it.

"Here," Ivy told her, switching places with her little sister and pressing her hand into Martin's. "I'll lead for a bit."

Cicely gave a last cough and fell silent. In single file the three of them groped onward, until the tiles beneath Ivy's fingers yielded to rough granite and they turned into the sloping passage known as Tinners' Row.

With the day-lamps lit, Ivy could have found Daisy's cavern

with ease. But in full dark it was hard to tell one door from another, and dangerously easy to lose count. Yet Ivy couldn't kindle her skin-glow, in case the guards spotted them. She could only hope that if she picked the wrong cavern, they'd be able to slip out again without being caught.

"Get ready," she told Cicely and Martin. Then she put her hands flat against the chiseled door and pushed.

Martin must have kept up his spell of silence, because it opened soundlessly, and the cavern stayed quiet as Ivy crept in. She let her skin glow just enough to see her surroundings, and spotted Thrift's favorite rag doll lying by a chair.

"It's safe," she whispered over her shoulder. "Come in."

Once the door was shut, they had no more need for secrecy. Brightening her glow, Ivy hurried to the smallest bed-alcove and pulled back the curtains.

Thrift lay curled up on her side, a picture of sleeping innocence. But the pillow next to her head was indented, and the covers formed a trembling lump at her back.

"I know you're there, Pearl," said Martin in a warning tone, and the little spriggan whimpered. She sat up, knuckling her eyes as she turned visible.

Thrift woke with a cry. "Mam!"

The door to the adjoining bedchamber flew open. Daisy rushed out, pulling a robe over her nightgown—and stopped, aghast, at the sight of Ivy and Martin. "What are you doing here?" she exclaimed. "Betony will kill you!"

"We came for Pearl," said Ivy, gesturing at the little spriggan.

Daisy gasped. "Thrift, you wicked child! Get up this instant!"

With guilty meekness the two girls climbed down, and stood clutching each other's hands as Daisy scolded them. "Why would you do such a daft, reckless thing? However did you—"

"That's not important right now," Ivy cut in. "What matters

is that no harm's been done. But we need to get Pearl out of here right away."

"No!" Thrift flung her arms about the spriggan girl. "You can't have her!"

"Thrift!" Daisy chided, but the child only clutched Pearl tighter. She turned to Ivy with a sigh. "She's been like this ever since we got back. I don't know how to manage her, without . . ." Her voice hitched, and she pressed a hand to her mouth. "I'm sorry. I just miss Gem so much."

Ivy was taken aback. She'd thought that once Mattock returned with the women and children, Betony would let the men go. "You mean he's still a prisoner?"

"Betony said they needed to learn their lesson. So they're all locked up in the diggings, except . . ." She hesitated. "Never mind. The point is, she won't let any of us see them. I don't think they even know we're back."

Meaning that all those men thought they were about to die, with no hope of pardon. And Betony wanted it that way. Smoldering anger kindled in Ivy, but she forced herself to stay calm. "You said they're all there except someone. Who?"

Daisy looked stricken. "Mattock," she said in a small voice. "And Mica. She's got them chained up in a cave halfway down the Great Shaft . . ."

Martin made a hissing noise, and Ivy stiffened. They both knew that dank, lightless hollow too well.

". . . and tomorrow she's going to execute them."

There was an awful silence in the cavern as Daisy's words sank in. Cicely spun to Ivy, wild-eyed. "I can fly down to them. Please. Let me help!"

"I wish you could," said Ivy heavily. "But if you try to get their chains off, you'll end up trapped down there with them. We've both been out of the Delve too long to touch iron without losing our magic."

Cicely looked stricken. "But so has Mica. And he's half faery too."

Ivy caught her breath. She hadn't thought of that, but by the bleak look on his face Martin had. "We need the key, then," he said. "And I'm guessing Betony has it."

In which case it might as well be on the moon, for all the chance they had of getting it. Stomach tight with anxiety, Ivy started to pace the dark, mottled granite of the floor. There had to be a way to save her brother and Mattock. But how?

"Gem," said Daisy abruptly. "He could break in and strike off their chains with a thunder-axe. Any of our men could, if we set them free."

Thrift perked up. "Daddy!" she squealed. "He's big and strong, he can do it!"

Ivy had no doubt they were right, but how could they free Gem and the others, let alone rescue Matt and Mica, without Betony knowing? A silencing spell could muffle sound, but not vibrations. Even if they didn't hear the stone door shattering, every knocker in the Delve would feel it.

"We need a distraction," Ivy said. "Something to force Betony and all her soldiers up to the surface."

Martin stood silent, gazing at his folded arms. At last he said, "I might be able to provide one. But it depends on how much Betony knows." He looked up at Daisy. "Did she question you when you came back to the Delve?"

Daisy made a sour face. "She didn't need to. Copper, that old fool, told her practically everything."

A chill rippled through Ivy. That meant that Betony not only knew Martin was a spriggan, she knew there were other spriggans living in Kernow as well. She might not know where to find the barrow yet, but she knew it existed, and all it might take was the threat of fire to get one of Ivy's followers talking . . .

Ivy turned to Martin in distress, but to her surprise he was smiling. "Excellent," he said. "Cicely, get up to the surface, find Thorn, and get ready for my signal. Ivy, go around the tunnels, and bring as many women and children here as you can."

"Teasel?" Ivy called as she stepped into the older woman's cavern. "Wake up."

Without Cicely to keep her invisible or Martin to silence her footsteps, avoiding the Delve's guards hadn't been easy. Ivy had nearly been caught twice, and only escaped by darting around a corner at the last minute. But though her route through the tunnels had been longer than she'd hoped for, Ivy had managed to visit Fern, Moss, Clover, and nearly all the other women she trusted. Teasel's cavern was her last stop.

"We're going to save Hew," Ivy continued, rapping on the door of the bedchamber, "but we need your help. Teasel?"

There was a rustle in the bed-alcove that had once belonged to Keeve, and the curtains parted as Teasel poked her head out. Her eyes were red-rimmed, and Ivy's heart panged for her: she must have been lonely sleeping without her husband, and crawled into her late son's bed for comfort. "You oughtn't to be here, me bird!" the piskey-woman gasped. "If Betony finds you—"

"I know," Ivy said. "But I can't let her execute Mica and Matt. That's why we're going to break out your husband and the others tonight."

Teasel broke into a racking cough. For several heartbeats she wheezed and thumped her chest, then sagged against the wall of the alcove in exhaustion.

Ivy had seen a few coughing spells tonight, but none as bad

as this. "Have you seen Yarrow?" she asked, hurrying to help
the older woman down. "Or is she out of medicine?"

Teasel sank into an armchair, dabbing her eyes. "She's
locked in her quarters. No one sees her unless a guard brings
them, and they won't do that without Betony's say-so."

And of course Betony wouldn't give such an order for
Teasel, or any of the other women who'd left the Delve. That
would be too much like mercy. Ivy's nails dug into her palms,
and she had to breathe deep to quell her anger before she
spoke. "All right, then. Get dressed and come with me."

By the time they got back to Daisy's cavern, all the other
women were waiting. Their hair was in knots, their eyes dim
with weariness, and with their children clinging to their skirts
they couldn't have looked less like an army. But if they had the
will to come here and the wits to avoid getting caught, they'd
proved their mettle already. Gathering them around her, Ivy
explained Martin's plan.

"I know you're afraid," she told the women. "I'm scared
too. But we can't let Betony bully us any longer. We have to
stand up to her and fight for the people we love."

Clover's oldest boy straightened up proudly. "I'm ready
to fight. My dad gave me a knife, see?" He pulled the little
blade from his belt and waved it, as the women exclaimed and
scuttled back.

"And a fine blade it is," said Martin, putting a hand on the
boy's shoulder. "But there are better ways to use it. Come over
here with me, and I'll show you."

The boy looked hesitantly at his mother, who nudged him
to follow Martin. Relieved, Ivy continued her speech. "So I'm
asking you to dig deep for the courage that I know is in every
one of you. When you hear the signal, you have to go down
and find your men, free them, and tell them what we need
them to do."

If Ivy could tell them the safest route to take, what spells they should use, and all the challenges they might encounter on the way, she would have. But she didn't know any of those things. She wasn't even sure how they'd get the men out of the diggings once they got there, if they were chained like Matt and Mica or trapped behind some great slab of rock. All she could do was hope the women would be clever and determined enough to work it out.

"I'm giving you this task," she told them, holding each of their gazes in turn, "because I trust you. I believe that if you work together, you can do amazing things—bigger and braver and better things than I ever could. You don't need me to do this for you. You can do it on your own."

When she finished, a hush fell over the cavern. Then Teasel spoke, her voice no longer raspy but strong and clear. "Ayes, you've said it. We've cowered and cringed before Betony these past twenty years, and what good has it done us? The more we give her, the more she takes, and now we may as well be so many sheep for her wolf's teeth to gobble. But you, maid . . ."

She reached out, clasping Ivy's hand in both her seamed ones. "You've done all you could to build us up, for all it cost you dear to try it. You may not have the fire of a true Joan, but you've surely got the heart of one. If you think we can do this, then I for one believe you."

"And I," said Fern, stepping out from behind her. "I'm not letting my Mattock swing from Gossan's gibbet, whether anyone else joins me or no!"

"I'll join you," Moss said. "I've still got the keys to the treasure cavern from the last time we had a Lighting. We can arm our men, and ourselves too, if it comes to that."

Bramble gave a little cough, and Ivy tensed, but the old auntie was only calling for attention. "I'm too old and slow to run about the tunnels," she said, "but I'll do my part. I'll stay here and care for your little ones."

The younger women's faces cleared at that, and Daisy put

down the wriggling Thrift. "Then I'll come," she said, and Clover nodded her agreement.

"Don't forget to find Yarrow," Ivy said. "If she has any medicine left, make sure you all take some, and give it to the men too."

"They'll need it, no doubt," agreed Teasel. "The air's worst down in the diggings." She inhaled slowly and looked about, frowning puzzlement. "Though it's fine here, odd enough. I've not breathed so easy since we left the barrow. What's your secret, Daisy?"

Thrift's mother looked surprised. "None that I know of. I've not done a thing different since we came back."

Yet no one had coughed for several minutes now, and Teasel was right about the freshness of Daisy's cavern. There wasn't a trace here of the throat-clogging haze that filled the tunnels, and now that Ivy thought about it, she hadn't heard Daisy or Thrift cough since she and Martin got here. Let alone Pearl, who was smaller than any of them.

But they only had a short time left to save Mica and Mattock, so that mystery would have to wait. "Once Martin and I get back to the surface," Ivy told them, "it won't be long before Gossan sounds the alarm. Wait until he and his men come after us. Then go."

The women nodded, determined. Ivy searched their faces—old, young, and in-between—and it grieved her to think of losing any of them. But if their story and hers had to end, at least it would be a brave ending. "Good luck."

"Are you all right?" Ivy whispered, as she and Martin crept through the tunnels. He'd recovered his poise in the light of

Daisy's cavern, but he'd been unusually quiet while Ivy was talking to the women, and since they stepped back into the darkness he hadn't spoken at all.

"I've been better," he replied in a low voice. "But I've also been worse. Don't mind me."

Behind him, Pearl sniffed a little. Daisy had been forced to pry Thrift away from her, and the piskey-girl had howled so noisily that Martin had to spell her to sleep. But when Ivy and Martin left the cavern, Pearl had followed without resistance. She knew she'd been foolish to run away, and she'd been weeping quietly ever since they set off, ashamed of herself.

But she still wasn't coughing, despite the smog in the tunnels. And though she could hear him breathing fast with dread, neither was Martin.

Oddest of all, Ivy wasn't either. The last time she'd sneaked into the Delve she'd been coughing in minutes, but tonight she hadn't felt so much as a tickle in her throat. No dizziness or weakness—in fact the opposite: she felt almost as clearheaded now as she had when Martin kissed her in the Earthenbore. Why?

A thought flashed into her mind, and Ivy nearly tripped over her own feet. Could Martin and Pearl be immune to the Delve's poison? Could they even—unlikely as it seemed—have the power to cancel it out?

"I'm still fairly attached to that hand, Ivy," said Martin in a strangled voice. "So if you'd stop trying to crush it, I'd be grateful."

Embarrassed, she let go. "Sorry." But she was so distracted that when Martin took her other hand, he had to nudge her to move on.

If spriggans had some kind of natural cleansing magic, it would explain everything. The strangely fresh air in the barrow and Daisy's cavern, how Martin had healed Mattock when Broch couldn't, the reason Cicely had stopped coughing immediately when they switched places in the Upper Rise. Even the tingling energy Ivy had felt when Martin kissed her made sense now: it hadn't been passion, it had been his power flowing into her.

Excitement leaped up in Ivy. If only one or two spriggans could make such a difference, what about thirty? Her people wouldn't need to look for a new home if Martin and the children could purge out the poison and make the Delve safe again. And then the piskeys would *have* to make peace with the spriggans, because they literally couldn't do without them.

Yet Ivy would never have discovered any of this if Pearl hadn't run away. It was enough to make her wonder if there might be some all-knowing power behind everything, like the Shaper, or the Great Gardener, or Rhys the Deep. Or perhaps just the same being called by different names, working in Martin's life and Thorn and Broch's as well as her own.

Though that unseen power could also be leading Ivy to her death tonight, for the sake of some greater good that she would never see. But it heartened her to think that all she'd suffered could be worth something after all, and that she and Martin might still be able to make a difference.

Steps quickening, she tugged the spriggans after her, up the Hunter's Stair to the Earthenbore. The sooner they reached the surface, the sooner they could carry out the rest of their plan.

"There they are," she whispered as the guards came into view, silhouetted in the tunnel entrance. It was still night, but the faint glow from outside was dazzling compared to the absolute blackness behind them. "Martin?"

Martin stepped forward and made a sweeping gesture. The guards stilled, frozen in time again, and Ivy, Martin, and Pearl darted past them. Together they ran out onto the hillside, up the path, and collapsed in the shadow of the Engine House.

In the moonlight Martin looked colorless, limp with strain

and exhaustion. But when he sat up and turned to Pearl, his face was stern and commanding as a king's. "Leap back to the barrow at once," he said, "and stay there with Jewel and the others. If I see *any* of you again tonight I will be very angry, do you understand?"

Pearl gave a little whimper and vanished. Ivy turned to Martin, eager to tell him what she'd discovered, but the bleak look in his eyes forestalled her. "What's wrong?" she asked.

"*It is a melancholy of mine own, compounded of many simples,*" said Martin. "I've got a lot to think about, and it's been a long night. But we've come this far, so let's ring up the curtain for Act Two, shall we?" He cupped his hands to his mouth and let out the eerie, piercing screech of a barn owl.

If the knocker guards heard the call, it didn't trouble them. The doorway of the Engine House remained empty until a black nose poked around the corner and a badger snuffled in, blinking at them with small, rheumy eyes.

"Are they ready?" Martin asked, as it unfolded into Broch.

"As they'll ever be," said the faery man. "Cicely is better at glamours than Thorn, but once they split up and start flying, even she finds it difficult to hold the illusion steady."

"That won't matter," said Martin, and privately Ivy agreed. It was dark, to begin with, and once they lured Gossan and his soldiers into the wood, the flickering shadows would help hide any weak spots in the glamour. The main thing was to keep their enemies chasing phantoms as long as possible before they realized it was all a trick. "Just tell them to be ready for my signal. I may need to improvise."

Broch nodded, changed shape again, and waddled off. "What do you mean, improvise?" Ivy asked, as Martin turned to her.

"Do you trust me?" he asked.

"You know I do."

Martin slid a finger through the chain of her pendant and

drew it out from beneath her sweater. "Then trust that I'll do everything in my power not to make you regret it." He kissed her lightly and disappeared.

Ivy closed her fingers around the stone, frowning. She was still wondering what he'd meant when she heard him call out to the guards in the rich, rolling voice he used on stage:

"Tell your so-called Jack that the king of the spriggans has come to challenge him. Tell him to come out of his coward's den and fight!"

Panic stabbed into Ivy. She rushed to the doorway, staring down the hill in disbelief.

Martin had materialized a mere stone's throw from the guards, arms folded and feet planted arrogantly wide. Shocked, they reached for their thunder-axes, but he raised a warning hand. "I wouldn't try it, if I were you. Soldiers, arise!"

Wind rippled the gorse behind him, and a host of spindly figures rose up with sinister smoothness. They looked nothing like Martin or the children back in the barrow, but they were chillingly like the spriggans Ivy had grown up seeing in her nightmares: gaunt, pale and hungry-looking, swathed in ragged cloaks and hoods that hid all but their glittering eyes.

The guards backed up, faces slack with fear. Their ancestors had led countless raids against the faeries and spriggans of Kernow, but these men had grown up without seeing a real enemy, let alone having to fight one. Even their skirmish with Ivy's people hadn't prepared them for this.

"Go and fetch your leader," commanded Martin. "Or we'll march in and drag him out. If he wants to keep calling himself Jack of the Delve, he'll have to fight me for it."

"But a spriggan can't . . ." The youngest guard trailed off, stammering, as Ivy walked down the hill to join them. Her mouth felt dry and her knees shaky, but if Martin could improvise, so could she.

"He can if he's *my* Jack," she said. "You heard my lord king. Go."

"My lord," murmured Martin. "I like the sound of that."

Ivy suppressed the urge to smack him. How could he make such a reckless challenge, especially after what had happened to Mattock? Martin might be quicker on his feet and better used to treachery, but he was still no match for Gossan.

If only she could tell Martin what she'd guessed about spriggans! But the guards were listening, and there was no chance now. All she could do was pray this mad scheme of Martin's would work.

The guards huddled together, whispering urgently. At last the oldest straightened up, hefted his thunder-axe, and thumped it three times on the tunnel floor.

The sound was muffled, but the vibrations would carry. The next guard to feel the signal would echo it, and soon everyone in the Delve would know the mine was under attack. With a last nervous glance at Martin the younger guard raced off down the Earthenbore to relay his message, leaving the older one behind.

He did his best to look defiant, but his eyes were watering with terror, and Ivy's heart went out to him. "Don't be afraid, Wolfram," she said. "It's not you we came to fight."

The knocker's mouth worked, and he spat on the ground between them. "Traitor! Siding with spriggans against your own folk? You're as false as the Joan said."

Martin stiffened, but Ivy touched his hand. "Think what you like," she told Wolfram. "You'll find out who's false soon enough."

They'd waited on the hillside for several minutes, and Ivy was starting to wonder if Cicely and Thorn could keep up the illusion much longer, when they heard boots marching up the tunnel and the younger guard returned, followed by a host of knockers, hunters, and a few doughty old uncles. As they stepped out onto the hillside, Ivy silently counted them: three, eight, twelve, fifteen . . .

By the time they'd fanned out into position, weapons drawn and gleaming in the light of the low-hanging moon, there were forty-two Delve soldiers—equal to the glamoured spriggans, and ten times more than the allies Ivy and Martin actually had. Stony-faced, they formed a living wall across the mouth of the tunnel, then parted briefly as Gossan and Betony strode through.

Ivy clutched Martin's arm, but he gently removed her hand and stepped forward. "Jack O'Lantern," he declaimed, "you see my army, as I see yours. Will you do as before and send your soldiers to fight while you amuse yourself torturing children? Or will you face me in single combat and prove yourself the better man?"

Mattock was hardly a child, but the flare of Gossan's nostrils proved Martin's taunt had struck home. "You're no man," he retorted. "You're nothing but a foul, thieving spriggan."

"Then I should be no great challenge for you either," said Martin brightly. "Consider this your chance to prove once and for all, to my people as well as yours, that you're the mightiest warrior in Cornwall. Defeat me, and my army will flee to the border of Devon, never to be seen by you or any other piskey again. But if I win"—his mouth curved—"I become Jack of the Delve, ruling piskeys and spriggans alike."

Betony gave a cold laugh. "You'll never be *my* Jack," she said. "Touch me and I'll burn you to ashes."

"No fear, Lady Macbeth," said Martin. "I'd rather die than touch you anyway. And I have a better Joan than you already, so there's no need." He turned to Gossan. "But since your wife seems concerned you might lose, I'll let you choose the weapons for our challenge."

He picked up a pebble off the ground, tossed it in the air and caught it again as a dagger, flicking it from one hand to the other so fast Ivy's eyes could barely follow it. "Knives? I like those. Or would you prefer swords?" Another toss, and the blade lengthened; he swept it in a shining arc around and behind him. "Spears, perhaps?" Once more the weapon changed, to a wooden shaft spinning in his hands. "I'll even play at thunder-axes, if you like."

With one last flash he swung a steel-headed pickaxe onto his shoulder and arched an eyebrow at Gossan. "But whatever you choose, we'll stick to it. No changing weapons mid-fight, like you did to poor trusting Mattock. What do you say?"

Gossan's gaze raked over Martin's slim faery build, then flicked to the troop of spriggans behind him—who looked far more intimidating than their king did. He leaned toward Betony, listening as she whispered. Then he smiled.

"No weapons," he said.

Martin, who had been juggling daggers, stopped abruptly. The knives vanished, and three stones pattered to the ground. "I beg your pardon?"

"No weapons," Gossan repeated. "That is my choice."

"Boxing!" Martin sounded relieved. "A little inelegant, but I approve. Shall we—"

Gossan shook his head. "Wrestling."

The piskey soldiers broke into grins and nudged one another. There could be little doubt who would win that contest, and by the blank expression on his face, Martin knew it too. "To three falls?" he asked. "Or yielding?"

In the light of his skin-glow, Gossan's teeth gleamed like bones. "To the death."

20

The silence that followed Gossan's words was so absolute that Ivy could hear Martin swallow. Then he lifted his chin and said, "Agreed."

"No!" Ivy burst out. "Don't, Martin!"

"It's already done." He turned to the illusionary spriggans behind them. "Retreat, all of you. Do not approach again unless I call."

The ragged figures backed down the hillside, melting into the shadows of the wood. Martin watched until they vanished, then turned to Gossan. "I'm ready," he said. "Where shall we fight?"

At a glance, the answer was obvious. The only place flat enough for a wrestling match was the floor of the Engine House. Betony led the way, stepping proudly with her skirts gathered in both hands. Ivy and Martin followed, with Gossan's soldiers behind them.

Ivy's stomach churned and her feet felt like lead; every instinct screamed at her to seize Martin and leap away. But they had to drag out the performance as long as possible, to give Teasel and the other women time to save their men. She glanced anxiously over her shoulder, but there was no sign of the faeries or Cicely. She hoped they were hiding somewhere, recovering their strength so they'd be ready when Martin needed them.

Yet what could they do? Once started, the challenge could not be interrupted until it came to its lawful end, quick and brutal though that end would probably be. Martin's best assets were his speed and his cunning, but neither would help him once Gossan got those big hands around his neck.

When they reached the Engine House Gossan's men set to work, clearing away the charred branches that littered the floor and hacking up the turf with their thunder-axes. Soon they'd turned the former dancing green into a patch of dark, gravelly earth, framed by knocker soldiers. They linked their arms to form a ring, eager to watch their Jack crush the upstart spriggan.

Gossan threw off his jacket and pulled his shirt over his head, revealing a broad chest and shoulders like an anvil. He handed the clothes to Betony, who smiled triumphantly and leaned to kiss him. Her gleaming eyes met Ivy's across the Engine House, and Ivy had to look away.

Martin plucked fretfully at his shirt-cuff. "In this cold? Is that necessary?"

The knockers smirked, and the nearest one leered at him. "Don't worry, little spriggan. Once our Jack gets a grip on you, you'll warm up soon enough."

"And by the time he's done with you, you won't care," chimed in another, and they all laughed.

There had to be a way to stop this, Ivy thought. Martin had suffered enough for her already without having to lay down his life as well. But he'd dropped his coat and started unbuttoning his shirt, so he clearly meant to go through with it.

Half-dressed he looked thinner than ever, with jutting collarbones and skin so pale she could see the blue veins running through it. Not weak or flabby—Martin had never been that. But he seemed like a mere boy compared to Gossan, especially with his hair ruffled like an owlet's feathers. Fighting grief, Ivy reached up to brush it out of his eyes. "Please don't do this," she whispered. "You've survived so long—you can't give up now."

Martin drew her close and kissed her wet cheek. His hands cupped the wingless blades of her shoulders as he murmured, "Don't cry, love. You know me. When could I ever resist a dramatic exit?"

"Enough," called Gossan. "Stop hiding behind your woman and come fight."

Martin held Ivy's gaze a moment, like a silent apology. Then he turned to the knockers. "Well? Are you going to let me in, or do I have to wrestle the lot of you first?"

The men guffawed and unlinked their arms to let him pass. But as Martin stepped forward, one stuck out his boot in front of him; he stumbled and nearly fell.

"That's foul play, boys," Gossan warned, but he was smiling. He smacked his hands together, bouncing from foot to foot, as Martin watched him warily.

"The rules of the challenge are as follows," declared Betony, her voice echoing through the night. "You may not conjure weapons or cast spells of self-protection; you must defeat your opponent by wits and strength alone. Only one of you may leave this ring alive—"

"And that one will be the unquestioned Jack of the Delve," Martin chimed in, "in case anyone was forgetting. Or would you rather just surrender now and spare yourselves a long and tedious view of my stomach?"

Betony's jaw tightened, and her eyes grew cold. But she made no retort, only raised her arms high. "On the count of three, the match will begin. One. Two. Three!"

At once Gossan exploded into action, hurling himself at Martin. But Martin spun aside, ducking the bigger man's grasp and popping up behind him. "Cuckoo!" he sang.

Ivy gripped her elbows, watching him anxiously. If Martin could keep dodging Gossan for a few minutes, that would buy their allies in the Delve more time. But it had to come to grappling at some point, or the match would never end.

She'd barely finished the thought when Gossan whipped around like a striking adder and cuffed Martin across the face. He reeled back, stunned, and Gossan grabbed him around the waist. He heaved Martin skyward as though he weighed nothing and slammed him full-length to the ground.

Ivy winced, but she couldn't look away. Gossan had flung himself over Martin, grabbing his arm and jerking it up at a hideous angle—but with a writhing twist Martin slipped free and leaped to his feet again. They circled one another, panting, for a long moment. Then the Jack rushed at Martin, and to Ivy's shock, Martin made no attempt to dodge him. He ducked, seized Gossan's leg and yanked him off-balance, sending him crashing onto his back.

Hope flared in Ivy. Perhaps Gossan's size didn't give him as much of an advantage as she'd thought? If Martin could keep out of his crushing grip, he might wear the older man to exhaustion, then leap onto his back and bring him down.

Yet without a knife, could he actually kill Gossan? Could he muster the strength, let alone the ruthlessness, to try?

Gossan lurched to his feet and lunged forward, grabbing at Martin. But the spriggan moved like the breeze, slipping out of his stony grasp. No matter how many times the Jack clutched at him, he couldn't seem to keep hold, and even Betony was beginning to frown before Gossan finally got both arms around Martin's ribs, hoisted him in the air, and began to crush him.

Martin's face reddened, and he let out a whistling gasp. The knockers roared, and Ivy clapped her hands to her mouth. But then, impossibly, Martin slithered free and dropped to a crouch at Gossan's feet.

The Jack staggered back, teeth bared in a snarl. "You cheating spriggan worm. Stop changing shape!"

"Am I?" panted Martin. "I just thought you were slow and clumsy."

Gossan glared at him. Then he took a deliberate breath, wiped his hands down the front of his trousers and straightened up. "You won't win that way, and you know it. Why are you wasting time?"

Ivy clutched her elbows, fighting panic. If Gossan guessed this was only a distraction, he'd call off the match and send his soldiers into the Delve at once. But Martin only tossed back his hair and gave Gossan a feral grin.

"Why not? After all the years your people made sport of hunting mine, it seems only fair to play with you a bit. And surely you can figure out how to kill a spriggan without me making it easy for you?"

Gossan spat in his hands and stalked forward, his chiseled features ugly with hatred. He lunged left, then right, blocking Martin before he could dart aside. Then he seized him by both shoulders—and instead of dodging, Martin thrust his arms up between Gossan's and shoved them apart.

That was raw strength, not trickery, and by the shock on his face Gossan knew it. But he set his teeth and snatched at Martin again. Arms twined and muscles straining, they staggered in a circle, staying upright longer than Ivy would have dreamed possible. But then, they didn't seem quite so mismatched as before . . .

With a start, Ivy realized what was happening. Instead of shifting smaller, Martin was making himself subtly bigger and heavier to hold the Jack at bay. But Gossan was no fool, and no stranger to changing size either. He began to grow as well, and soon he and Martin had reached human height, lurching about the Engine House like grappling giants. The final round, the test of strength, had begun.

At this size the ring was still large enough to hold them, but barely, and the soldiers scuttled back to give the champions more room. Betony stood her ground, but she looked more impatient by the minute, fingers drumming her arm as she waited for the match to end.

Yet incredibly, the two men kept wrestling. They scrambled back and forth, clutching at one another, and now and then the Jack managed to throw Martin down. But though every fall seemed fit to crush him, he always leaped up again. Even filthy and bruised all over, he refused to give Gossan the upper hand.

Then a rook flapped over the Engine House, croaking, and Ivy's heart bounded. It was Broch, giving the signal she'd prayed all night to hear. Their plan had succeeded. Mica, Mattock, and the other men were free.

Yet their triumph would be short-lived unless Martin won this contest, and she could see him starting to falter. Distracting him could be risky, but if it gave him the heart to keep fighting, it would be worth it. "Martin!" Ivy shouted. "They've done it!"

His eyes flashed to hers, bright with sudden joy. Then the Jack's tough skull cracked into his, and he fell down stunned with Gossan on top of him. Before he could recover, the older man grabbed him by the throat.

Ivy screamed, but the knockers' cheers drowned her out. Wildly she started forward, but firm hands seized her. "Don't be a slag-wit!" a familiar voice shouted. "You can't stop the fight now!"

It was Mica. Grimy from two nights in Betony's dungeon, reeking of sweat and worse, but alive. And on Ivy's other side, his eyes full of pity, stood Mattock.

"You can't interfere, Ivy," he said.

Ivy struggled to free herself from Mica, but it was no use. The soldiers crowded closer, eager to see their Jack's triumph, while Martin lay helpless with the life half-choked out of him, face purpling as he fought for breath.

Then Gossan shied back, his grip broken. The slender neck he'd been throttling had rippled into bullish muscle, Martin's fine features swelling to monstrosity as he changed to his ancestors' treasure-guarding shape. He heaved himself upright and clapped one ogreish hand around Gossan's neck.

Martin had told Ivy that the spriggan boys had taught him a few tricks, but she'd never guessed he knew that one. His lips curled, baring peg-like teeth, and the Jack's eyes bulged with terror as he scrabbled to get free. But Martin only gripped him tighter, and a blue tinge crept over Gossan's face. He squirmed, batted weakly at the spriggan's hand, and finally went limp.

Martin spoke then, his voice like a gravelly earthquake. "I could tear your head from your shoulders," he said, giving the Jack a shake, "and there's little doubt you deserve it. However, I am heartily sick of killing, so I'll ask you: do you yield?"

Gossan squeezed his eyes shut, tears striping his dirty cheeks. "I—"

"Let go of him, spriggan!" Light flashed through the Engine House as Betony shot up to human height and strode forward, flames crackling around her knotted fists. "The contest is forfeit!"

Martin sat back on his haunches, small eyes wary in the bulbous mask of his face. "How so?"

"You cheated! Tricked him with a false face, hiding your true nature—"

"He did not." Ivy wrenched free of Mattock, stepping over the startled knockers as she too grew to human size. "Martin fought with his own strength, as the rules said, and his faery shape is as real as the one he wears now." And nearly as strong, or he couldn't have wrestled Gossan as long as he had before changing. "It's not his fault you underestimated him."

"How dare you interrupt me." Betony's tone was venomous. "You speak as though you were my equal? A wingless, weak, half-faery child? If you weren't my brother's daughter—"

"You'd do what?" challenged Ivy. Her heart beat frantically, and her skin was crawling with fear, but this could be her last chance to expose Betony. "Banish me? Burn my mother half to death? Murder my best friend in front of my eyes? How many more ways can you punish me for telling the truth?"

Betony barked out a laugh. "Truth, you say! All you know are the lies your spriggan lover tells you. If you had the right to dethrone me, the Joan's fire would have passed to you long ago. But you have no power, only ignorance and pride." She raised her arms menacingly. "Stand aside, Ivy. I won't ask you again."

Ivy shook her head. "You've lost, and threatening me won't change that. Martin is Jack of the Delve now."

"Not while I breathe," Betony spat. "Drop my consort, spriggan, or I'll boil the blood in your veins. You haven't won yet."

"Technically true," admitted Martin, still holding Gossan at arm's length. "But I'm still waiting for him to yield. I think we ought to give him a chance, don't you?"

The Jack sagged, turning hopeless eyes to Betony. Then he sucked in a rattling breath and gasped, "I—yiel—"

"No!" Betony shrieked, lunging at Martin. But Ivy leaped in front of him and grabbed her aunt's flaming wrists instead.

The pain was instant and excruciating, searing through her hands to her whole body. She could feel fire racing up her arms and across her chest, her betrothal pendant flaring white-hot and the wool of her sweater withering to expose raw skin beneath. Ivy's knees buckled, and she clamped her teeth shut, biting her cheek so hard she tasted blood.

This was nothing like the little flame Thorn had conjured on the hillside or the tingling of Valerian's spell-fire. This was the infernal power of Betony's wrath, the same dark magic that had scorched Jenny to ash and left Shale a charred husk on the Joan's stateroom floor. Yet Ivy clung doggedly to her aunt, refusing to let go until either the flames died or she did.

She couldn't look down, couldn't bear to see the horror she was becoming. Surely her agony should have faded by now, as the fire flayed past skin and nerves to the muscles beneath. Yet the fire burned hotter than ever, scorching through Ivy's very bones. How was she standing? Her legs should have crumbled long ago.

Ivy threw her head back and flung her arms out like wings. Then with the last of her strength she hurled herself at her aunt.

Betony shrieked and toppled, her whole body convulsing. The fire in her hands died—and with a shout of triumph Ivy leaped to her feet, gloriously reborn.

She'd staked her life on the hope that Betony's power might not be all it seemed, and she'd been right. The searing pain that had wracked Ivy was only a glamour, like the smoke and heat she'd felt in the barn. Betony hadn't just warded the farmstead to keep Ivy and her followers from using it; she'd done it to keep them from seeing the lack of fire damage and guessing the truth.

Yet the air around Ivy seemed strangely bright, full of shimmering waves and ripples. Her ears roared, and she could hear something crackling nearby. What was that writhing shape at her feet? She squinted through the brightness but saw nothing she recognized, and in a moment it stopped moving and crumbled away.

"Ivy."

Martin's voice cut through her daze, and she turned to look at him. No longer monstrous, he knelt beside Gossan, his eyes shining silver with awe.

What was he staring at? Bewildered, Ivy glanced down—and

gave a little cry of astonishment. Her whole body was covered with flickering tongues of fire.

"My mad, magnificent queen." Martin climbed to his feet, a little unsteady, but smiling. "You never could learn anything the easy way. But could you put that out before you burn anyone else to charcoal?"

For a confused moment Ivy had no idea what he meant. Then horror seized her and she spun around, looking for Betony. But there was nothing left of the older woman but ashes and charred bones.

The fire Ivy had kindled died, and the cool night air rushed in around her. She stood trembling on the trampled soil of the wrestling ground, eyes blurred and chest knotted with grief. She hadn't meant to kill Betony, only to expose her aunt's trickery. After all her efforts to make fire had failed, she'd never dreamed the power of a true Joan would come to her now.

But by enduring fire, Ivy had also learned to wield it. And now Betony would never hurt anyone again.

Martin's hands closed on Ivy's shoulders and she turned to him, burying her face in his chest. He flinched as her hands touched his bruised back, but when he wrapped his arms about her there was no smell of dirt or sweat on him anywhere. "It's over," he murmured, pressing a kiss to her temple. "We've done it, my love. We won."

Until now, Ivy hadn't realized just how many of her people were watching. But once she'd wiped the tears from her eyes and looked around, she found the whole Engine House full. After freeing the trapped men, Daisy, Clover and the other women had raced about the tunnels, rousing all the other piskeys and urging them up to the surface. So nearly everyone in the Delve had seen Betony's fire die out and Ivy rise in a blaze of newfound glory to take her place.

"Don't be frightened," Ivy called to them. She could still

sense the Joan's power inside her, glowing in her bones and tingling beneath the surface of her skin. "You're safe now."

Wolfram took a hesitant step forward. "But lady, what of the spriggans?"

"You mean these ones?" Martin nodded to Cicely, who sat in one of the upper windows, and the piskeys all jumped as the false army materialized behind him. "I hate to disappoint you, but my people don't look anything like that." He waved his hand, and the apparitions vanished into smoke. "The real spriggans are twenty miles from here, tucked up in bed. Once you meet them, you'll see there's nothing to be afraid of." He bared his teeth in a slow smile. "Unless it's me."

Ivy winced. It would be hard enough getting her people to accept a spriggan Jack without that sort of thing, and the nervous silence that followed seemed to prove it. But then Ivy's brother shouldered though the crowd toward them, with Mattock following close behind.

"I was wrong about you," Mica said gruffly, then took a deep breath and sank to one knee before Martin. "My Jack."

Mattock started to kneel as well, but Martin stopped him. He caught Mica's hand and pulled him to his feet. "I forgive you," he said. "Just don't try to beat me up again."

"No fear of that," said Mica, with a short laugh. "I'm lucky you didn't pound me to gravel the first time."

If Martin had known about his spriggan heritage back then, he likely would have. But it wouldn't hurt to let her brother think he'd got off lightly. And after spending days in the same dank cave where he'd once chained Martin, Mica had other reasons to regret his rash behavior as well. Suppressing her bitterness, Ivy held out her hand.

Mica took it warily, as though fearing she would burn him. Then he gave a wry half-smile, and pulled Ivy in for a clumsy hug instead. He didn't apologize or ask forgiveness; perhaps he never would. But he was trying to make amends, and for now, that was enough.

Behind them Gossan stirred feebly and dragged himself upright. He still lived, thanks to Martin, but when he saw where Betony had fallen, his haggard face showed how little he cared for such mercy. He covered his eyes with his dirty hands.

"You killed Shale, didn't you?" Ivy asked. "And then you burned his body, so it would look like Betony had done it." No wonder Martin had called her Lady Macbeth. She'd lost the power to make fire when she burned Jenny, so she'd turned to deception and dark magic to keep her power instead. And Gossan had gone along with her, even to the point of murder.

Once he'd been like Mattock, not just loyal but honest and fair-minded. But fear had corrupted him, just as it had Betony. And now there was nothing left of either of them but an empty shell.

"You have your life," Ivy told Gossan. "But I exile you to beyond the Tamar, outside the border of Kernow. You will never see another piskey as long as you live."

The former Jack struggled to his feet, not looking at Ivy or even taking the clothes Martin held out to him. Head bowed, he stumbled off into the darkness and was gone.

But a rope of scarlet was unrolling along the horizon, and in the distance a rooster crowed, greeting the new dawn. Her people were free, Martin stood beside her—and at long last, Ivy was home.

ℰPILOGUE

"We've never had a Lighting this late in the winter before," mused Cicely, as she and Ivy watched the spriggan children setting the tables for dinner. "Or started so early in the evening, either."

"Do you think people will be offended?" Ivy asked, but her sister only laughed.

"After you and Martin saved the whole Delve? I'd say you can do anything you like."

Ivy would have liked to believe that, but old piskey habits didn't change so easily. Most of her people still hesitated even to speak to the spriggans, let alone welcome them into their homes. Yet the children had proved their worth already, by doing for the Delve what they'd done in their own barrow. Only yesterday Ivy had gone down to the diggings and found scarcely a trace of poison.

Martin had spent days healing the piskeys who'd been worst affected, and though no magic could restore the old uncles' missing teeth or smooth the wrinkles from the aunties' skin, they all looked a great deal better. No one coughed anymore, not even the youngest children, and the contrite Yarrow could lock up her store of herbal remedies and sleep untroubled for the first time in years.

But of all the spriggans only Pearl had found a permanent home yet, and only because Thrift had begged so piteously that Gem and Daisy had no choice but to take the girl in. Though Teasel was still giving Jewel regular knitting lessons, and Ivy suspected she and Hew would offer the girl a place in their cavern soon. But for now Jewel shared the Joan's quarters with Ivy and the other spriggan girls, while the boys camped out in the Market Cavern with Martin.

Yet things in the Delve *were* changing, as tonight's celebration proved. Now that they were all free to visit the surface, Ivy's people no longer needed a wakefire: they could recharge their fading skin-glows just by spending a few hours outdoors. But a Lighting always cheered the piskeys' hearts, and Ivy hoped it would soften them toward the newcomers who'd be sharing their feast as well.

"We've got twelve bottles of piskey-wine," announced Feldspar, jogging up with a handcart. "Where d'you want 'em?"

After the fearful awe the piskeys had shown when she first touched fire, Ivy had worried they might always be shy around her. But they'd soon realized that their Joan's newfound powers hadn't changed her heart, and now they were almost back to their old casual selves again.

"Wolfram's dug a cold-hole by the back wall," Ivy told him. "They can go in there."

With a cheerful thumbs-up, Feldspar trotted off. Ivy turned back to Cicely. "What did Mum say when you talked to her? Are she and David coming?"

"Not this time," Cicely said. "He's got some work thing they have to go to. But she sent her love."

Ivy nodded, privately relieved. Much as she liked her stepfather, she wasn't sure her fellow piskeys were ready to welcome a human on top of everything else.

"You didn't tell her what happened," Cicely added, a little reproachfully. "Or what's happening tonight, either."

It was tempting to ask her, *Did you*? But Ivy didn't want to dwell on her sister's mistakes, or act as though she expected her to repeat them. "Not yet. I only told her the parts I thought she'd want to hear, like Betony being dead and the Delve being safe again. But I told Molly everything."

"What did she say?"

"She screamed," said Ivy. "Right into the phone." Her ear still buzzed from that shriek of delight, but at least she had no doubt of her stepsister's feelings. Molly had been half-wild with frustration that she couldn't come tonight, but Ivy had assured her that the Midsummer Lighting would be a much better time.

And it would be. Because in the flowering warmth of that June night Ivy and Martin would be married, and he—who'd once been guilty, despised, homeless, and last of a dying race—would be crowned Jack of the Delve.

Ivy scanned the bustling crowd in the Engine House, spotting one familiar face after another: Mica furrowing his brow in concentration as he tuned their father's fiddle, Dagger staggering toward the wakefire with a pile of wood so high he could barely see, Daisy scolding Thrift for muddying her dress while Pearl stood meekly by. Hew was hooting and slapping his thigh over a prank Quartz had just played on him, while Teasel piled wedges of nettle cheese onto plates and passed them to Jewel and Ruby to serve.

Meanwhile old Copper sat in the corner with a face like a wet week and a few of the knockers who'd followed Gossan huddled guiltily against the back wall. They'd pleaded for mercy and Ivy had granted it, but they were still ashamed to look her or Martin in the face.

But they'd come here instead of hiding, so there was hope yet. It would take time to undo the damage Betony and Gossan had done to their people, but bringing them all together was a start.

"Ivy?"

Cicely turned crimson and scuttled away as Mattock walked up, a basket hooked over his arm. "You came!" Ivy exclaimed. "Are you all right?"

He made a diffident gesture with his half hand. "Well enough. You look . . . nice."

Teasel had made the gown for her, knitting its draped neck and long sleeves from wool she'd spun and dyed a deep cornflower blue. Then she'd passed it to Jewel, who'd embroidered it with silver vines that twined from Ivy's wrists to her elbows and up both sides of the softly flaring skirt. It was the loveliest thing Ivy had ever worn, and deliciously warm—though the fire she carried inside her meant that she was never really cold anymore.

"Mica told me you weren't coming," she said, as Mattock walked to the dessert table and began to unpack his basket of saffron buns.

Matt blew out an exasperated breath. "Mica thinks everyone's as moody as he is. I never said that. I only said . . ." His eyes became distant. "I'm not sure what good I'm doing here anymore."

"You don't have to do anything," Ivy told him. "I'm just glad you're here." But Mattock shook his head.

"I *want* to do something. I just don't know what."

Ivy's heart went out to him, but she had no answer. Matt was learning to use his left hand, but he was still clumsy with it, unable to wield a knife skillfully or do most of the other tasks that had once filled his days as a hunter. He'd never swing a thunder-axe like his knocker father, or cut and craft gemstones with the older piskey-men. He still loved baking, but as tonight's well-laden tables showed, there were plenty of good bakers in the Delve.

Cicely plucked her elbow. "Thorn wants to talk to you outside. It's important."

Ivy knew her little sister was only doing her duty as the Joan's attendant, but it was hard not to be frustrated at her timing. "We'll talk more later," she promised Mattock, and hurried out the door of the Engine House.

Thorn was waiting on the path, arms folded over her swollen belly—it was big enough to notice now, and her unbuttoned jacket and loose tunic did little to hide it. "Is it true?" she demanded. "You invited Queen Valerian and didn't tell me?"

Well, at least one person wasn't in awe of her. "I sent a message, but she didn't answer it. Why?"

Thorn jerked a thumb over her shoulder. "Because she's here."

Despite all the wards Ivy had laid around the hillside to keep unwanted guests at bay, a car was driving slowly toward them, headlamps sweeping the lane like searching eyes. It crunched to a stop above the Engine House, and a tall blonde woman jumped out of the passenger seat to open the back door.

It was Peri McCormick, the one the faeries called Knife.

Thorn went rigid, fists clenched at her sides. At piskey height, surrounded by gorse and bracken, she and Ivy were all but invisible; Thorn could have leaped away in an instant, and Knife would never know she'd been there. But as Queen Valerian stepped out of the car she looked straight at the two of them and beckoned.

Thorn swore under her breath, but she was too loyal to disobey her own monarch. She squared her shoulders, grew to human size, and stomped up the slope to meet them. Feeling awkward and a little apprehensive, Ivy followed.

"Queen of spriggans," said Valerian warmly, stretching out both hands to Ivy. "And now Joan of the Delve as well. Do you forgive me?"

"Of course," Ivy told her, clasping the queen's fingers in her own. Hurt though she'd been by Valerian's reluctance to help her, she understood it now. It wasn't faery soldiers or spells that Ivy had needed, it was her own readiness to die for the people she loved. Only the belief that she had nothing left to lose had given Ivy the courage to face Betony, and that strength, not Valerian's, had made her the Joan.

"And Thorn," said the queen, turning to the faery woman. "You fought bravely to help Ivy when I could not, and bring peace where it seemed most hopeless. I am proud of you."

Thorn stood with head bowed and lips pressed tight together, while a fat tear slid down her cheek. Then she swiped furiously at her eyes and said to Knife, "I know this isn't fair. I never wanted this, and you wanted it so much—" She heaved a breath. "I'm sorry."

Knife regarded the faery woman, distraught. Then she stepped forward and wrapped Thorn in a fierce embrace. "How gnat-witted do you think I am?" she demanded, as the shorter woman blinked dazedly against her shoulder. "I knew something was wrong the minute Wink told me you'd left the Oak. It drove me half-wild that you ran away to Cornwall before we could talk. When Timothy told me he'd seen you and thought you were expecting . . . I wasn't even surprised."

"Well, I was," said Knife's husband Paul, leaning out the window of the car. "Of all the Oakenfolk, Thorn, how on earth did *you* end up being the first one to get pregnant?"

Thorn's lips quivered, and Ivy braced herself for an outburst. But then Knife snorted, Thorn spluttered, and they both burst out laughing.

Paul watched the two of them in consternation. "I need a drink," he muttered, which for some reason only made Thorn and Knife laugh harder. It was a long time before the two of them stopped giggling like piskey-girls and straightened up again.

"It really isn't fair, though," Thorn said, as Knife wiped her eyes on the sleeve of her winter jacket.

"Stop feeling guilty," Knife told her. "You haven't stolen anything from me. I helped raise Linden and Timothy, and if you'll stop trying to avoid me, I'll be glad to help look after your child as well." She stepped back, taking Paul's hand through the window. "If there's one thing I've learned from becoming human, it's that missing something doesn't mean you can never be happy without it."

Thorn looked skeptical but said no more. Knife turned to Valerian. "Paul and I will be going now, but we've booked a cottage close by. If you need anything . . ."

The queen smiled at her. "You have done all I could ask, Perianth. Go with my blessing, and rest."

"This is the Draft of Harmony." Ivy's voice rang across the Engine House as she lifted the bowl of piskey-wine, the wakefire she'd just lit blazing behind her. The pendant Martin had given her hung openly around her neck now, its green depths dancing with golden light. "As we pass it from one to another, piskeys and spriggans and faeries alike, may we put aside all past divisions and hatreds, and drink to friendship and peace."

"To peace," her people echoed, but it sounded feeble. They hadn't expected to find Queen Valerian of the Oak at their feast, and they weren't sure what to make of her. Thorn and Broch were almost as good as piskeys in their eyes, but Valerian was the image of the lovely, perilous faeries in their droll-tales, and they were all waiting for her gracious facade to crack.

Well, they'd be waiting a very long time. Ivy wasn't sure how wise or good a Joan she'd be compared to Betony: only time and testing could prove that. But she knew what kind of ruler she hoped to be, and she could find no better example than Queen Valerian. Ivy sipped the draft and handed it on to Martin, who stood up and held the bowl high as well.

"A blessing on the Delve!" he called out, his voice resonant, and Ivy's people sat up at once. Those words at least were traditional, and something they could all agree on. They shouted back the blessing as Martin drank, firelight glinting on the signet ring that had once been his father's and the silver vines Jewel had embroidered on his doublet. But instead of handing the draft to Mattock, who sat on his right, Martin walked across the circle to Valerian.

"Your Majesty," he said, and lowered himself to one knee.

The piskeys gaped, and Dagger started to his feet in outrage. But Valerian shook her head, smiling, and rose to take the bowl from Martin's hands.

"You honor me, king of spriggans," she said. "But tonight I am only a guest, and your servant." She touched his cheek with a mother's tenderness, then crossed the stones and offered the draft to Mattock.

Hesitantly he accepted it, his face full of wonder—and when he had drunk, Valerian took it back and offered the bowl to Mica. Patiently the faery queen carried it around the circle, presenting it to each piskey and spriggan in turn, and holding their gazes with her own until they either drank or looked away. Not until she'd attended all of them did Valerian drink and hand the bowl back to Ivy. Then she returned to her seat.

So many had sipped the piskey-wine, there was only a few mouthfuls left. Encouraged, Ivy drank and poured the dregs into the wakefire. She handed the empty bowl to Cicely and was about to announce the start of the feast when Martin stepped in front of her, offering his arm.

She'd almost forgotten—there was one more important ceremony to come. Blushing, Ivy let Martin lead her to the back of the Engine House, where a throne stood on a wooden dais. She stepped up onto the platform, feeling small and strange, and turned to face the crowd.

There was a minor eruption at the back of the ranks as Thrift and Pearl squirmed through, clutching a lumpy cushion between them. Together they trotted over the grass, heedless of Daisy's protests, and held up their gift to Ivy.

It was a golden circlet, so beautifully crafted that only piskeys could have made it, but with a slight dullness that hinted it hadn't been used in many years. Three equal-sized gemstones adorned its center, one airy blue, one moss-green, and the middle dark as granite; while all around them the gold was shaped like tiny, leaping flames. Ivy had never seen anything like it before, but she knew what it must be: the ancient, long-lost crown of the Joan.

"We found it in the treasure," announced Thrift, and Pearl added hastily, "Not in the Delve. In the barrow."

"Of course." Martin looked solemn, but his lips were twitching. "Spriggans might be grave-robbers, but let it never be said that we're thieves." He lifted the circlet and set it on Ivy's head, then stepped back and swept his arm toward her. "All hail Joan the Wad, queen of the piskeys, knockers, and spriggans!"

"All hail our Joan!" shouted Mattock, clapping loudly, and Hew and the other rescued men joined in. They kept it up until the whole crowd was cheering with them, and Ivy's blush grew so hot she thought she might burst into flames right there. Shyly she lowered herself onto the throne that had once been Betony's and waited for the noise to die down.

"*'Tis Joan, not we, by whom the day is won*," Martin quoted, putting a hand on her shoulder. "*For which I will divide my crown with her.*"

Ivy laid her hand over his and smiled. Then she called out, "Let the feast begin!"

Ivy was sitting with her empty plate in her lap, wiping the last crumbs of saffron bun from her fingers, when Broch walked up to her.

"I've found something that may help unite your people." He opened his hand and showed her a smooth, dark gray pebble with a few crumbs of mortar clinging to it. "It seems all those stones in the entrance of the barrow weren't just there for decoration."

He dropped it into Ivy's palm, and she started in astonishment as a moonlit landscape appeared before her eyes, and a lilting voice began to speak: "In the days of the good Joan Chalcedony, there lived a piskey who had lost his laugh . . ."

"Lorestones." Broch took back the pebble, and the vision faded. "My people, the Children of Rhys, used seeds for a similar purpose—to record stories and events that might otherwise be forgotten. I haven't had a chance to study more than a few of the stones in the barrow yet, but if you need more proof of how things used to be . . ."

Ivy nodded, grateful. Her people might not be great readers, but they loved stories, and viewing these lorestones would do more to convince them that spriggans, piskeys, and knockers had once lived together in harmony than Ivy's words, or her crown, ever could.

"You've given me a precious gift," she told Broch. "I owe you and Thorn more than I can say." The words knotted her throat, but she had to speak them. "I'll miss you when you go back to the Oak."

Broch looked puzzled. "Are you sending us away, then? I

know you'll want someone to help negotiate the peace treaty, but I thought you had someone else in mind."

He gestured to a bench by the wakefire, where Queen Valerian sat talking quietly to Mattock. His half hand lay relaxed on his knee, and he was listening to her with obvious interest. Not in a romantic way, or at least Ivy hoped not: despite her youthful appearance the faery queen was far older than he was, and showed no sign of wanting a consort. But if Mattock could talk to Valerian, then he might not mind becoming the Delve's ambassador to the Oak as well.

"I do now," Ivy said, with a smile. "And if you and Thorn want to stay with us, I'd be honored."

A pointed cough made Ivy look around. Martin stood behind her, firelight washing his skin with gold and gleaming in his white-blond hair. He'd lost his pinched look, and the embroidered doublet and fitted breeches suited him; he no longer moved like a fugitive but with the calm dignity of a king.

"My Joan," he said, holding out one hand. "Will you honor me?"

Ivy followed his gaze to the mossy square at the center of the Engine House, where a few couples—Daisy and Gem, Ruby leading a red-faced Dagger, and to her faint surprise, Mica and Yarrow—were dancing. Then she put her hand in Martin's and let him lead her to the floor.

She'd always been a good dancer, light-footed and graceful as her faery mother. But her lack of wings had always hampered her, and she'd seldom danced with anyone but Cicely until tonight. Now with Martin's arm about her waist, she could finally leap and twirl as a piskey-girl should. And with the airy grace of his spriggan heritage he matched her steps flawlessly, smiling at her all the while.

Joy swelled in Ivy, warming her chest. It had been worth everything—all the doubts and fears that had tormented her, all the hardships she'd endured—to come to this place, this moment. Her people were free, her home truly safe again. And as Martin gathered his strength and threw her high into the air, Ivy felt as though her heart was flying.

THE END

ACKNOWLEDGMENTS

I was eager to write this third book of the trilogy as soon as I'd finished *Nomad*, but it took a few years longer than I'd anticipated. Thanks to the many faithful readers who sent e-mails begging for more about Ivy and Martin in the meantime, reassuring me that I wasn't the only one to think there should be more to the story!

Still, this book wouldn't exist without a lot of other generous and hard-working folk behind it. I am deeply grateful to Steve Laube at Enclave Publishing for giving *Torch* the chance to shine as a published novel, Lisa Laube for her thorough and patient editing, and Lindsay Franklin for her great work as copyeditor (any errors that remain are entirely my fault). Thanks also to Jordan Smith and Trissina Kear for their mad marketing, publicity, and Instagram skills, Kirk DouPonce for the beautiful covers, and Josh Adams for agenting above and beyond the call of duty.

Love to my fabulous first-draft cheerleading squad of Deva Fagan, Rosamund Hodge, and my brother Peter Anderson, plus Erin Bow who made Encouraging Noises about the early chapters over tea; and my heartfelt thanks for the sharp-eyed critiques of Chawna Schroeder (author of the wonderful *Beast* and *The Vault Between Spaces,* also from Enclave!), Kerrie

Mills, Leng Malit, Rebekah Brown, Emily Sather, Aubrey Heesch, and Erin Fitzgerald.

Kelsi Johnson and Liz Barr read the revised draft and gave me crunchy delicious feedback, while E.K. Johnston took me out for crunchy delicious chicken and waffles (an essential part of a balanced author). My mother Joan lived up to her queenly name and supported me with daily love and prayers, while my brother Mark and sister-in-law Lisa checked in on me regularly to find out how the writing was going. Thanks to you all.

And finally, these books would not exist, let alone be published, apart from the grace of my Heavenly Father, Saviour, and Guide. If there is anything of lasting worth in these stories, it comes from Him.

ABOUT THE AUTHOR

Born in Uganda to missionary parents, R.J. (Rebecca Joan) Anderson is a women's Bible teacher, a wife and mother of three, and a bestselling fantasy author for older children and teens. Her debut novel *Knife* has sold more than 120,000 copies worldwide, while her other books have been shortlisted for the Nebula Award, the Christy Award, and the Sunburst Award for Excellence in Canadian Science Fiction. Rebecca lives with her family in Stratford, Ontario, Canada.